sometimes
never,
sometimes
always

for my students, for the poems in each of them—

sometimes never, sometimes always

ELISSA JANINE HOOLE

Woodbury, Minnesota

First Edition
First Printing, 2013

Book design by Bob Gaul
Cover design by Lisa Novak
Cover photo: "For a Rainy Day" by Brian Oldham

Flux, an imprint of Llewellyn Worldwide Ltd.

Library of Congress Cataloging-in-Publication Data
Hoole, Elissa Janine.
   Sometimes never, sometimes always/Elissa Janine Hoole.—First edition.
      pages cm
   Summary: "When seventeen-year-old Cassandra Randall can't think of anything interesting about herself for an English assignment—to write a poem that celebrates herself—she starts an advice blog that has unintended consequences"—Provided by publisher.
   ISBN 978-0-7387-3722-5
[1. Self-perception—Fiction. 2. Bullying—Fiction.] I. Title.
   PZ7.H7667So 2013
   [Fic]—dc23

                                                          2013023054

                              Flux
                    Llewellyn Worldwide Ltd.
                      2143 Wooddale Drive
                    Woodbury, MN 55125-2989
                        www.fluxnow.com

             Printed in the United States of America

Acknowledgments

Thank you to my family, to D and the boys, for mostly holding it all together while I'm writing and even making sure that I occasionally remember to drag myself away for an adventure or two. Thank you to all my family and friends for their enthusiasm and their love and for letting me know that they support me in this dream. Unending thanks to the musers, for their everything.

So many thanks to my agent, Sarah Davies, whose unwavering belief in me as a writer is only a steady email away, for her calm British voice on the phone talking strategy and hope even as she tells me the truth about what I need to work on.

Thanks to my editor, Brian Farrey-Latz, for loving these characters and this story, for his understanding and his vision. To Mallory Hayes, Sandy Sullivan, and the whole team at Flux, who are amazing and helpful, and for the breathtakingly gorgeous cover art and this whole awesome experience.

Thanks also to Melanie Kroupa, for her revision notes that helped strengthen this book immensely, and to my beta readers, whose advice is always the best. Thank you Cat Hellisen, Kari Olson, Ryan Gebhart, Amanda Thrasher, Amelia Volkman, Jenny Pinther, and all who read excerpts and talked me through plot problems and helped me interpret tarot cards!

Most of all, thanks to YA readers, and to the teens who stand up to be selves worth celebrating!

———

Post your answers
and share with your friends.

———

Trapped by your voice, which cuts me in a
  hidden vein,
My heart is imprisoned, writhing in pain.
Your indifferent eyes, not even a glimmer?
My lonely heart twists; my hope grows dimmer.

Seriously. The whole thing goes on like that—forty-two sets of anguished couplets. I'm no poet, as evidenced by my weekend failure, but there's no way I'm submitting this to the newspaper. Even if I kept it anonymous, I don't think I could handle hearing Britney and Annika mock it, knowing that Drew wrote it. It would feel too mean. Besides, what if they thought I wrote it? That I wanted my stupid poetry in the school newspaper?

Newspaper. I promised the princesses of perk that I'd come by the office during lunch tomorrow to start doing the layout for this week's issue. I wonder what it'll be like to have somewhere to go for lunch. I wonder if they'll actually talk to me.

Will I always be the lonely one, hiding in my cell?
Everyone hates me—will you as well?
The way your dark hair frames your face,
My captive heart commences to race.

I'm going to commence to throw up. What is this crap? And who is she writing to? I unzip the top of my backpack and shove the page into the gap, where it joins the neglected ranks of candy wrappers and old homework and dead pens at the bottom of my bag. Thank god I don't have any classes with Drew except for last-period study hall.

I see Kayla waiting for my bus outside of school, which is completely abnormal. Usually she makes me find her, track her turpentine scent down to the basement art room, where she'll be huddled up with her music in her ears, scribbling away at her tiny black ink worlds that I never quite understand. Today she glares at me through the little hole I've scraped in the frost on the bus window as we pull up.

"Your stupid church is trying to ruin my life," she says, by way of greeting.

I raise an eyebrow, hitch my backpack over my right shoulder, and step off the bus. "Join the club?"

"They want to cancel the Winter Carnival. *Cancel* it. Cancel my first and *last* act of extracurricular leadership and nullify the entire reason I ran for junior class student council representative and gave that ridiculous speech that still makes me break out in hives if I think about it too much."

"And ruin your chance to get Martin Shaddox to turn straight and decide to make out with high school girls who wear too much eyeliner?" I smile. I'm not overly worried about the church succeeding in canceling the Winter Carnival. The carnival is a tradition at Gordon High that school board members have fond memories of, and many businesses in the community sponsor booths and events on the midway, along the shore of Sterling Lake.

"He is *bi*, for your information, and I wear exactly the right amount of eyeliner." Kayla glares at me with her raccoon eyes. "And yes. Exactly so. And you *must* make them stop."

1. The three words that best describe you ...

I find out on the first day of the New Year that I am the least interesting person I know.

Okay. So there's this stupid survey that Kayla sent me. Everyone on my friends list is doing it—tagging each other, competing to be the coolest, the wittiest, the craziest, the wildest. Even my kid sister Dicey's answers are more original than mine, and she's only thirteen. She has her horseback riding and her spelling bees or whatever. What do I do? Or, maybe more accurately, what do I do that is only mine?

I frown at the screen. I've been stuck on the first question forever. *What have you done this year that you have never done before?* There's Kayla's answer, bold and sassy in front of me. Kayla, who not only got her own car (okay, so it's an old hearse, painted purple), but also lost her virginity *and* got to go cliff-diving in Jamaica for her dad's wedding (okay, so the virginity thing sounds like it wasn't all that great, and now she has to put up with the evil stepmother, but *still*).

Looking at her answers on this survey, I feel less like her best friend and more like an inexplicably drab accessory.

"Cassandra, let's go. We'll be late. And what are you doing on that computer again? I know you've been on longer than an hour today."

Yes, my mother still restricts my computer use, as though I'm in preschool. I had a tiny hope that some things would change when I turned seventeen—maybe my parents would start treating me like an almost-adult—but so far it's been almost twenty-four hours and nothing has changed.

"Yeah, I'm logging off."

Dicey sticks her tongue out at me, but when Mom looks over, she's prim as can be, her pink leather Bible carrier clutched to her chest. "What about Eric?" she says, bouncing on her heels. "Aren't we waiting for him?"

Mom's lips purse together, a sure sign she's lying. "Eric doesn't feel well this evening, honey. We'll go without him this time."

Yeah right. Okay, stupid Internet survey. What's one thing I've done this year that I've never done before? How about walking in on my brother giving his boyfriend a blow job? No need to wonder why Eric doesn't feel like sitting through Fire and Brimstone Hour three times a week at the Joyful News Bible Church.

"Let's go, Cass." Mom hands me my church coat, a navy blue wool with silver frog fasteners up the front that makes me look about twelve. "Don't forget your Bible like last time." I nod. My Bible is safely ensconced on the bookcase beside

my bed, where it's been for the last two months. Gathering dust.

Dicey smiles at me, crossing her eyes for the tiniest of moments before trooping out the door after Dad. Dicey's all right, if a little silly. Her presence in my life feels sometimes like a promise of good things to come—like I can see what kind of sister she'll be to me when we're both older, when we'll be better aligned, somehow.

I'm still thinking about the survey when Pastor Fordham stands and launches into his Neverending Sermon. *What was your biggest achievement this year?* Making it through a semester of Trigonometry without asking Ms. Mueller why she doesn't wax her mustache? Speaking a nearly coherent sentence to Flynn Roberts while making eye contact? (Okay, so I actually looked at his eyebrow, and the sentence in question was more of a fragment—"Broken pencil?"—which was fairly idiotic anyway, since he was standing there behind me in line for the sharpener. It was no surprise that Flynn raised an irritated eyebrow and said, "Are you done, then?" instead of whispering seductively the exact time I should ask for a bathroom pass to meet him for a secret make-out session in practice room three, as I may or may not have fantasized about him doing.)

I mean, Eric and I have our foster pigs—right now a sweet pair of sisters named Pumpkin and Nutmeg—but fostering the guinea pigs was Eric's idea, a service project for youth group, actually. And I did manage to get a job of sorts doing the page layout for the church newsletter, but that's only because my mom is computer illiterate. Is that

it, then? My greatest accomplishment this year? Not stellar SAT scores, not building housing for homeless with my bare hands (okay, so Emily Friar probably didn't use her bare hands or even really build anything, but you wouldn't know that by reading her precious, self-congratulatory, long-winded answer to that stupid question), not winning a graphic novel contest like Kayla did and getting flown out to Seattle to meet all the artists she worships. Not making first-chair violin like Cordelia Mandelbraun wrote about, but like, does she realize that nobody in the entire violin section is any good? Most of us only pretend to play.

Dicey's sharp elbow digs into my side and I sit up with a start. "I wasn't sleeping," I whisper-hiss, elbowing her back.

"Daydreaming," Dicey murmurs, her eyes fastened piously on the preacher, or rather on the projection of him that fills the front wall of the church, since Pastor Fordham is prowling the aisles—his holy spittle raining down on the sinners in his wake.

"I'm contemplating various methods of suicide," I whisper back. Dicey smirks and pulls her eyes away from the front for a brief moment.

"You're going to hell, Cass," she says. She's teasing, but she also believes it, a little bit. Or she's too scared to *not* believe.

I nod slowly, looking around the gigantic church. Heads sway rhythmically in time to the preacher's rocking cadence. "I'm already there, Dice," I say.

It's funny, okay? A joke. But in truth, it's like all of this is part of it. Part of this feeling, like nothing I am, nothing I *want*, is coming from me alone, from some essential core of

who I am as a person—what makes me my own. Church is my parents. Church is this family, my sister. My brother, in a way that gets a little messier. But it's not me.

My sister gives me a long look. "Melodrama," she says, her whisper barely audible. "I'm telling you, you need to try out for the school play."

"Girls." Dad glares at us from the end of the pew, but I see the angle of his frown and I can tell it's all for show. He reaches his arm around my mother and squeezes my shoulder lightly, his eyes fastened to the screen ahead. I try to shrug away from his hand—from this patriarchal display of possession. But he's my dad. I watch his profile until Mom glances over and nods pointedly at the screen, where Pastor Fordham speaks fervently about the sinfulness of what he calls sorcery. What normal people call fiction.

2. One thing nobody knows about you …

Terry, our youth group director, sits at the head of the table, clutching his guided discussion questions, ready to lead our discussion on the topic of tonight's sermon: fantasy books. "I've read all of those vampire books," confesses Drew Godfrey, slipping into the chair next to me. Her hair, as usual, is not quite clean.

I force myself to smile. Terry notices I've "forgotten" my Bible once again. The muscle beneath his eye pulses twice, rapidly, and his mouth turns down.

"We can share," Drew says quickly. She scoots her chair a few inches closer, her elbow brushing mine. I try not to recoil.

"It's okay. I'm an auditory learner." One hour of this, followed by cookies and paper cups of warm, watery Kool-Aid and I can go home. One hour. Anyone can endure one hour, right?

Terry directs the discussion toward the "literature" that Pastor Fordham referenced in his message. A few kids, Drew

included, tentatively defend the vampire books, and they talk for what feels like forever about wizards or maybe werewolves.

I don't know. I don't read those books. I don't read much at all beyond what we're forced to read for English class, not anymore. I start books sometimes, and it's not that I don't like reading, not exactly, but it messes with my head, with my feelings. With *me*—I get all tangled up in the head of this character, and let's face it, it's not all fun and games to be a character. I hate the way my thinking starts to fall into the patterns of the book, like I'm nothing on my own. Books trick me into caring for someone—someone who isn't even real—and then *bam,* awful things happen to this fake person, to me, and there I am, feeling real grief for a made-up sorrow, a tragedy built of words. Kayla's always talking about how great it is to lose herself in her books, but I worry. If I lose my*self,* what will be left?

I barely follow the discussion, but Terry wins, or whatever. Yay for the righteous. Magic—real or imaginary—is a tool of the devil. Reading about it is a step toward the lip of a gaping chasm of debauchery. A slippery slope of sin. Terry adopts a particularly ominous tone as he describes the dangerous places an unsuspecting teen could find herself in if she "opens the door to these terrible temptations."

First, unsuspecting young people might start reading vampire books. The power of darkness consumes them, and they become unable to tell right from wrong. They begin disrespecting elders, believing themselves to be in possession of power and wisdom, believing themselves knowledgeable beyond guidance. They dress and talk inappropriately. Before

you know it, a silly, wish-fulfillment story about a sexy vampire leads the vulnerable youth to kill puppies and drink their blood, basically. Whatever. I've heard this tirade before.

What's the biggest risk you've taken this year? Kayla taught herself to skateboard. Dicey helped "break" a colt at her stable. Emily Friar ventured nearly alone into the projects to deliver Christmas donation baskets to the poor. (Okay, so she called it a "socioeconomically disadvantaged neighborhood," and seriously, Emily, what do you think this is, Chicago? As if there's a place in Sterling Creek that could be considered truly dangerous.) But really, what risks do I take? I search my memory for daring endeavors and come up empty.

"But don't you guys think that God would be willing to forgive someone for reading a book about vampires, as long as that person, like, *knew* it was fake? Like, that it's just a story?" Drew leans forward over the table, toward the rest of the group, and I can almost feel her earnestness like the scrub of a washcloth on my morning face. I guess I admire her, a little, for at least asking the questions. She's not afraid of Terry, with his watery eyes and unwavering stare. So even Drew Godfrey takes more risks than I do.

"But why read such stories?" Another girl speaks up, her voice so breathy and sweet that I imagine she must sit in front of her mirror practicing, watching her eyes widen in the perfect semblance of purity and innocence. "Why fill your mind with evil when you could read stories about God's love?"

I don't remember exactly when I stopped believing. It wasn't like one day I was this earnest girl and the next I was transformed into an evil atheist. It was more like a gradual

realization that I only believed in a sort of safety-net kind of way. Like, if all else fails and it turns out there is a God, my ass will be covered. Okay, so I'm pretty sure that's not going to fool Him. Or Her. It? Whatever.

I still don't quite know what to do with this, though—with my lack of belief. It's not like I'm going to advertise it. I'm the only one in my family who isn't fully convinced that God exists, and I wonder sometimes, why didn't it stick for me? I was only nine when we started coming here, and I know I believed back then, and even before that, when we were normal Lutherans like everyone else.

I think my parents assume that none of us remember when the baby got sick and Mom spent all those months crying, and then when it was over, we were all wrapped up in this Joyful News business—wrapped up with the kindness and the consolation and the community and the prayers—wrapped up snug like being trapped in the sheets after a feverish dream. At least, that's how it sometimes feels to me. My parents don't ever talk about it, in any case. But they're happy, so I sit here in youth group, and even though I do stupid stuff like leaving my Bible at home, I generally try not to make waves.

Still, when this girl across the table speaks, with her baby voice and her eyes all shining with faith, I almost can't keep myself from taking her by her rounded shoulders and shaking her, hard. I can't explain the desire, and of course I don't do it. I can't. I bite the inside of my cheek and keep quiet. Like usual.

3. If you could change one thing...

Eric's the only one who ever knocks on my bedroom door. Dicey acts like it's her room too, and Dad never comes in; he sends Mom. Mom's a total barger.

"Hey," Eric says. He leans on the door frame with his hands in the pockets of his jeans, waiting until I motion him in before he crosses the threshold.

"Hey," I say, handing Pumpkin over to him. I scoop Nutmeg out of her bedding and cuddle her to my chest. The guinea pig makes soft happy noises in my arms. "Missed you in youth group. Had to sit by the Shrew."

He smiles a little, but his gray eyes are serious. "Drew's all right, you know? I mean, she needs to learn how to dress. And fix her hair. And—"

"And stop smelling like a linebacker after a long game?"

"Cass." He points to his *What Would Jesus Do?* bracelet.

I roll my eyes. "Fine, I'll be nice."

Eric and I have both known Drew practically all our lives,

like everyone else in Sterling Creek, and to be honest, even when she was little she was the kind of kid who walked around with a target on her head. The girl who never gets any of the jokes but laughs anyway. The one who makes strange and fairly unbelievable claims about her family and defends the lies staunchly when she is found out. Oh, and then she used to have this tic; maybe she still does, I don't know. She'd lick her lips, top and bottom, after almost every word she spoke, her mouth ringed by a circle of chapped skin.

"Were Mom and Dad pissed that I stayed home?" Eric sits beside me on the pink carpeting and drops a little blanket over shy Pumpkin as he sets her gently on the floor. Her pink nose twitches adorably, and then she burrows deeper under the blanket where I can't see. I could write about the pigs in my stupid survey, but none of this was my idea. Eric's the one who researched small mammal fostering and how to care for them. He's the one who begged me to help him, who promised to clean all the cages and deal with all the medical needs. Eric's the one who gets to take the credit.

I shrug. "They weren't thrilled, but you know. Mom made excuses and Dad grunted." They're hard on Eric in general, but they wouldn't let me off so easy. Probably, when it comes to him, they've got the sense to know that they don't want to know.

Eric and I haven't talked about the day I came home sick and found him with Gavin. He knows it's not an issue with me. I couldn't be mad at Eric if I tried. We're just ten

months apart, and neither of us can remember life without the other. He knows me—maybe better than I know myself.

"Hey?" He's the only person on earth I could possibly ask. "How would you describe me, you know, like in a couple of words?"

He examines his perfectly shaped fingernails—a neat row of blushing half-moons. "Having an identity crisis, sissy?" He smiles as he says it, but he only calls me sissy when he's feeling protective, big-brotherly. So what's he protecting me from? "Aren't we all supposed to be finding ourselves anyway?" He watches Nutmeg sniff at the edge of Pumpkin's blanket from my cupped hands.

If you were someone else, would you be friends with you? Why?

What do you want people to remember you for?

What do you stand for?

"Eric." He can sense my desperation; I can tell by the way the tip of his tongue slides over the back of his front teeth, lightly grazing the edges. It's one of his tricks for speaking fluency, from his stuttering days.

"Cass."

"Well? You're not helping."

"I'm pretty sure if I help you discover yourself, that actually defeats the purpose of self-discovery." He grins, and this time it's such a smartass grin—I know he's not going to tell me anything.

And...okay. What he says makes sense, especially since

I'm trying to separate who I am from who Kayla is and who Eric is. "I hate it when you're right," I mumble.

"Get used to it." He slips his hand into the pocket of his jeans and pulls out a crumpled twenty-dollar bill. "This is for you, by the way. Or whatever."

"What's this?"

"Birthday." He folds my fingers around the cash. "I wanted to pick something out for you, but I didn't... I wanted you to be able to choose what you wanted. I thought maybe something for the pigs? Or for you. Your choice." He shakes the hair out of his eyes and puts the pig back in the cage almost like he's embarrassed. He couldn't decide on a gift for me. Eric—the pathological shopper—couldn't pick out a gift for his own sister.

I smooth the bill against the floor. Andrew Jackson and his oddly coifed hair look up at me with some kind of challenge. "I'm going to buy something for myself," I say, but so quietly that nobody else can hear. I tuck my chin down into Nut's soft brown fur and breathe in the warm aliveness of her, and I'm a little jealous of her simplicity. A pig never has to find herself. A pig just exists.

Eric closes my door behind him, and I look around my room as if I'm a stranger, a scientist making a hypothesis about the girl who lives in this room. A biographer looking for clues. A big loser discovering herself.

"I'm going to figure this out," I say to Andrew Jackson, who smirks up at me. Nutmeg's happy chickering against my neck gives me strength. It's a promise. I'm going to find myself if the cliché of it kills me. I'll start tomorrow. I'll start with this.

I lean the twenty against my alarm clock as a reminder from Right This Moment Cassandra to Sometime Tomorrow Cassandra. A reminder of how things are going to change.

4. Your best friend
would say you are …

Kayla won't give me a ride to school, although it's what the best friend with the car (okay, hearse) is supposed to do, right? She's supposed to pull up and honk, with the music blaring, ready with gossip to report or homework to copy or a crazy madcap plan to drive across the country instead of going to school today. That's how this is supposed to work. Except I live, according to Kayla, "in God's Armpit," so until Mom and Dad give in and let me get my own wheels, it's the bus for me, waiting at the same stop as my little sister. Eric's (boy) friend Gavin picks him up every morning like a best (boy) friend should, except my parents won't allow the whole pull-up-to-the-curb-and-honk business.

Morning Prayer Circle.

How I wish I were making this shit up.

Dicey squeezes my right hand. "Thank you, God, for the first day back. Please help us remember how to listen and

obey our teachers, and please be with our teachers, too, as they get back into the swing of things."

"Your turn, Cassandra."

My eyes are open. The usual smile has settled over Mom's features, and I hate this moment. "Pass." I've passed every morning for almost two years now.

"Maybe tomorrow you'll find Jesus in your heart, princess." She says the same thing every time. Her smile dims the same way, too. She never opens her eyes.

I don't answer. I never do. (Boy)friend Gavin is on my left, his hand warm and dry—his palms are never anxious and sweaty like mine. He sighs that breathy little sigh like every morning and says his "thank you" and "please" and all that. He plays it safe, but I know how his other hand clutches at my brother's fingers. I know the twisted yearning of their grasp.

"Amen," says my father. He exhales, an audible whisper of breath that carries his love and his loss and his hope up to heaven.

"Amen," says everyone else. I suck my bottom lip inside my mouth to keep it still.

In God's Armpit. Because of this, I have to ride the stupid bus.

5. Your favorite after-school activity…

Kayla holds one index finger in front of my face. I yawn. "Hear me out before you say no," she says.

"Lemme put my stuff away."

She removes her finger but doesn't step away from the locker we share.

"Come on, Kayla, the stupid bus was late. If I'm tardy for homeroom, Ms. Franklin will make me come in during lunch."

"Listen, though. I need a favor." Kayla always needs a favor. And I always do what she needs because… well, why not? She's my best friend.

"Yeah, and I need to put my crap in the locker." I try to shove her out of the way, but K's like twelve feet tall and made of granite. Okay, so she's really an inch shy of six feet tall and supermodel thin. Still, I can't move her.

"You're so hilarious when you're irritable, Midget." She smirks, folding her arms across her chest.

Midget. As Kayla makes a big show of looking over the top of my head like she can't even see me, I push her with my backpack. "Are you going to stop bullying me and tell me about your stupid favor so I can crush your fragile dreams and get to my freaking homeroom already?"

She rolls her eyes, which are thickly lined in black. "Bullying, *right*. You're such a retard, Cass." She steps aside, barely.

"Midget? Retard? Seriously?" I shove past her. The lock spins beneath my fingers. "What's next? You gonna start calling me gay too, like we're in middle school?"

She smiles. "I need you to do page layout for the school newspaper."

I look up—she's serious. "What happened to what's-her-face?" As if I don't know her name like everyone else in the entire school. (Okay, so I usually call the whole group of them the Vomit Vixens, and I know that's insensitive, but it's not my fault Jenny's got an eating disorder. It's not like snide nicknames between me and Kayla are injuring her popularity.)

"Jenny Hilderman?" Kayla lowers her voice. "Treatment," she whispers. "They're saying eight weeks minimum. Cass, they need you. I told them you're a wiz at page layout."

Them. She means the senior editorial staff, who are somehow the most influential people at our high school despite what seems to me to be an obvious lack in important traits. Like... the human emotions of empathy and compassion. And blemishes. And body fat.

The Gordon High Gazette is actually kind of a big thing. Like, adults read it. I'm not sure why, except maybe there isn't really any other kind of local paper and the editorial staff of

the GHG is … well, *selective* about who gets to write for them. Annika Nielson and Britney Summers know everyone's business. And they know how to make it into a good story.

"No way would they let me do that. I have no experience." Really, I do. It's just not the kind of experience I want anyone to know about. The church newsletter. My church has a reputation for being weird and controversial—the kind of thing that Britney and Annika would definitely turn their nose up at. Still, K's right that this could be a great opportunity if I'm interested in the newspaper—get on the staff as a junior, maybe even get an editorial position by my senior year.

So, am I interested in the newspaper? It would look good on my college applications, if nothing else. Which … well, it would make my parents happy. But is it what I want? I put my hand into my pocket, feeling the edge of the twenty-dollar bill, my promise to discover myself.

Kayla snaps her gum, twice. "Cass, they're desperate. Not one of those bitches can run a freaking computer, so I told them about that bulletin thing you do at church. Come on." Not even looking back to see if I'll follow, she starts down the hall. My homeroom is in the opposite direction. I stand helplessly looking after her for a moment. She's a formidable sight, it's true—ever since she grew out of that slouching phase in eighth grade—and I can only withstand the tug for a moment before I'm sprinting down the hallway after her, a trailing puppy skidding on the wet tile floor.

"Kayla, I'm gonna be late again!" Whine, whine. Follower Cassandra is a follower. Sigh. I trot up beside her. "Seriously,

K, I gotta go if you want to see me at lunch. Franklin's going to—"

"You must be Cassie!"

"It's soooooo good to meet you!"

Squealing. Cooing. These girls are like rabid or something. They pretty much attack me when I reach the top of the junior stairs. Annika Nielson and Britney Summers claw at me enthusiastically with their bubble-gum-pink fingernails, smother me with their perky perfume. I pull back, stumbling into Kayla, who steps to the side and lets me fall. The tardy bell rings, and I go down.

I mean, for real. I'm so overcome by the fawning attention of the senior editors of *The Gordon High Gazette* that I fall on my ass and slither down seven marble steps on my backside right in front of everyone.

"OMG, Cassie, are you okay?" Britney scurries down the stairs and hovers over me on the landing, her fringe of perfect blond hair hanging in my face. She actually says "oh em gee." And she calls me Cassie. Ew.

"I'm soooooo sorry!" squeals Annika, directing people to pass around me.

"We'll take you to the nurse!"

I scramble to my feet, but my butt really hurts, and I can barely stand up straight. "No, I'm okay, it's just..." I look for Kayla, but she's nowhere. The final bell rings. Pain shoots up my spine. I try to laugh, but it's unconvincing.

"Cassie, you could have a broken tailbone!" Annika's eyes are wide, each thick, curled lash visible. "My neighbor broke

her tailbone ice skating once, and she had to carry around a little blow-up donut pillow for, like... *ever.*"

Britney gathers my books from the floor. I try to help her, but a sensation like a scalpel slicing open my spinal column from the bottom up stops me. "Well..." At least it would get me a pass into homeroom. "Okay. But I don't really think I broke my ass." I wince. "God, I hope not."

"Wow, Cassie, you say 'God'? I didn't think people who go to your church would say that," says Britney, her face a caricature of surprise.

"And 'ass.'" Annika's eyes are wide, too, but there's something else there. Admiration. For swearing? How lame is that.

I roll my eyes. "Yeah, I'm a real believer... in the idea that words are words, you know?" I limp toward the nurse's office, flanked by the two perkiest girls I've ever met. They link arms behind my back, practically forcing me to lean on them for support on the walk to the nurse. At least I can't smell any vomit on their breath.

6. Your most embarrassing moment...

The nurse's eyes are bored. "Do you want to ice it?" she says. No inflection. No concern. Thank god she doesn't want to examine it, is all I can think.

"Uh, sure." I look around. "Like, can I stay here?" I'm not wild about the idea of icing my ass in homeroom. Besides, I'm not sure I can make it up the stairs at the moment.

"Do you have one of those blow-up donut pillows?" Annika leans over the nurse's desk, her face serious. "She could have broken her tailbone. I mean, I watched her hit, and she hit hard. The whole floor shook."

Was that a crack about my weight? Because, whatever. I'm perfectly happy with my body. Okay, so maybe not my broken ass. At least I'm not a Vomit Vixen. Their newspaper may look good on my college applications, but is it worth this? Is it worth this to *me,* to Cassandra?

"No, we don't have any of those," says the nurse. She

sighs. "Look. You ladies need to head to class. You're already tardy."

"*What?* We were helping our friend get here after she fell! You *have* to give us a pass to homeroom." Britney is indignant. I can see her writing up the story now—a shockingly honest exposé on the woeful state of the health care system at Gordon High.

The nurse sighs again, dragging a small blue pad of passes out of the drawer of her desk. "You could *ask*," she says, her cursive angry and cramped.

"And you could take some lessons in bedside manner," snaps Britney.

The nurse doesn't respond; in fact, she looks past Britney as though she's not standing there. Then her apathy slips away into a warm concern, and she stands up and starts toward the door. "Oh, Drew honey, you poor thing. Need your pills again today?" Am I imagining the smug look the nurse points at the perky twins? "I'll get you a glass of water right away, hon, and let me know if you need anything else."

Seriously? Drew is here? Eff my life, I can't escape this girl.

"Hi, Cassandra," she says. Her voice is small and her eyes dart over at Britney and Annika nervously. "Are you all right?"

I smile. "Yeah, I fell on the stairs in the junior hall." *Lame.*

"Drew Godfrey?" Annika's voice is syrupy. "How *are* you?"

Drew's answering smile is thin but hopeful. "I'm okay," she says. "It's just…normal stuff." She waves a pudgy hand in the air aimlessly. For a moment her sleeve falls up around her elbow, and the skin on her arm is red and scabby. Quickly her

fingers tug the sleeve back down, over the backs of her hands. I try to remember if I've ever seen her arms before.

"Oh, *good*," says Annika, smiling even more. "I was worried for a minute that you might have head lice again." She and Britney take the blue pass and they both waggle their fingers at me. "See you soon, Cassie!" they say in perky harmony.

"Sorry you got injured on the stairs!" says Annika.

"Maybe you should sue the school," says Britney. "They totally didn't have a wet floor sign out!" And then they're gone. And Drew and I sit here in the hard plastic chairs, both of us nursing our humiliation in silence.

"I never had head lice," she says after a while.

Okay. I try to think of something to say. "So you're taking some pills?" Obviously, I don't think long enough before speaking.

Drew is one of those people who never look you directly in the eye; instead, her eyes search and search along my hairline like a confused newborn. "It's my eczema," she says. "It's all over my body. It's itchy, and I have anxiety, and then it gets itchier, so then I scratch, and it gets scabby, and that makes me anxious, so I pick at it, and that makes it get itchier." She rubs her hands over her arms.

Gross. I struggle for an appropriate response to this level of oversharing. "Um. That sucks." I mean, it's not like I'm judging her for having eczema. She can't help that, I guess. But ... I don't know. I didn't really need to know about her scabby rash, that's all. I feel terrible, but seriously, do I need to know about anyone's scabby rash? I'm not a freaking dermatologist.

The nurse hands her a paper cup of water, and Drew swallows two pills before her eyes roam my way again. They're muddy eyes, a leftover color like dried paint stuck to the art room tables, a color without any brightness in it.

"Yeah," she says. "It does suck." She crushes the paper cup in her fist. "But I *never* had head lice."

7. In your spare time…

The pain is less by math class, and my butt is only slightly sore by the time English rolls around. This is the first class I have with Kayla—well, the only class, actually—and I'm pissed. I accost her at the door with a barrage of complaints.

"How could you leave me like that? You disappeared. You totally dodged out of the way and let me fall down the stairs, Kayla, and then you were… gone. Do you realize I may have broken my fucking tailbone?"

"Cassandra," says my English teacher, stepping between us on his way into the classroom. "I don't need to hear that kind of language in my workplace." He raises an eyebrow, but his tone is indulgent. He's not the type to get hysterical about an F-bomb, luckily. Ms. Franklin would have emailed my mother. Which… well, I'd rather not contemplate that scene. She'd probably make me go in for counseling with Pastor Fordham or something. I shudder at the thought.

"Oh, relax," says Kayla, sweeping past me into the room. "It's not like I *meant* to abandon you." She shrugs. "The tardy

bell rang. I thought you were right behind me. How was I supposed to know you'd go over backwards?"

Mr. Dawkins stands at the front of the room and claps his hands twice, his customary cue that we should shut up and get down to business.

Right. So she's trying to get me to believe she didn't *notice* that I fell down half a flight of stairs? I make my way to my assigned seat, which is inconveniently across the room from Kayla's, and take out my notebook. She's not going to brush me off like this, not about this. She dragged me all the way across the school and then left me to die on the stairs. I start scribbling a note, my hand quickly cramping up from my angry grip on the pen.

"Cassandra, really. You're not impressing me today." He keeps his voice quiet—Mr. D is not the type of teacher who believes in public humiliation—but he holds his hand out for the note. "You know my thoughts on notes. No reading, no writing, no folding, no passing." He leans in closer. "Please, Cass. Can you put this out of your mind, at least for the next fifty minutes?"

I nod and hand him the page from my notebook, grateful to him for immediately crumpling it up into a little ball. And then, when he actually walks across the room and drops the ball on Kayla's desk, I'm blown away. I see him lean down and speak to her, and she nods, shoving the paper into her pocket without reading it.

"*I celebrate myself, and sing myself,*" says Mr. D, in that voice that means he is quoting some writer he loves. "*And what I assume you shall assume.*"

"Narcissistic much?" mutters the boy next to me. He doodles in the margin of his literature book with a heavy black pen. I turn my head, startled to hear, for the first time, the voice of this kid I've been sitting next to for weeks.

"Exactly so, Darin," says Mr. Dawkins with a smile and a nod. "And many people at the time were shocked, outraged by Whitman's poetry. They called it indecent." Mr. D continues reading from the poem, cradling the heavy textbook in his arms as he stalks around the room, quietly tapping the page of the books of students who aren't listening as he walks by, never pausing in his reading. He drops a clean sheet of drawing paper on Darin's desk as he strides past. Darin shrugs and moves his doodling to the approved medium without a word.

"Whitman talks about celebrating himself, and indeed the speaker in this poem is named Walt Whitman, but the details here are not all autobiographical." Mr. D jots some phrases on the white board and I copy them into my notebook: *Praise of the Individual. The Collective Experience. Democracy. The Boundaries of Self and World.*

Poetry is pretty, but I'm not very good at making sense of it on my own. Luckily, although Mr. D wants us to think for ourselves, with a little prompting we can always get him to tell us his own thoughts. Which I then write down and regurgitate in a similar form on the tests, in the essays. Easy peasy as long as I take notes. As long as I know the requirements, I can manage to keep straight A's.

"Instead of the usual analytical essays, I thought it would be exciting for us to write some poetry this semester," Mr. Dawkins says, turning from the board to face us. He claps his

hands again for emphasis. "You will each write your own 'Song of Myself'—celebrating yourselves and singing yourselves."

He goes on to explain the requirements and things, but my brain screeches to a halt. Not this. I can't write poetry. This is American Literature, not Creative Writing. We're supposed to read things and write essays on them and take tests. Things I can manage. Things I can control. Around me, people are opening their notebooks, chewing on pens, scribbling away. I can't catch my breath. I don't touch my pen.

"Cassandra?" Mr. D taps my notebook, where I've dutifully written all the notes, up to the point where he gave us the assignment.

"I can't write poetry," I say.

"Of course you can," he says.

No. I can't. "Well, I can't write poetry about myself."

"Of course you can."

I sigh. This is so stupid. I push my open notebook away from me. Not much, a couple of millimeters or so, but it's enough to make my point.

"Well, what are you interested in? Do you have any hobbies? Goals? Special abilities or talents?"

I shake my head. What, am I supposed to collect butterflies or something? The pigs—that's Eric. The music I listen to—that's Kayla. The clothes I like—that's Kayla. Goals for the future—Mom and Dad. Church? That's … not something I can write about.

"Sports?" Mr. D sounds so hopeful.

I laugh. "I played softball one summer in eighth grade."

"Well! Write about that!"

"So I should celebrate how my own teammates chanted 'easy out' every time I got up to bat?" It's a true story, but even then I was careful not to let it be important to me. *I'm not good at sports*. I checked the box and moved on.

Mr. Dawkins can't help chuckling. "Cass. What do you like to do in your spare time? How would you describe yourself? What are you proud of? What makes you different from everyone else in this room?"

"I—" I don't know. I don't *know*. I look around the room, and it's like … it's like the stupid survey all over again. Desperation crawls up out of some hole deep inside me, and this awful hiccupy thing happens inside my lungs that makes me gulp for air like a guppy. I can't breathe. In my spare time? I go to the mall and pretend to shop. I go to church and pretend to listen. I go to football games and pretend I know the score. I asphyxiate in the middle of English class. Mr. D takes a step back.

"Cassandra?" He does that weird crouching thing next to my desk that teachers do when they want to ask you a personal question or correct your spelling. "Are you okay?"

Oh yeah, totally. I cover my gasping mouth with one hand and nod to say I'm okay. Of course I'm okay.

"I don't understand, Cass. You *must* have something to write about. Something about you that's special." It's like he can't get past that question, like he can't believe a person could possibly exist who doesn't have a hobby or a talent or a passion or whatever.

"I'm not special," I whisper. I can breathe again, in shallow little puffs, but I can't look at him or anyone else. I'm not

sure if he hears me. He continues to survey me, searching for substance.

"Do you like to read, maybe? Write? Draw? Go fishing? Ski? Play Monopoly?" I shake my head no. "Start fires? Mutilate kittens?"

I can't stop myself from smiling. The desperation passes. Around me, most people are bent over their papers, laboring over their songs. They talk and laugh as they work, and a few of them are reading each other's poems out loud. Teasing. Arguing. Asking for help. Mr. D nods to a group in the corner by the computers. "Be right there," he says.

"I'll be okay." My voice is still stuck in whisper mode, but my lungs at least seem to have regained normal functionality.

To my horror, he reaches out his bony English-teacher hand and pats my shoulder, and then he withdraws his hand and shifts his weight on his heels, searching for a better view of my eyes. Even in the noisy classroom, I can hear his knees popping as he crouches there.

"Cassandra. There's something inside of you that's worth celebrating, that's worth singing about. If you think about it long enough, you'll find it."

"If I think about it too long, I'll fail this assignment," I mutter. The due date looms from the white board. Two weeks from tomorrow, also midterms.

"It's not about the assignment," he says, hauling himself to his feet. "It's about life." He turns toward the group of kids who are waving him down from across the room.

"But..." *Life.* The panic returns. "What if there's nothing?

What if there's nothing to write about?" He can't leave me. I can't write this poem.

"Well, I guess you'll have to make something up then," he says, in a tone that implies he's done all he can do for me.

Make something up? "Something for my poem?" I persist, half-rising out of my chair, as if to follow him.

He shrugs. "Or something for life," he says.

I sit. *Make something up.*

Darin pauses in his doodling and looks at me through his shaggy bangs. "It's okay," he says. He looks like he's about to elaborate, but then he tosses his hair back. "I mean, I would read a poem about mutilating kittens." And then he laughs, but it's a nice laugh—not a mocking laugh and not the creepy kind of laugh that would make me suspect there was some truth in the statement.

"Thanks, I'll keep that in mind." My voice is shaky, but his eyes are a steady gray, and he smiles at me.

"Relax, Cassandra. It's a stupid assignment." He hands me his paper, which I can see now has a few lines scribbled in among the sketches: *I celebrate myself, and sing myself, but I won't let you watch while I play with myself.*

"You're disgusting," I say, sliding the paper back across the desk. My cheeks tingle a little. I hope I'm not blushing.

"It's what makes me special," he says, and then he does the weirdest thing. He reaches across the table and takes my hand, but before I can pull it away, he draws this stupid little smiley face on my index finger with his pen. And then he holds up his hand—each finger has a little face like mine— and he waves at me.

All I have to do is smile, lift that one finger, and wave back. The bell rings, and my hands are still clutched into fists in my lap as he tosses his hair back and stands. "Lighten up," he says. And then he's gone.

8. The biggest risk you've taken...

I'm not sure I've ever gone to the mall alone. Eric's twenty is in my pocket and it makes me mad. I can't believe he couldn't pick something out for me, for his own sister. I want to walk directly over to my favorite things and say, "Look, this is what I like, this is the kind of gift you should get me." But as I stand here in the crowded food court in the middle of the Sterling Creek Shopping Center, I can't even decide which direction to go, which store to walk into, much less what I want. I'm not sure I know how to even walk without Kayla leading the way.

Make something up. I can do this. Out of habit, I turn left, toward the music store and the store where the skater kids hang out, but I can't get myself to go all the way into the skater shop. I flip my hand listlessly through the rack of black T-shirts near the door and pretend like I'm checking out the orange suede sneakers on display. I feel so dumb. I don't know these people. A boy with a pink-and-blond faux hawk and

black eyeliner nods, but he doesn't smile. I can feel him judging me. I tug the sleeves of my sweatshirt over my fingers and wish for Kayla, for her confidence. The boy scowls, his brow heavy with metal barbells.

Okay. So not that store. I keep moving, roaming the corridors like a tourist in a foreign city, my eyes wide and uncertain. Colors swirl around me—an endless stream of trendy fashions spinning on racks and colorful banners proclaiming sale prices and neon signs and television monitors with music videos flashing—herds of people pass me, their conversations loud and unintelligible to my dizzy ears. I stumble a little, and even the air feels strange surrounding me, artificial and busy, too full of motion. I stop and lean against the wall for a minute. When I look down, there's that little smiley face on my fingertip. *Lighten up.*

I laugh. Indeed. A deep breath, and I'm ready to dive in again, into the chaos. *Make something up.* Stupid self-discovery.

I'm sure I wouldn't have seen them if I'd been with Kayla, or with anyone else. There are things you see when you're with your friends and things you see when you're alone.

I wander into the bookstore—the big one that my mother hates because they came into the mall and drove out the smaller chain that was there already, leaving only the used-books place downtown. Like I said, I'm not a big reader, but sometimes, I can't explain why, I just like to go into a bookstore and look at the covers. I trace my fingers across the paperbacks on the display tables, all the different colors and textures and typefaces. Even though their stories don't appeal

to me, I can see why people want books, why they want to hold them in their hands and stack them on shelves and run their thumbs over the edges of the rough-cut pages.

I find the cards in the bargain aisle, half price. I'm not sure I would have picked them up if Pastor Fordham hadn't just been talking about the tarot, about witchcraft and sorcery and the dangers of the occult. It's kind of funny, and I wonder what he'd think if he knew that his warnings against the evil are what draw me to it.

The box is heavy in my hands, compact and wrapped tightly in plastic; I can see the bright spine of the guidebook and the dense rectangle of the deck itself. I've never even seen tarot cards before. On the front of the box is a picture, bright and alluring, a picture of the Fool. Like the book covers, this artwork captures my eyes, holds them hostage. I can't put it down, this box of sin.

"Thank you, Eric," I find myself whispering. Sometimes I do that—I speak my thoughts out loud, or maybe I'll move my mouth to the words in my head. It catches me off-guard every time, and I look around the store to make sure nobody heard, but I'm all alone here, clutching this secret. My birthday present. My riskiest moment.

I pay for the cards, staring down at the counter as I shove the twenty toward the guy at the till. I half expect him to narrow his eyes at me, maybe quote Scripture or something. Possibly pick up a phone and dial my mother. Instead, he smiles and taps the spine of the book.

"I like this one," he says. "Good for beginners, but it doesn't talk down to you."

I don't answer. I don't talk to people who work cash registers, not because I don't want to but because my brain can only process one thing when I'm standing in line to pay for something, and that one thing is handing over my money. Sometimes I leave the checkout lane and hold a conversation in my head—the conversation I should have had if only I could pretend to be a human for a minute.

I feel my face heat up. "Thanks," I mumble. I grab the bag off the counter and duck back into my fluffy down jacket on my way out the door.

My plan is to walk home from the mall, which isn't a perfect plan, but it's not like I have options. This town is too small to have a city bus, and my parents won't even let me get my stupid license yet, much less a car. It's not that far and I've walked it before, but it's already dark, and the wind is colder than I expected. The heavy lump in the plastic bag bounces against my leg as I half walk, half jog along the highway. Okay, so "highway" is an exaggeration, but it's the main road that cuts through town.

I'm crossing at the second light when I hear the honk— not an angry, get-out-of-my-way kind of honk, but more like a hey-I-know-you tap on the horn. Still, it startles me, and I spin around to see a semi-familiar minivan pulling over to the curb and a manically waving woman at the wheel. Mrs. Johnson, my old Sunday School teacher. Hallelujah. She leans over and pops the passenger door open.

"Cassandra, good gracious, climb in, darling! What are you doing out here, walking in this weather?"

I slide up onto the seat, tucking the bag underneath my

feet. "I—I was hanging out at the mall." I stammer a bit as I search my brain for an appropriate response. If she asks me what I bought, what do I say? Besides, there's no "if." She will totally ask.

"Whatcha got in the bag there, honey? Buying books for school?" Mrs. Johnson leans toward me though she keeps her eyes on the road. One mile, maybe a little less, and we'll be at my house. I slide my feet backward, wishing I could make the bag disappear.

"Oh, you know. I have … an English project." True, in a way. Won't hold up under scrutiny though. "And how about you?" I stumble into a subject change. Talking to adults can be so freaking awkward. "Did you enjoy your holidays?" Holidays, yes. Totally safe topic.

"A blessed time, to be sure," she says with a happy sigh. "The kids all came home, except for Mark, of course. You know he's doing missionary work in Ecuador, right?" She chuckles. "Oh, silly me, of course you know. You were at the sending service, weren't you?"

As if she doesn't know. At the Joyful News Bible Church, church attendance is a matter of great importance. I would bet that Ruth Marie Johnson could tell me exactly how many times I've missed services since my baptism.

I nod. "Oh, yes, it was a beautiful send-off. Is he doing well?"

"Very well, hon. Doing the Lord's work." Mrs. Johnson clears her throat and my stomach plunges. I can tell that something is coming—something tart and slightly unpleasant, which she will try to roll in sugar before serving to me. "But

tell me, Cass. You can tell me. Is something wrong at home?" Her foot lets off the accelerator a little as we approach the turn-off for God's Armpit, delaying the end of this conversation.

I shake my head and smile, my right hand sweating around the plastic handle of my shameful birthday burden. "No, everything's great at home!" My voice is bright and chirpy, oozing with happiness. A baby bird on Prozac. Three blocks. Two and a half. The car slows down, impossibly slow. A toddler on a big wheel could pass us up.

"It's just…" She lowers her voice and leans closer until I have no idea how she can see out the windshield. "We've noticed your brother has been staying home sick an awful lot. I know your family has been through a lot already, so we've been worried… is there… something *serious*?"

I scoot a tiny bit closer to the door. One more block. "Oh, no, nothing serious, really." A smile, a nonchalant toss of my hair. Nothing serious, but I also can't let her think he's not coming because he isn't a good churchgoer. "He's got, like, a sinus infection or something? Headaches. Lots of head-aches."

Mrs. Johnson makes a clucking sound and straightens up in her seat. She nods slowly as she makes the turn into my driveway. "He's in our prayers," she says, serious and stern—is it a promise or a threat? "We've been worried about you all."

I have no idea who "we" includes. Has the entire church been worrying about Eric's absence, about the lamb straying from the fold and the family that's failed to shepherd him? Or is this a more personal "we," maybe Mrs. Johnson and God?

I fold the top of the bag down as I switch hands and tug at the door handle, forcing another smile. "Oh, we're fine, Mrs. Johnson, but thanks for your prayers. I'll tell my family you're thinking of us. And thanks for the ride."

I'm out of the car and up the drive before she can respond, praying in my own way that the path to my room will be clear.

9. Something new to you …

When I peel the plastic off the box, I am half expecting the screaming chaos of a legion of demons. That would certainly get my attention. Just because I'm not the world's most faithful flock-member doesn't mean I wouldn't listen if the evidence were in front of me. But the cards slide out of the box without so much as a whisper from the devil, and they feel, in my hands, like any other new deck of cards. Slick and springy under my fingers, and slightly oversized.

I set the cards on the floor, tucked behind an old stuffed pony pillow of mine, and pull Pumpkin out of the pig cage for some floor time. "Hi, girls." I wave my little finger-face at them and imagine that they're amused. Pumpkin squeaks a few times until I get her settled on the floor with a newspaper on top of her head and a treat. For a moment I feel bad about not getting something for the pigs with my birthday money. Still, the deck of cards calls to me from behind the pillow. I take it out and flip through, admiring the pictures.

Despite the seemingly simple artwork—line drawings and what looks like colored-pencil shadings—the pictures are

so compelling. I slide the thin guidebook out of the cardboard sleeve and start looking through it randomly. The meanings read like nonsense to me, strings of simple words. *Prudence. Circumspection. Attraction.* The book lists some of the cards in four suits, like regular playing cards, except the suits are Cups, Wands, Swords, and Pentacles. I frown at that last one. Pentacles—the five-sided star makes my hand shake a little. It looks like a legitimate devil worship symbol.

I pull a card from the deck and try to match it to one of the meanings. It's a picture of three smiling women, each of them holding up a big golden cup. I assume this means it's in the Cups suit, so I look up the three of cups in my book. *Fulfillment and abundance*, it says. I guess that makes more sense when I look at the corresponding picture. The three women are dancing or celebrating, and they have flowers in their hair and bunches of grapes and gourds around them. *Abundance. Fulfillment. Celebration. Partnership. Marriage.* A nice card, this three of cups. I turn over another card.

There's a tap at my door and my heart lurches; my hands race to shove the cards, the book, the box out of sight behind my pony pillow. Pumpkin squeaks in annoyance at my sudden movements.

Of course, it's Eric. Anyone else would already be in here by now, staring at me with shock and horror as I sit here surrounded by sorcery and evil. Maybe this was a bad idea. I'm going to have to be more careful if I want to keep the balance of peace I have going with my family. But there's something about this—my jumping pulse, my flushed cheeks. It's exciting. It's *interesting*. It's all mine.

"Cass?" Eric hovers in the doorway, biting his lip. "You weren't in study hall."

"Went to the mall." I wave him into the room and he pulls the door closed behind him.

"The mall?" He laughs. "Is the Armageddon approaching?" He takes Nutmeg out of her pen and cuddles her close.

"Yeah, pretty much." I feel my eyes slide over to the pony pillow. "I bought myself a birthday present."

"That was lame of me, Cass. I didn't mean to make you pick out your own present, but...I don't know. Things change, and I probably haven't done the best job keeping up with you and your interests. I know I've been...preoccupied with Gavin. Did you get something for the girls?" He tries to wave Nut's little paw at me, but she squeaks.

"She'll nip you." I turn my hands over on my lap, searching for a hangnail or something to worry. Again, the smiley face grins up at me, and for some reason I think of Darin's eyes. My heart makes a crazy move, like a fish flopping in the bottom of a boat, and I have to catch my breath. "Apparently I haven't done the best job of keeping up with my own hobbies and interests lately," I say. "I was thinking that a lot of what I'm interested in is really me following along with your interests, or Kayla's. So I'm taking up a new hobby." I force my voice to levels of brightness that rival my Mrs. Johnson tone. Maybe I *should* try out for drama.

"Oh yeah?"

"Can you keep a secret?"

"Cass, of all people."

"Well, maybe there's, like, a limit on secrets. Too many and you pop like a balloon, you know. Ka-pow."

He shifts on the carpet, and this time it's Eric who examines his hands, as if he could ever discover an imperfection. "About that," he says.

"About what?"

"About my secrets."

I shake my head. "Eric, no. Not yet. Seriously, just get through high school, okay? Go off to the Cities or to Madison, like you planned."

It's too hard, making a change. Here in Sterling Creek, everyone knows you, but they also know all the yous of the past. Yesterday Eric. Fourth-grade Eric, in the neatly tucked white polo in the Christmas show, his palms skimming the legs of his pants. My thoughts stray for a moment to the tarot cards, to my promise. It would be easier to find myself if I could escape the connotations of all those Other Cassandras.

Eric shakes his head. "I've been talking about it."

I take his hand. "I can't..."

I can't protect him from this town, from our church. It's not like there aren't any gay people here in Sterling Creek, Minnesota, but it's no San Francisco either.

"I needed...I needed to talk to someone about my faith, about what's right."

"I can tell you what I think, but you already know I don't buy the idea that God hates gay people," I say. "It doesn't make sense that a loving God would set you up for failure like that. Fall in love, commit a grave sin. I hope you're not talking to Pastor Fordham about all this, because he's the kind of guy

who would send you off to be reprogrammed or something." I shiver. I'm exaggerating, but there's a bit of zeal in our new minister's eyes that makes me nervous.

"Cass. You're not being fair."

"And you're not being logical."

Eric shakes his head. "God doesn't have to be logical. It's all a part of the mystery, little sis." He sighs, as tired as I am of this repeat conversation. "So, what's your secret?" He nods toward the pony pillow.

"No way. You'll tell the God Squad about me and they'll send over an exorcist. Pea soup everywhere. It will completely ruin the décor. Probably better keep it to myself." I feel my eyes dart over to the pillow again, even though I'm willing them not to.

"That bad, huh?" He shoots a hand behind the pony and pulls out the tarot cards. Nutmeg squeaks in alarm. "Cassandra, seriously. Do you know how crazy Mom would go if she saw these?" He drops the box onto my floor as though it burns his hands, and I wonder if maybe there *are* demons, fire and brimstone. Maybe the cards can't hurt people who are already going to hell.

"She's not going to find out." I reach out my finger and touch Nutmeg on the top of her head, the spot between her ears that calms her. I'll have to do a better job of hiding them from Mom than I did hiding them from Eric.

"But if she does."

"She won't. And don't worry. If she does, I'll make sure she knows you had nothing to do with them."

"Because I don't." He stands up. He runs his hands down

the legs of his jeans, the nervous gesture left over from child-hood. "I don't want any part in it."

I stand too, reaching for his arm, but I only catch the edge of his sleeve for a second and then he's halfway across the room. "I could ask the cards about you," I offer. "About your secret." I look at the box on the floor between us. "About how you can tell them."

He stops.

I could do this. Just to see.

"It's only a game, a parlor trick," I continue, picking up the cards and showing them to him. I know he's wavering because his hands are back on his jeans, and I can remember him as a little boy, twisting from side to side in Sunday School as he struggled to recite his weekly verses, his mouth refusing to form the syllables, his hands running lightly up and down across the navy blue corduroy as he squeezed his eyes tightly shut to keep in the tears.

He shakes his head. "I can't, Cass. You know it's not right. Even if you don't believe in sorcery, you have to see that this isn't the kind of decision I should entrust to a deck of cards. It's more important than that."

"What are you going to do, pray over it?"

I don't mean to say it, really. I especially don't mean to sound so sarcastic. Okay, so I wish my brother would see how messed up this whole church situation is. I can't understand his insistence on believing in something that basically con-demns him to a life of suffering or self-denial or whatever. But I do love him, and I try hard to respect the fact that these

beliefs are, for him, very real and reasonable. I try to hold my tongue. Sometimes it slips.

"You can be a real jerk, you know that?" Eric says. He slams my door behind him, but a half second later he opens it again and sticks his head in to glare at me. "This is why I can't talk to you about this. Because you have to act like anyone who believes is completely stupid." He narrows his eyes, and for the slightest of moments I see his mouth working on his words, and I wonder if he's going to stutter.

My stomach clenches. "Eric—" Of course he's not stupid. He's my brother. He's the only one who ever treats me like I have my own thoughts and opinions, or the only one who ever bothers to find out if I do. "I didn't mean—"

"You play your card games, Cassandra. But games can get serious sometimes without much notice. And please. Keep me out of it."

10. If you were to describe your style...

Except for the WWJD bracelets and the fact that we gather together on Wednesdays and Fridays for team-building activities, discussions of "teen issues," and occasional acoustic guitar sing-alongs, the members of my youth group have very little to do with each other outside of church. In Sterling Creek, the Joyful News Bible Church remains a sort of fringe operation —an oddity to the stolid Minnesotans, whose habit of worshipping in the same congregation as their parents and grandparents and great-grandparents means that sometimes there are four or five church services occurring on a single block, several of them the same denomination.

So, we at Joyful News are thrust together not because we are alike but because we are different: mostly newcomers like my family (okay, so in Sterling Creek that means we can't trace our roots back three generations or more; in our case, my parents moved here when Eric was a baby and my mother was pregnant with me), or, in some cases, recent converts to Christianity.

In any case, Drew Godfrey is not my friend, no matter how nice I am to her on Sundays, Wednesdays, and Fridays. If only she would figure this out, youth group might actually be tolerable.

"I heard you got on the newspaper staff," she says, and then she giggles, like it's funny. She pulls the end of her messy ponytail over her right shoulder as she sidles up to me, her fingers twining into the split ends. "That's so cool. I heard Annika and Britney are really exclusive, so, you know? Instant awesome."

See, that's another reason Drew will never be popular. She makes it obvious how much she longs for it—her desperation speaks to those with power over her, makes it clear how easily she could be used.

I turn slightly from her. A normal person would see this, but Drew presses closer. "They barely ever involve juniors on the staff of the paper. They must really like you," she says. "And it's a good thing, you know, to be on the good side of those two."

I remember the way they looked at Drew last week in the nurse's office. "Well, they're pretty desperate for help, what with one of the Vomit—uh, Jenny—in the hospital or whatever. I'm not really on the staff, like writing or anything. I'm just filling in to do the page layout." I edge away from Drew, but she takes a step closer for every step I take back until I'm up against the Kool-Aid table, with no other options besides taking a cup of red sludge for myself and one for Drew.

"Thanks," she says, tipping her cup back and drinking

deeply. "I was, like, dying of thirst for some reason tonight. We had pizza for dinner, so that might be why."

She looks at me for a response, but what is there to say to that? I can't even. I make a sound that I hope seems vaguely agreeable and take a tiny sip out of the cup in my hand, while searching for Eric among the people gathered around the fellowship hall.

"Your hair looks really pretty like that."

"What?" My non-Kool-Aid-bearing hand wanders up to touch the nape of my neck, where I've spiked up the back of my hair with gel. "It's the same as always," I say, and then, almost despite myself, I keep on talking to her. "It's probably time for a new style or something, but I don't know what to do with it." I bring my hand down, uncertain. "I could grow it out, but really, I only like long hair when it's super amazing. Otherwise it's sort of…" I look at her and her sad, dishwater-blond mess. Oh, damn it. I don't really want to be that mean girl, you know?

Drew doesn't notice my jab, or at least her smile doesn't falter as she flips her ponytail back over her shoulder and leans in a little closer, reaching past me for another cup. "No, keep it short," she says. "It emphasizes your face this way. You could actually do some really wild highlights, like… black or red or purple. My mom does a bunch of different colors all the time." She pulls her ponytail again. "She always wants me to do something wild, but… you know. I hate having attention on me." She colors and takes a step back, occupying herself with her cup for a moment, and then she looks up at

me again, but this time her muddy brown eyes are strangely intense.

"Cass? Can I ask you something stupid?" Her cheeks and the hollow of her throat are pink, and I catch a subtle wave of nervous body odor. I look away, my eyes landing at last on Eric, who has noticed my predicament.

He waves. "Time to head out, Cass!" I flash him a grateful smile.

"My brother," I say, moving away from her. "I guess I'll see you Friday."

Drew's face falls. "Oh. Sure," she says, and then she shakes her head quickly. "But wait a sec. I've got... I've got this thing... I was hoping..." She sets her two soggy paper cups on the table and digs in her shoulder bag. "Wait a minute, Cass. Please."

I wait. Of course I do. I'm not a horrible person.

"Will you take a look at it, and maybe, if it's not too stupid, you could pass it on to Annika or Britney? Not, like... not with my name on it, you know. Anonymously. I mean, I'm pretty sure it's totally stupid, but like, maybe you could read it?" Drew takes a final look at the notebook in her hands, and then she tears a page out and hands it to me—pink pen on gray, lined paper, all her i's dotted with tiny circles.

"It's a poem?" Somehow I'm holding it, trying not to seem like I'm actually accepting it. Like I'm going to read it and pass it on to the newspaper, hand it to Britney, to Annika. What if it's terrible? Worse, maybe—what if it's actually good?

"Sort of." Her face is in a deep blush now, and the pungent

smell of her nerves wafts up at me. She smiles, and it's almost painful. "It's this thing I wrote, you know? But like, maybe if it's any good, it could go in the newspaper?"

"Oh, I don't know, Drew. I'm not... I'm not really involved in any of that." I wave the pink scribbles vaguely in front of me, still trying to decline the proffered page.

"Well, maybe you could just... read it then? And if you think it's worth publishing? Maybe..." She's picking at her ponytail again and makes no move to take back the poem, so I fold it in half to keep the pink poetry inside and take an uncertain step away from this awkward exchange.

"Bye, Cass. See you." She nearly whispers the words, into her hair, and I don't quite know what to do.

"Yeah, see ya," I say, and then I nearly bowl Eric over on our way back to the minivan, where we wait for the rest of the family to arrive.

"What was that all about?" His eyes linger on the folded sheet of notebook paper.

"What? Oh, it's nothing." I shove the poem into my coat pocket. *Nothing.*

11. Your definition
of a good friend …

Monday morning is always pure chaos, and I'm already on the stupid bus when I realize I forgot to grab food or money for lunch today. "Beautiful," I mutter, regretting that last punch of the snooze button and the stupid Morning Prayer Circle playacting. Okay, so it's not like I'm going to starve over the course of one day without a lunch, but it's still annoying.

I spent the whole weekend worrying over that stupid Song of Myself assignment, and I've got nothing to show for it. Okay, so it was sort of hard to concentrate on writing when I think I was really waiting on Kayla to call. That's stupid, right? Waiting on her. But we used to do something every Saturday night, and every week she swears that *this* Saturday is going to be the one that we get back to our old routine.

Maybe she'll buy me lunch for once. We used to eat together every day, the two of us, plus Emily and Cordelia and a few others. We used to giggle over inside jokes and squish our chicken-patty buns flat and Kayla would show us

her angsty dinosaur comics and I would tease her until her disdainful-of-everything face would crack into a slow smile. Not anymore, though. Not since she talked Mr. Cavner into letting her lurk in the art grotto, crouching in the dark like a bat with her tortured fountain pen, all misunderstood. I scrunch down into the bus seat. Now Kayla doesn't eat; she lives on charcoal and paint fumes.

I pull my glove off with my teeth and slide my hand into my coat pocket to check for spare change. Maybe I can at least get a candy bar out of one of the vending machines in the student center, if I feel like walking past the stupid football team perched on the ledge throwing out ratings of every girl's ass. Well, it doesn't matter. Nothing but a half-used Kleenex in my pocket. Gross.

I check the other pocket, expecting more of the same. Instead, I pull out Drew's poem and smooth it against my legs, which are braced up against the seatback in front of me. I check to make sure nobody's looking, but everyone on the bus has that Monday morning look, wrapped up in their headphones and sleepy thoughts. I spread the paper out and skim over the loopy pink writing. I was wrong—the i's aren't dotted with circles, they're dotted with tiny hearts. Gag me.

The poem is called "My Imprisoned Heart," and a quick skim tells me all I need to know about this poem: it's grosser than the Kleenex in my other pocket.

"Why do they want to cancel the carnival?" The event kicks off our winter break, which is the first week of February, and the whole community participates in the cross-country ski race around Sterling Lake at the center of town. Instead of classes that Friday, there's ice skating, games, food stands, a bonfire with a big outdoor dance, and this year Kayla's getting this famous illustrator guy to come up from Minneapolis to judge a snow sculpture contest where teams sculpt their favorite comic book heroes. Eric apparently has a team working on a sculpture of Northstar, one of the first openly gay characters. Which is probably not a good idea, but whatever. He's not going to take my advice about anything, obviously.

"Why else? Because it's fun." She stalks off ahead of me toward the school, fleeing the light of the morning sun. "They object to the bonfire, for one thing, or to the dancing happening in conjunction with the bonfire, I don't know. They say it has some kind of pagan significance, and they've also got their undies in a bundle about some of the proposed snow sculptures. Like, of course they're going to be 'scantily clad.' Hello? They're superhuman crime-fighting heroes. Isn't that synonymous with wearing your underwear in public? The church is saying that the school has to have a Bible study or something for kids who choose not to go to the carnival."

"A Bible study? At school?" Um, separation of church and state, how about.

"Oh, I don't know. I don't have all the details, but they're making demands, Cass, and you have to talk to someone over there. I've gone through a lot of trouble to make this all come together. Martin Shaddox is coming all the way up here in the middle of nowhere because of me, and I *cannot* have Jesus on the welcoming committee."

"I'm nobody. Joyful News is not going to listen to me, Kayla. Why don't you get your newspaper friends to—"

"Cassieeeeeeeee!"

"Speak of the devil." Kayla purses her lips around a fresh coat of black lipstick and rolls her eyes.

"You're coming to work at lunch tomorrow, right?" Annika touches my arm, almost possessively. Her perfume is so bright, so instantly recognizably *her*—an exclusive atmosphere that makes me giddy. In spite of my professed scorn for all of the Vomit Vixens, Annika's intoxicating, a little. I imagine what it would be like to have my own scent, a signature in the air around me that would announce to the world who I am. Or maybe to remind myself.

"We have to get this issue ready to go by Thursday," says Britney. Even though both girls want the same thing, her eyes are softer than Annika's, less confident. "You can stay after school on the nights we need help, right?"

"Of course she can! I'll even give her a ride home." Annika bats her eyes at me until I nod yes, then rewards me with a winning smile. No need to tell them about youth group until there's a conflict. "You're amazing, Cassie!" she adds as they depart, leaving me feel like I'm spinning in their wake.

"How can two ridiculously tiny people feel like an entire swarm?" I'm standing, reeling, next to our locker as Kayla spins the lock. She looks a little pissed, actually, but that might be her normal face. It's hard to tell sometimes with her.

"A plague of locusts, more like." Her voice is dark.

"I thought you guys were like this." I hold up my crossed fingers.

Kayla tugs a bag of gym clothes out of the top of the locker and shoves a bunch of junk that comes out with it back in. "Yeah, well, you know how it goes with those girls. You're in until you're not. Queen Annika has decided to hate all over *Tyrone Thesaurus Rex*, so now we're mortal enemies." She slams the locker shut, ignoring the fact that I am waiting to get in. "It's complicated and shit."

"So they're not printing it? What are you talking about? *Rex* is brilliant." I actually have no clue what her comic is about, but she has assured me many times that it's brilliant. Something about a dinosaur with a big vocabulary and a plot that parallels the Oedipus story. "Everyone loves your comic." I, for one, know my lines as best friend.

"They don't get it. No one does. The philistines."

I almost ask her if I should quit working on the paper. It seems the natural thing to do—the act of solidarity. It's in the script. It's the drama of our friendship. But then it occurs to me: Why should I quit just because Kayla isn't into it anymore? Okay, so it was all her idea for me to do this in the first place, but still. Now it's mine, this chance, and even though I haven't officially done anything yet, what if I actually *enjoy* being a part of the paper? Maybe it's something I'm good at. I'm not her puppet. Or worse, her puppy, trailing after her heels.

Has it always been this way? This one way? I can't picture it, sometimes—I can't see our friendship in the past. I can't put the pieces into their places to see the whole picture. Instead of connections, events drawing us ever closer, which is what I imagine when I think about best friends, I remember being sort of peripherally tossed into the seats next to each other. Twin outliers. Maybe I'm the only one who could be friends with someone who spends more time muttering into her ink-stained pages than confiding secrets. Maybe she's the only one who could be friends with me. But ... maybe not.

The night I was born, the last night of the year, there was a new moon. My dad drove to the hospital all hunched over the wheel of our car, peering through the dark night. My mother hoped I would be born on New Year's Day because then my picture would be in the newspaper and I would win a big basket full of prizes from the local merchants. I would be a fresh sign of new beginnings—the promise of change. Instead, I came into that dark night at exactly 11:56 and became the last baby of the old year. Like I was born into a quietly fading history.

I don't want to be popular, not exactly. People like Annika and Britney—they aren't real. They can't be real, I suppose, or they'd be vulnerable. But maybe I can find the real beneath the act, you know. Maybe I need to be more ... I don't know. *Active* about making the connections.

Kayla wouldn't quit the paper for me. I realize this even as I realize that it's what she expects from me, or maybe she doesn't even bother to expect it, doesn't even question it, the same way she always walks ahead of me and never looks back to check if I'm following. It's not her fault, like it's not Eric's fault for not being able to choose a birthday gift for me. It's me. I've conditioned them all to expect me to follow along, to form myself into their ideas of who I should be.

As if to prove my point, off she goes without waiting for me to get my stuff out of the locker. I watch Kayla walk away, hoping she'll pause or look back, but she doesn't.

Whatever. I shrug and go back to gathering my stuff for homeroom. I don't notice Drew until she speaks.

"Cass?"

I jump, rapping my elbow on the door of the locker. "Oh. Hey." I check the wall clock, hoping I can tell her I have to rush, but oddly enough, I still have seven whole minutes until the tardy bell. "Did you need something?" I wince because it sounds too mean.

But Drew doesn't react, just takes a step closer. Her cheeks are pink, and she's chewing on the side of her index finger. Her cuticles are ragged—I look down and compare them to my own. I can't help it. I'm relieved that my nails look better than hers. And then I feel guilty for even comparing.

"I was thinking," she says. "Wondering, like, if you had read my poem yet. I was thinking..." She lapses into an uncertain silence. She's too close.

I nod. "And?" There's an entitled impatience in my voice that comes in part from how I feel about Kayla right now. I'm sick of trying—to be a nice person, to be a good best friend, to be interesting. I'm sick of it.

Her bottom lip drops open a little and I regret the tone. "Sorry, Drew," I say quickly. "I...I don't mean to snap at you. I just...need to go ask a question about my pre-calc home-work." It's a total lie. "Do you still want me to show the poem to Annika and Britney?" Why am I asking this when I have zero intention of doing it? Isn't it meaner to keep on acting like I'm her friend, when I hate being near her? I start walking toward the math room. I hope she doesn't follow me all the way there because I don't even have my math book, much less a question about the homework.

"So you liked it?" Her face brightens.

Oh god. I feel like the scum of the earth, basically. And now I'm going to lie to her some more.

"It was really heartfelt. Really...nice rhymes." I smile at her, trying to be generous. I feel bad for her; I can't help it. "I mean, I guess the speaker of the poem really likes some guy? I think...people can relate to that."

Drew shakes her head, her eyes bouncing off my hairline. "Or maybe it's not even a boy," she says. "Maybe...a friend. I don't know." She looks down at her hands twisting together in front of her. "It's kind of a lonely poem, you know?"

"Cassie, come heeeeere!" It's Annika, of course, standing by the door of the math room beckoning to me, an insistent look on her face.

I glance at Drew. "I have to..." I gesture in Annika's direction.

"Great! Introduce me?" And Drew steps closer to me. For a second I think she's going to take my arm like we're best friends, but at the last second her hand jumps up to fiddle with the end of her ponytail. She's so eager it makes me queasy.

"Um." I don't move. I'm such a coward.

"Cassie, I've been looking for you *everywhere*," Annika

says, and she *does* take my arm, steering me deliberately away from Drew. "We have to talk."

I'm totally confused. Of course she wasn't really looking for me everywhere. She talked to me like two minutes ago. I follow her lead and step away from the now crestfallen Drew. "About what?"

Annika turns, looks over her shoulder at Drew. "Aw, honey, don't look so sad. Top secret newspaper business, you know. And I'm sure your skin will clear up when you start washing your face more regularly." Her winning smile is so solicitous that I don't even know if Drew realizes how cruel she is.

To me, she hisses a low warning. "Cassie, OMG, we do not associate with greasy cows like that girl. What were you thinking? Surely you're not actually friends?"

I know I should stick up for Drew. Annika's being needlessly mean. The girl has *eczema*, not leprosy. Okay, so I don't really like Drew the Shrew either, and I've made fun of her greasy hair and her acne and the lumbering way she walks. But privately, not to her face. And not with that awful pretend-niceness.

"Oh, she's this girl from my church." My voice is hollow, a duplicitous Judas-voice. "She's always hanging on me."

Annika wrinkles her nose. "She smells bad."

"Were you really looking for me?"

"Looking *out* for you, that's all. We like you, Cassie." She smiles, her bright green eyes with their perfectly curled lashes crinkling up a little at their perfect corners. "I mean, I know you're thinking that this job on the newspaper is only tempo-rary until Jenny gets back, but like, this is your chance. You play your cards right, and who knows what could happen."

She squeezes my arm again and spins toward the math room, her high blond ponytail wagging behind her. "See you at lunch tomorrow, Cassie."

If I play my cards right. I think of the cards buried in the back of my closet. *This is my chance*—so maybe I should take it. What if I used the tarot cards and wrote a column for the newspaper? It could be an anonymous advice col-umn, except it gives advice about the future, based on read-ings I'd do for people. It would be something to write on that stupid survey, and in the Song of Myself, too. Some-thing risky. Something all mine.

12. Your parents wish that you …

Mom corners me as soon as I walk in the door, which isn't really her style. Normally she's more of a strike-fast-and-retreat type, like a shark with a distaste for messy carnage.

"Cassandra, we need to talk." She holds out her hands to take my backpack from me while I remove my coat, but I hesitate before handing it over, doing a panicky mental rundown of its contents before surrendering it to her. Mom says that teenagers have no rights to privacy, that until I'm an adult with my own space, my property belongs to her and is subject to search and seizure at any time, with or without cause.

"What?" Stalling. I skim through possible sources of contention. Did I forget to clear my browsing history on the computer? Reveal confidential data while talking in my sleep? Oh god. Not the tarot cards. My stomach drops through the floor and then rapidly resurfaces somewhere in the vicinity of my throat. I can't breathe.

"I was hoping you'd pray with me, Cass." Her mouth is

a thin line, moving around her crooked teeth. She notices my stricken face and tries to smile. "It's nothing terrible, Cassandra, honest. I just want to talk." She hangs my backpack on the hook by the door without opening even one zipper, clearly a record. Despite what she's saying, this has to be serious.

"Can I get changed first?" I have to check on my hiding place. I have to be sure of the bomb she's going to drop on me.

She looks away, then toward the front window, and for the slightest of moments, my mother's face looks old in the bright afternoon sunlight reflecting off the snow. She doesn't have wrinkles, but her skin seems softer, somehow. Like it's lost a little snap, a little glow. "Sure, honey, but hurry. I want to talk before Eric and Gavin get here. I'll make us some hot cocoa."

Oh god, *cocoa*. Mom is always on a diet. The only time she indulges in anything even remotely resembling sugar is when she's majorly stressed out. Like majorly. I slip away to my room and close the door behind me, leaning against the thin, hollow barrier. My eyes sweep across the room, but I don't see anything out of place. No mess, nothing disturbed. There aren't even any signs of her being in here for her usual activities: no clothes folded on my bed, no lingering scent of furniture polish. Pumpkin and Nutmeg are quiet and calm, hidden in their piggy tunnels. I dart over to the closet and crawl quickly to the back, where my old luggage set is stashed. Tucked one inside the other like Russian dolls, they made a perfect hiding place for the cards, which fit neatly into the smallest bag—a little purple zip-up "ditty bag" that I keep my makeup in if I stay overnight at Kayla's house.

I keep my eyes on the door while I stealthily unzip the outermost suitcase. My cover story is wedged into my mouth, at the ready: *I was trying to hang up my dress, but it slipped off the hanger.*

This would be a way better cover story if I wasn't still wearing the damn dress. I wiggle it off over my head and throw it into the bottom of the closet as evidence. The truth is curled up, hidden in a scandalous smother of lies.

Zip, unzip. They're still there. Everything is still there, untouched.

"Cass?" Footsteps, and I straighten up, letting out my breath in a hiss. "Oh sorry, honey, didn't realize you weren't decent."

Yeah, because I told you five seconds ago that I was going to get changed. How utterly incomprehensible that I would have my clothes off. "My dress is on the floor," I blurt. Okay, so clearly I'm brain damaged. "I mean, I...I'll hang it back up." Lame.

Her eyes slide around the room. "I brought you your cocoa," she says, and she holds the cup out as though I'm going to take it, like I'm going to stand there in my bra and underwear holding a steaming mug of cocoa.

"Um, you can set it on my dresser, I guess," I say. "Thank you."

This ridiculous mental malfunction I've got going on almost makes me forget my manners, which would be a grave error. I feel acutely vulnerable right now. I grope for my dress on the floor of the closet, hoping I can keep the unzipped luggage hidden, and successfully manage to hang up the dress and pull on some sweats and a long-sleeved T-shirt. "That feels much better," I say, smiling brightly as inane words continue to trip off my tongue.

"Cassandra, is...is Eric...*carnally involved*?"

"Whaaaat?" Carnally involved? Unwanted images of that time I walked in on him and Gavin flash in front of my eyes, and my face burns. "Mom!"

Carnally involved? I mean, really. Who says that? Who even *thinks* that? I shudder, trying to impress upon my mother how incredibly mortified this whole discussion is making me, but she doesn't look at me. Instead, she sinks down right there on my pale pink carpeting and buries her face in her hands. I imagine she's crying, though she doesn't make any noise. Oh god. I take a step closer to her. "Mom?"

"I found...a *condom*...in his trash can," she says. She keeps her hands over her face, hiding her eyes, but she's not wallowing in it; I can see her pulling herself together, piece by piece, like a jigsaw puzzle of poise. She lowers her hands and waves them in front of her face in little motions, as though the air in front of her is the source of her discomfort. Onion fumes, maybe. "I'm so sorry, Cass. I didn't mean to lose it like that. Really, I'm all right." Her thin mouth pulls into that smile again, a stick-figure line-smile that couldn't fool anyone.

"Mom, I don't know anything about this, really." And I don't, either. I have no details to report about Eric's sex life, or lack of one. That's between him and Gavin and doesn't need to involve anyone else's opinion, no matter what my family's church might say. I'm not sure if Eric is cool with God on this score, but personally I can't put faith in an unconditionally loving God condemning people for loving. Allegedly.

"I can't wrap my mind around why he would be disgracing himself like this." She dabs at the corners of her eyes with an index finger wrapped in the edge of her sleeve. I see the black mascara stain spread across the fabric in a little pool of saltwater. "Not to mention the poor girl." She looks up at me, wounded. "He hasn't even introduced us to her," she says.

"Well, you know Eric. He plays his cards close to his chest," I say. It's true, but she doesn't know how true, and I don't really want to tell her.

"But this is too close. What do you think, Cass? Should I have Dad talk to him? Or maybe if I say something to Gavin, do you think? Eric respects him, and even though Gavin isn't saved, I know he's an honorable young man. I'm sure he would talk some sense into Eric, if I could figure out a way to speak to him about it."

I shake my head. "No, Mom. Don't embarrass him by talking to his best friend about something like this. What if Eric was... *you know.* Experimenting, like. With..." Oh, god. This is too much. She stares at me without any glimmer of understanding in her eyes. My face heats up again.

"Experimenting?" She presses her lips together, and her eyes grow so liquid and fragile I can barely continue.

"You know. Like with himself." Okay, so this might be the most embarrassing moment of my entire life. I'm explaining masturbation to my mother. She may as well not even be human, and I may as well be dead.

Her voice is small and uncertain. "Oh." A frown, her eyes on her hands in her lap, twisting and twisting the band on her left ring finger. "Ohhh." She looks up, and her face is pink, too, but hopeful. "Do you think that could be it, really? Will you pray with me, Cassandra? Pray for strength for Eric and for guidance for me, as his parent?"

I squirm. She only knows that I'm uncomfortable praying in front of other people; I wonder if she suspects that I don't pray at all, if she speculates about what is or isn't in my heart. I've never really tried to tell either of my parents what I think—it seems like words better off left unsaid. Someday, when I'm an adult with my own place, won't they realize that I've got different ideas about what to do with my Sunday mornings? It doesn't have to be a big thing, a big conflict. We can go our separate ways, that's all. Later, once I'm out of this town.

"*You* can pray, if you want," I say. I think it's easier to keep the peace, mostly.

"Jesus, in your glorious name, we thank you for the many blessings you bring into our lives. Our children, each one of them a gift so precious. Help them, Lord, as they face the many temptations of this carnal world, and please be with me as I try so hard to interpret your will for them and guide them along the path to righteousness."

She ends the prayer and squeezes my hand, and I can't help it. For a moment, I'm awash in this awful sort of rueful sadness. It prickles up out of my chest and binds my throat, my mouth and nose, until I have to labor to breathe. It's not God, and it's not the Spirit, smothering me with vengeance.

It's pity—pity and compassion for my mother. She and I may have our moments, but right now all I can think of is how she's feeling as she watches her children careening off into the world, out of her reach. How it feels for her to be so powerless, and how comforting it must be to be able to hand it all to God in a prayer and trust that it will work out in the end.

Oh, Mom. It's not going to work out the way you hope. And if I were a praying person, I'd ask God to give you the flexibility to bend under the new shape of things. Jesus, help my black-and-white, literal-minded mother to understand that righteousness is a rainbow of different shades of gray.

13. Describe your family ...

Annika and Britney gossip the entire lunch period today about people I barely know, while I do exciting things like adjusting kerning and placing ads for community businesses in the margins of the sports section. I knew this newspaper was read by a lot of people, but I had no idea that there are companies all over town paying good money to get their little business-card-sized advertisements stuck in the side columns of *The Gordon High Gazette*. And somehow each and every one of those ads was created in a different program on a different platform, and for some inexplicable reason, they all look completely different on my computer screen from the way they look on the proof sheets the businesses send. This, apparently, is my (impossible) job—making the two match up.

So while Britney and Annika talk smack about the entire basketball team and more than half of the hockey team and discuss the sexual history of all the cheerleaders, I spend my lunch swearing and restarting and loading and reloading fonts. They hardly know I'm there.

Three things I did not know (or really need to know) about the jocks at my school:

1. Jack ("Off") Fuller, the captain of the hockey team, allegedly got his nickname from an act performed in the presence of the entire hockey cheer squad. (And according to my sources, performed while the squad gave their own rousing performance of the cheer "Strike! Strike! Strike!" altered to "Stroke! Stroke! Stroke!") Um, go Gordon Golden Gophers? So gross.

2. Felicity Forrest sat between twin senior forwards Cade and Connor Jacobsen on the basketball bus and is apparently equally talented with her right and left hands. So double gross.

3. That shadowy upper lip of Melissa Vigliotti, star athlete and top contender for valedictorian? *Steroids*, whispers Annika, *not just Italian*. So mean.

Okay, so this information seriously does not need to live in my brain. I feel dirty just knowing these details, like the knowledge of the used condom in my brother's wastebasket. Ew. Take a trip from my conscious memory, please.

Hours later, and I'm still trying to banish these thoughts from my head. Down the hall, I can hear my mom nagging Dicey to finish her math homework and the sounds of Dad's evening news filtering out from the den. I finish the dishes from tonight's dinner, my fingers sweeping across the bottom of the sink, checking for stray silverware. Everyone's home and getting ready for bed except for Eric, who's still at the library with Gavin. The library, yeah right.

Eric, seriously. What was he thinking? And he wants to tell them—to tell everyone about Gavin and whatever. I don't mind that Eric's gay, but I wish we could skip the part where everyone finds out and gets shaken up and upset and...complicated. I hate that part. I wish sexual orientation could be something quiet and personal, not the kind of detail that compels perfect strangers to think about it or talk about it or have strong opinions about what my brother and his boyfriend might do when they're alone.

There's no question about the stance of the Joyful News Bible Church when it comes to homosexuality. Pastor Fordham has even uttered that awful cliché about "Adam and Eve, not Adam and Steve," and this in an audio recording he distributed in one of the monthly mailings to the entire congregation. I mean, really? That's the best you can do?

Dad is harder to read—he's a reserved man who gives monosyllabic answers to most inquiries. A lot of the time I get the feeling from him that he's patiently waiting for his children to become useful in some way, and in the meantime he prefers to stay out of the way. He usually says all the right things; it's just that he seems sometimes like he's moving through life out of a sense of duty rather than following his dreams and passions.

I'm not sure how a man so rational and aware of his obligations will react to his son's revelation of *love* for another boy. I imagine him sort of frowning, like he does, drawing his eyebrows together and saying, "But Eric, what about having a family? What about a wife and children?" Deviation from expectations is simply not on his radar.

I pull the plug and watch the dishwater swirl down the drain. I still think Eric should wait to tell them until he's out of college, or at least out of high school. At the very least, he should wait until the end of next month when he turns eighteen. I can't really see my mom and dad sending him to one of those reprogramming therapy places, but at least if he's a legal adult, he could refuse to go. That kind of thing is terrifying to me, really. Even if Mom and Dad are okay with Eric being gay, the church people will be... more complicated. And what about the rest of the world, all those stupid people full of hatred—I know it's hard for him to hide, but I'm scared for him, too.

I slip into the quiet of my own room, the soft sounds of the pigs in the darkness. I kneel by their cage and watch, for a moment, their small comfortable lives.

"I wish we could skip the drama and go to the part where we're all fine." I say the words softly into the downy top of Nutmeg's head as she snuggles against my neck, and she makes her little purring happy sound. I sit with her a bit and then set her back down in her pen, where she crawls into her little tunnel to chill.

The tarot cards call to me from their hiding place. I can almost feel their snappy shininess in my hands, and I long to spread them out on the floor and mix them up, to search those intriguing pictures and those lists of inscrutable words for some way to help my brother.

I listen again, my ear pressed against my bedroom door,

trying to figure out if my parents have gone to bed yet. Maybe if I sit with my back against the door, I'll hear the footsteps approaching and have time to hide the cards before someone enters. It's past ten o'clock, and Mom has already stopped in once to say good night, so it's probably safe. Okay, so Mom's a bit of an insomniac, and there's still my nosy sister to contend with, but still. This was about risk-taking, right?

I get the cards from the back of my closet and grab my little garbage can from under my desk. If I keep the can right beside me, I can hide the deck inside it if someone comes in. It will have to be enough.

I slide the cards out, starry-side up, and read the directions in the guidebook. The querent—that's the person asking the question—is supposed to think about the question while shuffling the cards. Still, maybe I can sort of channel Eric as I shuffle, thinking about what kind of question he would ask if he were willing to try.

I close my eyes for the slightest of moments, holding the deck in both hands. *Eric.* The cards feel heavy in my hands, a weight of consequence. I smile to think of how I half expected a demon to emerge from the plastic when I opened them. *Eric.* I struggle to keep my mind on him, on the question I think he would ask at this time. *Should he come out to Mom and Dad?* I shuffle the deck, trying to concentrate, but my mind wanders as the cards slide past my fingers.

Okay, so: Am I more interesting with this secret? The cards in my hands are entirely mine—Kayla doesn't know about them, my brother doesn't trust them, and the rest of my family would believe it's a sin for me to sit here on my pink carpeting with these bits of plasticized paper running through my fingers. I spread them out on the floor, pushing them in circles. I remember my earlier glimmer of an idea—the tarot reading column in the newspaper. I sit up straight, my fingers tingling. I actually want this. Like, I want this, for *me*.

I wonder if the church would care, if they would protest a tarot column like they're protesting the Winter Carnival, like they protested the Gay-Straight Alliance or when Ms. Ross wanted to teach an elective class about Gothic literature. Would it get the newspaper in trouble if they did? Would they find out it's me?

Okay, so maybe I could make it a step or two removed from the school. Like, a secret message in the newspaper that would lead people to me. Lead them to me, but anonymously. What about the stupid side column ads I spent my whole lunch period perfecting? There are spaces left over where Annika instructed me to stick in snowflake clip art and hearts for Valentine's Day, stuff like that. I could put something into one of those squares, some way for people to get their questions to me. I could make an email address, maybe, and then they could send their questions, and I could write up a weekly column in the paper based on certain questions. Except… that's still leaving the newspaper open to criticism from the church for using the occult. Plus, at the newspaper, there would have to be at least one person who knew who I was, and assuming that at least one of those people would be Annika or Britney, it wouldn't stay a secret for long, even if I used a fake name. I let my fingers trace the path of the long river of blue starry-backed cards as I think.

My brain runs through possibilities of tarot reader names as I gather the cards into piles on the pink carpet. *Esmeralda. Zenubia. Clairvoyant Clarissa.* Okay, so the names need some work, clearly. Oh, *shit.* I was supposed to be channeling Eric!

I close my eyes again, centering myself on his plight rather than my advice column idea, and then I pull the cards together, slowly stacking them in my hands, mixing them up more and more until it feels like enough. I hear a footstep in the hall and freeze, my pulse quickening and my nerves on edge. I listen intently, but it's only Dicey passing by on her way to the bathroom. No big deal, but I wait, my hand holding the deck inside the garbage can, until I hear the flush and the footsteps retreating back into her bedroom at the end of the hall. I wonder if she saw the light shining underneath my door.

Pressing my ear against the door one more time, I make sure the hall is empty, then I quietly unfold the reading map that came in the guidebook and follow the diagram for a ten-card spread. The first card I turn over, what my book calls the querent's "present position," is called the Queen of Wands. I study the card: a woman in a yellow gown with a wand and a sunflower scepter. At her feet is a lovely black cat. The card is pretty, but I have no idea what it could mean in relation to Eric's present position.

The card crossing her is all full of wreaths and a guy riding a horse. Looks happy, sort of. Maybe that's Gavin? Or Eric himself? I flip the next card, the one that will go at the top of the reading and represent the "goal or destiny."

Whoa. In some ways, there couldn't be a happier, more perfect card—a beautiful couple and their dancing children.

A rainbow of wealth above them. A home and land ahead of them. Does this destiny include Gavin? I mean, I know plenty of gay men have children, but what if this card means the opposite—that Eric will change or deny himself, like the church would want him to do, and marry a woman and have two kids and this thing that looks like a perfect life? What if it *is* a perfect life? And yet, what if it's not, and in this future my brother is living a lie, not truly himself?

My stomach twists. There's no way for me to know what these cards mean, which interpretation is truth. There has to be truth here, somewhere, or at least some kind of guidance, some kind of insight.

I love my brother for who he is. I see how happy he is with Gavin. Heartache sweet. Still, I can't help but want life to be easier for my brother. I can't bear the thought of him being a target for every small-minded person on earth. And then there's the way his faith tears him apart, the way he wrestles daily with his belief and his identity. My stomach sinks. What if this card means that Eric changes for the church?

I flip the next few cards quickly. King of Cups, Two of Wands, and in the "future influence" spot a really interesting-looking card called Temperance. An angelic, robed figure pours water between two cups. There's this enormous set of blood-red wings and a large triangle on the figure's chest and a glowing circle in the center of its forehead. There's something paradoxical about the card, something about the way the water seems to float between the cups, the angelic halo of white around its head contrasting with the dark red of the wings. Creepy but also sort of reassuring, like.

The next four cards are supposed to stay face down until I finish reading the first six, so I slap them down on the carpet and look up the meanings of the first six cards in my little book, but it's frustrating. These lists of words could mean everything. It's like I'm missing a key to understanding, some code-breaker that will make the whole alphabet shift over and match up just right. *Victory. Conquest. Hopes Accomplished.*

Hopeful words. But hopeful for what?

I pick up the Queen of Wands, Eric's present position. The black cat is so dark in the otherwise yellow-dominated artwork, an inky familiar to this powerful woman. Sunflowers grow all around, even on the queen's crown. Who is she, and what part does she play in my brother's life? *A loving companion. Pure.* I study her face—it's powerful and chiseled, a face of strength. When I hold my hand over the bottom half, over the word "queen," the face is genderless. *A kind and caring friend.*

Oh. This card *is* Eric, and the boy with the wands on the horse who is crossing him has got to be Gavin. *Victory.*

I listen carefully before going back to my guidebook, but the hall behind the door is quiet. In the corner, Nutmeg and Pumpkin peep softly. I want to figure out this reading before Eric gets home tonight. I look up the meaning of the Ten of Cups—the happy perfect family under a rainbow of golden goblets. There's so much peace and love in the meanings, the card may as well be wearing tie-dye. So who is that happy family of Eric's destiny?

Family is difficult. I don't mean, like, the kind of difficulty you struggle through and then feel a sense of achievement when you surmount it. I mean the kind of difficult that goes on and on. But that feeling, like you're all working hard together to make everything work, it's sort of like happiness. Right? And love. And home.

Next comes the King of Cups—the book says the card represents a person in Eric's life who is educated, religious, and wise. The king in the picture has a kind of stern look, or maybe he's just world-weary. His hair is cut close to his head, and gray. His throne seems to be on a small stone square in the middle of a sea, and he has a heavy gold fish necklace. Could it be Pastor Fordham? Eric isn't all that close to him—not like he was with Pastor Jake Marshall, who was sort of a role model for him. And since the card is in the distant past position in the spread, I wonder if it could possibly have something to do with Pastor Jake.

A few years back, Eric went through a period of time where he thought he had a calling, like to be a minister. Despite my own lack of faith, I can envision that calling being important to him, but Eric hasn't mentioned the idea for a long time. Maybe not since that awful fire in the church that took the life of Pastor Jake's wife. Pastor Jake and his daughter never came back to the church; it was like they vanished into their grief. Eric grieved, too, at the loss of his mentor.

I flip through the pages, checking out the Two of Wands and then reading about Temperance, a card that very clearly seems to support my feeling that Eric should wait patiently until the right time to act. Yeah. This is exactly what I needed to see.

I'm thinking about how I'm going to tell Eric about this when a sharp rap on the door at my back makes me jump and lunge toward the cards. I try to scoop them up in silence. "Just a sec!" I call, hoping my voice doesn't betray my panic.

What about the last four cards? Their starry sides taunt me, cloaking the answer in mystery. It's probably Eric at the door anyway. I drop the rest of the cards into the garbage can and pick up the last row carefully, keeping them in order. I have no pockets, nowhere to put the cards in my hand. I shove my hand into my pajama bottoms, tucking the cards into the waistband of my underwear at my hip and pressing my arm against them to hold them there.

"Eric?" I open the door, but the face that looks down at me is not his. My father stands framed in the doorway instead, his brows gathered in the middle of his forehead.

"He's not in here?"

"What?"

"Eric. He's not with you?"

Something screwy happens to my heart, like a twitch or a spasm, and my hand presses into my hip, hard. "I ... I haven't seen him since after dinner, when he and Gavin left for the library." The library closes at eight, but Gavin and Eric often go up to the top of the iron mine dumps, to Plath's Lookout. The overview is technically closed; they don't plow the road up, but Gavin drives up to the gate and parks, and the two of them either hang out there in the car or hike up to the top if it's not too cold.

"I'm worried about him." Dad looks so perplexed, so uncertain. I've never seen him like this. Worried about Eric? That seems so impractical, for my dad.

"It's not even curfew." I squint at my alarm clock. "It's

barely eleven." Eric's usually home by now, but that doesn't mean anything.

"My heart is uneasy," he says. "My prayers. I keep..." He shakes his head as though he's embarrassed. "It's probably nothing, you're right."

"What is it?" Eric's okay. We're close. If he weren't okay, I'd feel it, wouldn't I? I think about the tarot, about how happy everything was in the reading. What if the last four cards were totally different? What if they got into a car accident on that awful hill? Kids have been killed on the lookout, though not since they put the guard rail up when that whole carful of teenagers slid over the edge a few years ago. "Dad?"

"It's just that..." He shakes his head. "All right. I thought I'd check with you. I'm sure he'll be home by curfew like always."

He closes my door behind him without saying good night and I lean against it, my hand on the cards at my hip. My heart races. I spread the cards out, a compact fan in my hand, and my first look at the pictures gives no hint of tragedy. I slide the rest of the cards back into the box and hide it before taking out the guidebook to check the meanings of this final run. My fingers are cold and tentative. Where is my brother right now?

The first card is the questioner, or his current perspective. The Knight of Swords. *A courageous and heroic youth.* Sounds fine. I skim the meanings for the next three cards, all of which refer to love and support and strength—good companions, wealth, business, and respect. How could anything be wrong?

The numbers on my clock glow red. No Eric.

I return the deck to its hiding place and tiptoe out into the living room, where my dad sits in his armchair in the dark.

"Dad?"

"I can't pray," he says.

"What do you mean?" He's always praying. "Just say, 'Hey, God, what's up? Where the heck is my son?'"

"Cassandra."

"I didn't say 'hell.'"

He looks at me, his eyes narrowed, but he doesn't push the matter. Which is when I know something is seriously wrong.

"Dad, what do you mean, you can't pray?"

He folds his hands and bows his head. "Lord, I honor you and I ask y-y-y..." He takes in a quick breath and lets it out, squaring his shoulders. "I ask your b-b-b-b...bl-bl..." He shakes his head. "I can't. It's like when he was a little boy." My dad's eyes are bright in the dark living room, reflecting like distant stars off the spill of light from the tiny bulb above the kitchen stove. I've never seen my dad cry, not even when the baby died. Crying, in his view, doesn't accomplish anything.

"Dad, nothing happened to Eric. Have you tried his cell?"

I can hear him swallow, as if he has to push the words past the lump in his throat. "No answer. No ring, actually. I called Gavin's phone too, and Gavin's mom. She doesn't know where he is either." His shoulders heave up and down, and his hands come unfolded and hang off the arms of the chair, uselessly. "It's so inexplicable, Cass. I have absolutely no idea why I'm feeling like this, why I'm worrying about him, why I'm stuttering every time I try to ask Jesus to look out for him. Stuttering like he did when he was a little boy. Do you remember it, Cass? Do you remember the way he would get so angry?"

I nod. Of course I remember.

"You've got to tell me where you think he could be."

Is it terrible of me to feel—for an instant—a tiny happiness? Not about Eric, but about the fact that my dad is talking —talking to me, like this? I don't want him to be miserable, and obviously I care about my brother, but this is the first real conversation my dad and I have had in forever.

I kneel down on the rug beside his chair and take one of his dangling hands in both of mine. It's cold, and the flesh seems loose on the bones—far looser than it should. Has he grown so old already? "Dad, wait until after his curfew is past. He'll be home, I swear."

It occurs to me to wonder if something bad happened to Eric because I used the cards, because of my dabbling in sorcery. My dad can't pray. A fear flickers at my lack of faith . . . maybe there is such a thing as demons, after all. Maybe we're being punished. My insides twist up in doubt.

"Do they go to some girl's house? Are they sneaking off to do drugs? I need to know, Cass. I have to go find them. I'll take my phone, so you can call me the instant he arrives home safe and sound."

"Plath's Lookout," I whisper, an involuntary shudder traveling across my shoulders as the horror of the idea hits me. People die on the lookout. I mean, people *choose* to die on the lookout. What if . . . what if this is all too much for Eric?

What if he and Gavin devised some kind of stupid Romeo and Juliet suicide pact or something? There haven't been any jumpers since my eighth grade year, not since this kid leaped and was found, still alive—horribly mangled but conscious and in pain—like ten hours later.

"Take me with you."

My father stands, tosses his keys once in his hand. "Let's go," he says.

14. Your biggest fear ...

Gavin's car is dark against the snow. I don't see any sign of Gavin, or of Eric. There's a tiny sideways sliver of moon—what Dicey always calls a banana moon—and the thick clouds are scudding across the black sky, offering only a brief glimpse of starlight here and there. "They sometimes hike up to the top," I say. My pajama bottoms are thin; they flap in the wind. I shiver.

The beam of Dad's flashlight cuts across the line of trees planted by the mining company to keep the red dust in place. Tree trunks flash bright blond against the blackness, their uniform spacing drawing attention to anything out of place. I can't see Eric and Gavin anywhere.

"I guess we'll have to hike up," says Dad. "Are you too cold?"

I try to hide the shivers by wrapping my arms around myself. "I'm fine." A lie, of course, a small sin borne of terror. I can't bear the thought of him leaving me here. The visions of what I could discover on my own chill me more than the January air.

What if they're making out or something, or stretched out on the backseat? My feet unwillingly trudge along in the wheel ruts toward Gavin's car. The windows aren't steamy at all, and when we're closer, we can see why.

"Whoa." The windows are broken. Okay, so not *all* of the windows, but the passenger side window, the windshield, and the little triangular window in the backseat. Not like, cracked. Broken, like shattered. Little beads of safety glass fill the bucket of the passenger seat.

"Did they hit something, do you think?" It's the only thing that makes sense to me—a deer, maybe. A moose? I search for blood or hair along the passenger door or dents in the fender.

"It happened here," says Dad. He reaches out a gloved hand and runs it across the edge of the window, and I can hear the tinkle of tiny glass chunks raining down and clinking softly against the frozen snow. It's so cold. Where is my brother?

"Footprints!" I point at the side of the road, where sure enough, two sets of boot tracks lead away from the car. I can't help myself. "Errrrriiiiiiiic!" My voice echoes. I wonder if the whole town can hear.

I expect my dad to shush me because he's an astoundingly quiet man, even in an emergency, but he adds his own voice and shouts too. Then we wait, in nervous silence, for some kind of answer.

Nothing. My shivering gets more pronounced, my teeth chatter audibly. There's no way I can follow that trail up to the top, not dressed like this. Dad hands me the keys.

"Wait in the car, Cassandra." His voice is grim. What does he expect to find? I fiddle with the keys in my cold fingers.

"But ... what if there's something out there?"

"I'll be right back." He squeezes my shoulder and shows me the tiny flashlight on the key ring. "You go get in the car and stay warm."

"Be careful."

Dad disappears into the shadows, and I circle around to the driver's side of Gavin's car and shine my tiny flashlight around, hoping to find something more, some clue to where Eric has gone.

What I find is disgusting on so many levels. At first I think someone sprayed the whole driver's side of Gavin's car with a squirt gun or something because it's covered in big streaks of half-frozen wet splatters, but then I notice the color where it's dripped down into the snow.

It's pee. People have peed on my brother's boyfriend's car, and in the snowbank beside the edge of the road, someone has spelled out a word. Okay. So. *Almost* spelled.

The yellow snow reads, *FAGGETS*.

15. One thing you've lied about...

Later, when it's all over and we're safe at home with hot cocoa and my mom fussing over Eric's black eye (which he says happened when he ran into a tree branch in the dark), it occurs to me that covering up the word in the snow was probably not the smartest thing for me to do. What if those assholes had *killed* Eric and Gavin instead of throwing ice chunks and peeing on their car? Tampering with the evidence might have screwed up any kind of case against them, but all I could think of was that Dad could *not* see that word, that poorly spelled accusation in the snow. That's not the way for him to find out.

Eric won't tell us what really happened. He says they pulled the car up like they usually do, sat there talking and listening to something on the radio for a few minutes, and then got out to go for a hike. He says they were a little way up the trail when they heard bass thumping and tires squealing. They hid in the trees while a bunch of guys shouted and carried on. When they heard someone throwing ice chunks at their car,

Eric says that Gavin wanted to go back and stop them, but he convinced Gavin it wasn't safe to go messing around with a bunch of drunk rednecks.

"I told him he has insurance for a reason," says Eric, holding an ice pack to the side of his face. "And besides, that's when we heard them starting up the trail toward us."

"And that's when you fell?" prompts my mother, hovering. She reaches out to brush back several strands of dark hair from his forehead.

"Yeah, pretty much. We were off the trail, not using our flashlights, and I ran into the tree, and everything got all sparkly. I slid down this steep part of the hill a little bit, but Gavin grabbed my jacket and kept me from going all the way down. I couldn't see. I think that's where I lost my phone."

"We'll go back tomorrow in the light," says my dad. He runs both palms of his hands up and down across his cheeks, scraping against the stubble. I'm not used to seeing him this disheveled.

Mom falls unsteadily into the chair across from me. "Yes," she says, "you and your father should go tomorrow, right after school. Together."

"No." Eric says it too quickly, and both Mom and Dad frown. I think of the word in the snow, and I'm glad I kicked it away. Mom presses her lips and taps all of her fingertips together, the way she does right before things get difficult.

"I found a condom in your garbage can," she says.

What? Seriously, Mom? *Now*? I want to disappear, but I'm sitting in my heavy wooden chair at the dining room table and if I move, even a little, the chair will scrape loudly against the wood floor, calling attention to myself. Anyway, I'm trapped back here against the wall like always. Someone would have to get up to let me squeeze past. I study my cuticles, but the silence is so thick and heavy that eventually I have to look up, to see why nobody is screaming or defending themselves or making shocked sounds.

Eric's face is grim beneath the ice pack but unsurprised. He looks my mother in the eyes and nods slowly. Her eyes are brimming with tears that she refuses to blink away or let fall. I turn my face to Dad, who sits at my right, his hands still on his cheeks. He looks a little stunned, but there's something else. Is it pride? Is he really *proud*, thinking of his son using a condom? Gross.

Finally, Eric sighs. "What would you like me to say?" He sounds tired.

"I think everyone has said enough for one night," says my dad, standing up with a scrape of chair legs. "It's late, and you two have school."

"I want you to say that I'm wrong in what I'm thinking. That it's some mistake." Mom's voice is small beneath the authority of Dad, but she isn't finished. She's obviously been wrestling with this all day, and now that Eric is talking, she doesn't want him to stop.

"It really isn't what you think, Mom," says Eric. "Trust me." He nods to my father and stands up, too. "Good night," he says, and both Dad and Eric leave the room, heading toward their bedrooms.

Now that Dad's gone, I have an escape route, but Mom's still sitting there with those tears hanging on the edge of her lashes and I don't know what to do. I stare at her shoulder, wondering if I should try to comfort her. She'll try to pray with me, when what I really want to do is race down the hall after Eric and demand that he tell me what really happened out there, who it was.

"So do I trust him?" Mom says, and she turns to me. "Can I?"

"Eric's okay," I say. And it's like I can make it true, even if it's just for tonight. I feel my breath come back to me, and I didn't realize I was holding it, rationing it out to a mere whisper of oxygen. I'm dizzy.

Mom nods, and though she never wipes away the tears, her face is flawless. "Thank you," she says. "I'm sure you're right." There's something else there, in her eyes, some kind of truth I'm not ready to see, not ready to talk about. I shove my chair back with a loud scraping sound.

"I'm going to bed," I say, and I stumble down the hall to my room. I want to know everything, but I leave Eric alone with his thoughts. He'll come to me when he's ready to talk. Until then, I'll trust him, like he asked.

16. Your best and worst nicknames...

I have to track Kayla to her cave, downstairs in the art room, this morning. She doesn't look up from her drawing, not even when I pick up a utility knife and scrape dried clay off the wood tabletop with an annoying grating sound.

"I'm pretty sure somebody punched Eric last night," I say. She keeps drawing, no indication that she hears me.

"And they broke out the window on Gavin's car."

She frowns at the page in front of her. "Cretins," she says.

"And they wrote hate mail in the snow with their piss."

Finally she looks up. "Shut up. They did not."

I shake my head. "Some asshole who can't spell the word 'faggot.'"

"They should die in a fire."

"Right?" Scrape, scrape, scrape. Kayla goes back to her ink world. We're quiet, the two of us, but I can't tell if it's our normal, best friend quiet—the comfortable, I-don't-have-to-talk-to-you-because-you-know-me-so-well kind of quiet—or if she's pissed at me for something. She gets like that.

Okay. "So, I'm starting an anonymous tarot card reading…thing," I say. "Maybe in the newspaper, or somehow *through* the newspaper. Like, secretly. Anonymously."

She puts down her pen for that. "Serious?"

"Serious."

"You're going to kill your mom," she says. She smiles as she imagines it.

"Hence the anonymous part." I pick at a string hanging from the edge of my sweater sleeve. I don't really know why Kayla loves to hate my family. Okay, so there are some differences in the way our families operate, but my mom and dad have always been nice to her, even when we were little kids and Kayla spent most of the time she was over at my house asking my mother to read the labels of our food to make sure there wasn't any high-fructose corn syrup or MSG, parroting her parents' politics at our dinner table, and scowling through the evening prayers.

"What you need is a blog," she says, picking up her pen again and opening to a page in our notebook, the one we pass back and forth with all our notes in it. "A pseudonym, a blog, and a new email address." She divides the page up into rows and columns, labeling each one. She takes charge. My idea is slurped up into the Kayla machine, and I sit here nodding, smiling. Agreeing. Telling her she's brilliant. My shoulders slump a little.

Well, I needed her help anyway. And I mean, it's cool that

she thinks it's a good idea. "Are you sure?" I say. "I don't really think anybody reads blogs."

Kayla rolls her eyes. "Look, do you want to do this or not?"

I don't know. I thought I did. "Okay, so I was thinking of names," I say. "What do you think of using an anagram of my own name?"

"I think that's an awesome idea. I mean, if you want everyone to figure out who you are in like five minutes." She taps the pen against her teeth. "Look, Cass. This is a cool idea, but you're going to have to do it right. People will read, if it's interesting and if you get the word out, but you can't let them guess that it's you."

I shrug. "Maybe it's stupid," I say. "Maybe it's a bad idea."

But Kayla smiles. "No, it's a perfect idea, and you're the perfect person to write it. Give your blog some personality and nobody will ever guess it's you."

Okay, so you know what? That's a crappy thing to say, and I wish I had the guts to tell her so. Instead I glare at the clock and say, "Time for homeroom." I want to leave her there, to walk away angrily, but my feet won't walk away. "Let's *go*, Kayla."

I badger her to hurry. She takes her time. I wait for her. She gets her stuff out of our locker first. I wait for her. Is this seriously how it is every day? It is, isn't it?

"You could be totally evil," she says, checking her makeup in the mirror on the locker door. "Every reading could be, like, a complete dream-crusher." There's a gleam in her eye. "I'll help you break their hearts, if you want."

"But what if the cards are good?" *Like the reading I did for Eric.* I think of his black eye, the yellow snow. Either I read the cards wrong or God's vengeance is fast-acting and unjust. I must have done it wrong.

"Good is boring." She takes one last look at her reflection and walks off, leaving me to scramble for my stuff and get to homeroom. *Good is boring.* So now I'm boring? So because I'm not mean, I have no personality?

I wonder how everything changed, how the two of us writing movie scripts and making animated music videos on her dad's computer slowly morphed into painting our nails black while Kayla rants about how stupid everything is and I try to get her to crack a smile. I miss that boring goodness, you know? When we could be creative and silly instead of always being darkly satirical or whatever Kayla's deal is now.

I take three or four steps down the hall after her, trotting like usual with my back curled around the books in my arms, when it occurs to me: I don't *have* to follow. I straighten, look around. The halls are starting to empty—a knot of blond hair and perfect legs in skinny jeans and mini-skirts lingers by Annika and Britney's locker, but I'm pretty sure those girls have some kind of permanent tardy-immunity or something.

"Cassie!" The squeal emerges from the huddle of breathy voices. I look at them, startled. I'm so used to passing these girls with my head down. Annika giggles. "You look like a deer in headlights," she says.

I am, pretty much. I feel myself curling up again, hunching over my books. "Um, hi, Annika." Throwaway words in a barely audible voice. I hate myself for this meekness, but I can't seem to find my real voice. If I even have one.

"Are you coming to work during lunch again today? Please, please, Cassie?" Britney moves closer and puts her arm around me and I try hard not to wince, my still-sore rear end reminding me of what happened the first time I was mauled by these girls. Britney laughs. "Are you scared of me, Cassie?"

"Aw, don't be scared," says Annika. "We like Cassie, don't we?"

The girls around her laugh, and it's not exactly mocking, but it's not exactly friendly either. It's sort of…automatic. Like the girls are some kind of mechanical friends, programmed with a built-in laugh track and maybe a few different modes of squealing, cooing, and gushing.

"I can come in at lunch today, but not after school," I say. I have church and youth group every Wednesday, but I'm still not going to tell them that. I try to disentangle myself from Britney's arm. "Or at least, I'll be able to make it at lunch if I get to homeroom on time. If I'm tardy, I'll be spending my lunch in detention."

"That's cute," says Annika with a laugh. "Let her go, Brit. Hurry, Cassie! We need you to get the file to the printer by Thursday."

They need me. Annika and Britney and their stupid little newspaper need me in order to get to press. I don't know whether to feel powerful or sick at the prospect of being all muddled up with them. I've spent most of my middle school and high school years wanting nothing to do with this group at all, and I know, okay? I know they're not real friends.

But they need me.

"I'll see you at lunch, then," I say. My voice is stronger than before.

"See you, Cassie!"

Cassie. I hate that nickname, and I always have. It sounds like a brain-damaged cow's name. A flash of daring, and I speak up. "Cass," I say.

"What?" Britney raises an eyebrow. The mechanical girls turn as one, their faces blank, waiting for their cue.

I clear my throat. "Cass. I like to be called Cass."

Her eyes grow round with surprise, and then she turns slowly to Annika. They burst out laughing, and the whole group follows suit. "Byyyyye, Cassieeeeee!" They all say the hated name in unison and then dissolve into giggles. It stings, a burning shame on my cheeks, but I keep my head up.

"Cass?" Everyone stops laughing and looks at the source of the voice behind me. I turn around slowly. Drew Godfrey.

"Don't you hate it when you smell something really horrible but you can't figure out where it's coming from?" says Annika.

"I smell it too," says Britney. "Maybe a sewer backup?"

"Maybe." Annika squeezes my arm, pulling me away from Drew. "Cassie, walk with us to homeroom?"

I hesitate. Drew's face is pink from the exertion of hiking up the junior stairs, and I can see a light sheen of sweat on her upper lip. "Cass, can I talk to you a minute?" she says. So earnest. Maybe she doesn't hear their comments.

"Come on, Cassie. It stinks over there." Annika tugs me away.

"Or... maybe it's you?" Britney raises one of her perfectly plucked brows, a smirk on her face.

"I—" I look back, and Drew waves her hand. She hears them.

"It's okay, Cass. I'll... tell you at youth group," she says. "No big deal."

I let Annika and Britney steer me away, but I'm torn. I can't quite figure out what happened, what I should have done, how I could have fixed the situation. I don't even like Drew, but I don't like being a part of something hurtful, either. It's one thing to call her the Shrew when I'm talking to Eric or Kayla, and it's another thing entirely to make comments about how she stinks when she's standing right there. Her sad little mud eyes follow me down the hall. I look back twice. Of course I do.

"Youth group? You go to youth group with that mess?" Britney gives me a fake-sad look. "I'd say *her* prayers aren't working." There's something in her voice—some little tone that I don't quite catch at the moment but that works in my head for hours afterward. Something that makes me suspect that Britney can't quite figure out why she's saying the mean things she's saying, either. Like she's scared of the idea of being a mechanical girl, squawking in concert. But maybe she's more scared of the alternative, of being a girl without a personality. Without a crowd.

The tardy bell rings. Damn it. "Now I'll be in lunch detention instead of newspaper," I say. I don't know why I have the one homeroom teacher who treats homeroom like it's an actual class.

"Tell her you were helping me," says Annika. "Tell her it was for the newspaper."

"She doesn't care."

"Trust me." Annika's voice has a final sound of authority, and I can see how she gets what she wants around here. "See you at lunch, *Cassie*," she says with a sly smile.

17. If you could
see into your future…

"Mom is pissed. Family meeting, right now." Dicey's brown eyes twinkle with mischief—both at the prospect of getting me in trouble and at daring to say the word "pissed" *almost* within the hearing of my parents. And on a Wednesday right before church, at that.

I'm not going. Neither is Eric, and this is most certainly the topic of discussion at this impromptu family meeting. Not that you could call what goes on at our family meetings a "discussion." Okay, so occasionally we're allowed to ask questions, but it's very clear that Mom and Dad are a united front, and any disagreement is quickly quelled by open displays of "Because I said so."

I don't care. I'm not going. Eric can give in, but there's no way I'm going to go. Not tonight, not after the stupidity in the hall this morning with Drew—I can't face her. What if she tries to give me more poetry? It's not my fault she can't write. It's not my responsibility to stick up for her when the stupid mean girls insult her. I didn't laugh like the wind-up girls. I didn't say anything to hurt her. It's not my fault, and I'm not going to be the next one they target either. I'm going to keep my mouth shut, mind my own business, and try to get the most out of this opportunity to be a part of the newspaper. For my college applications. For my Song of Myself, maybe, I don't know. Do I have to justify everything?

You know what? I didn't get a tardy from Franklin today, and it was all because I said I was helping Annika and Britney on the newspaper. See? Even the teachers play by their rules.

Okay, so I have to come up with a good reason to skip church. None of this anxiety headache crap like Eric tries to pull. What's making him so anxious every Wednesday and Friday night? So far, he hasn't figured out a way to wiggle out of Sunday morning services, but at least there's only fellowship and Bible Study Luncheon afterward, no youth group.

"I have homework," I say, failing at the creative work of excuse-making. "It's a huge assignment, and I've fallen behind on it already." It's a complete lie, unless you count that stupid Walt Whitman assignment, which I'm definitely not doing. It's not due until Friday. I'm not going to youth group, and I'm not writing poetry.

"So I can't go," I say. A zing of something daring lurches through my chest cavity, a tingle at the back of my neck. I don't think I've ever refused to do anything before, not like this. Sure, I've resisted passively—listening to family prayers without participating, forgetting my Bible—but I've never actually said no.

Dad sighs. It's clear he's frustrated by this pretense of

democracy and wishes he could order me to get in the damn car. "What's the project?" he says.

"Yes, and what do you mean, falling behind?" says my mother. "You're perfectly aware of your responsibilities as a member of this family, and one of those responsibilities happens to be attending church services. You should be able to schedule your homework well enough in advance to make all of your commitments."

The tiny thrill of my defiance keeps me from caving in, keeps my shoulders straight and my eyes firm. "I need to stay home."

"Leave Cass alone," Eric says, surprising me. I figured he'd save his defense for himself. "She's only missed, like, twice in the last five years." He sighs. "Look, I know you're upset with me, but you don't have to take it out on her."

"And you!" Mom moves seamlessly from one target to the next. "Eric, this is the third time this month you've been too sick to go to youth group. What am I supposed to say? What do I tell people when they ask about you?"

"Tell them to mind their own damn business." I can't help it. The words come out before I can filter.

Dad slaps his hand down on the dining room table, making the salt and pepper shakers jump and clatter together. "Fine," he says. "I've had enough of this. We'll all be late if we keep this up." He points at me. "You. Get your priorities clear. Got it?"

I nod, but I wonder what happens if my priorities are different from his. What if my priorities are all my own?

"And you," he says, turning to Eric. "You get yourself

to bed and don't come out for anything. Friday evening you *both* will be coming to church, no excuses. As a *family*." Dad brushes his hands together and stands up. He looks at Dicey. "Get your Bible and get in the car."

I sneak a sidelong glance at Eric. His eye has swollen almost all the way shut and the bruise is a colorful mass of tender-looking flesh. It looks like a fist hit him, not a branch. Does the fist belong to someone in our youth group?

The moment they're out the door, I log into the family computer in the kitchen and pull up one of the blogging sites I researched at school today. I type in the name I chose—Divinia Starr—and settle on a theme that has a dark blue background with little gold stars all over it. The blog set-up is easy compared to the crap I've been doing with the stupid newspaper, and now I'm ready to start. But how?

I guess I need to do some readings, so it'll look like there are already people who need my help. I set Mom's timer for one hour, which is plenty of time to get everything hidden away before everyone gets back from church, and then I go into my room for the cards, trying to think of the kind of problem or question a person might ask about.

Eric's standing there when I get back, looking at the screen. Reading my profile. "*Divinia?*" He makes those stupid air quotes when he says it. "Cass, what is this? Divinia Starr?" He lowers his voice. "The tarot? You aren't seriously doing this, are you?"

I shrug. "I'm making something up."

His eyes stray from my face to the cards in my hands. "Can I see them?" He bites his lip when I hand the cards over.

"Not going to burn me, are they?" His smile is too thin to show his dimples. Eric has two of them, twin divots that make it almost impossible to keep a straight face when he grins at you. I only have one dimple, on my right cheek, which just makes me look lopsided.

He slides the cards out in a little fan, face down, and looks at them. "Did you do that one reading you mentioned, then?" He says it so nonchalantly, like I was going to ask the tarot whether I should have a sandwich or cereal for a snack.

I nod. I can't take my eyes away from his face, from that awful bruise. "Who did that to you?"

"Ran into a branch." He flips over a card. The Ace of Swords. "Is this a good one?"

"Bullshit." I take out the guidebook. "It's obvious, Eric."

"Obviously good?"

"Obviously punched." I tap the book. "*Strength, power, victory, love.* Good things. Now tell me who did it."

He inhales slowly, flipping the card away toward the computer desk. "I don't like this, Cass, these cards."

"Come on, Eric. I know you. You believe in God, and I get that, but you can't convince me you believe in everything Pastor Fordham says. You can't believe there's such a thing as—"

"Dark magic?" Even his thin attempt at a smile disappears. "I don't know, Cass. I mean sure, obviously there are things I have to question, things about the Bible I can't believe, but that's because there's a good reason not to believe. Stuff like this, though... these cards. This is messed-up stuff.

It may not be sorcery like they say, but I can still see plenty of good reasons to avoid them."

I think about the reading I did, all those pictures of sunshine and rainbows and happy families. Right. I reach up and jab my finger into his cheek, which is purple and swollen. He doesn't flinch. "I saw the car. I saw what they did."

"It was nothing," he says, brushing my hand away. "I wish you'd stop."

"Stop what? Stop caring? Stop wondering which asshole punched my brother in the face and pissed all over his boyfriend's car?"

He sets the deck on the edge of the computer desk and shakes his head. "Stop messing with these cards," he says. "Stop trying to be someone you're not." He walks all the way down the hallway without looking back.

I remember his cards; I think of his face. And then I sit back down, double-check the time, and type up my very first reading.

18. Your first crush ...

English class is different now. My finger tingles where I scrubbed off Darin's smiley face, and even though I know it's only my imagination, I keep running the tip of my thumb across it. I'm dreading today because we're supposed to be working on the final drafts of our songs of ourselves, due tomorrow and shit, but when I slide into my seat and Darin shakes his hair out of his eyes, it's hard to deny the grin that forces its way onto my face.

"Hey," he says.

"Hey." Okay. So I can think of worse opening lines. Certainly there are better ones, but I can't find coherent words, at least not while his gray eyes are focused on me.

"Write anything yet?"

"Um." See? I knew I could do worse.

"I thought maybe I could help. You know, give you some ideas."

"What about your own poem?" He doesn't even have a notebook. Like usual, the only thing Darin seems to have brought with him to class is that ever-present black pen.

"Oh, that." He waves his hand. "I'm already failing this class for the semester."

"My parents would kill me." I feel a million shades of stupid for that remark, but it's true. My mom has a stroke if I get a B+ even on my midterm progress report. She makes me go around with a little note asking for extra credit; I have to get each teacher to sign it like I'm in middle school or something. If I got a C, she'd probably enroll me in summer school. Or maybe she'd ship me away to some crazy Christian all-girls school. In eighth grade I got a B- on my report card in Public Speaking, and I was grounded—seriously grounded, with heavy labor every day and no phone or Internet—for an entire quarter until the next grades were out.

But Darin just nods. "I did some research," he says, reaching into his back pocket.

"On what?" On Whitman? I lean closer to see the crumpled page he brings out on the desk.

"On Cassandra," he says. "The mythical Cassandra, from ancient Greece. Or ancient Troy, actually."

Wait—he was researching *me*? Okay, my name, but still. "Didn't she get killed in the Trojan War?" Something about Troy, anyway. "Was it something with the horse?"

He frowns. "Well, yeah, a bunch of bad stuff happens to her, I guess. But that's not the cool part."

"Obviously." I laugh.

"Yeah. So, she was given a gift of prophesy from Apollo," he says."

"She could predict the future?" I think of the tarot, and my hands start to sweat.

"Sort of. I mean, she could, but then she pissed Apollo off somehow and he cursed her."

I remember this story now. "Oh, yeah, she refused to sleep with him."

"So everything she prophesied was true, but the curse was that nobody would believe her until it was too late." Darin tosses his shaggy hair back from his face and fixes me with those eyes again. "Can you imagine how crazy awful that would be? To see all these terrible things, like your own death, or the death of everyone around you? And to have nobody believe you when you try to stop it?"

"Yeah." I grip the cool metal legs of the chair with my clammy hands. "That would really suck."

"So maybe you could write something about that," he says.

"What?" For a second, I almost think he somehow knows about the blog—about my ridiculous fortune-telling. But he couldn't know. Nobody knows about it except Eric, and he wouldn't tell anyone. "What are you talking about?"

He shakes his head. "I—I don't know, exactly. It's just that ... Dawkins says you should figure out something special about yourself, and you say there's nothing. And he says to make something up, but this other Cassandra always told the truth." He tosses his hair again, but it settles right back into the same tousled mess as always. "What if you wrote the truth? About yourself. Tell me ... I mean, tell your readers the truth about you."

"That's the whole problem," I say. What if the truth is something I haven't figured out yet? I could tell all kinds of truths in this poem, I suppose, but none of them would be worth reading about. None of them are mine alone. I don't know why I keep coming back to this—why I don't write about fostering pigs or listening to Kayla's favorite bands or watching her boyfriends do skateboard tricks on the library steps. If I'm going to celebrate myself and sing myself, it feels like I should *know* myself, like that Internet survey. I should know the answers. "There's nothing to tell."

"Maybe I don't believe you," he says. "Maybe nobody will."

19. A secret you wish you didn't know...

All they talk about, pretty much, is each other—the "popular" kids. Today is the last day to work on this issue; it goes to the printer today, and it'll come out sometime tomorrow morning. I'm wrestling with widows and orphans and fonts while Annika and Britney gossip about everyone at school.

"You know why she's switching schools, don't you?" Britney shakes a bottle of pink nail polish. She's been shaking it for at least ten minutes. I wonder if she's actually going to do her nails, or if she just likes to have something to do with her hands while she talks behind people's backs.

"Is it about that whole mess in the locker room?" Annika asks. "Because that was a mistake, actually. Jamie told me personally that they meant to put that deodorant on Drew's lock, not Jillian's."

"No, it's more than that. And I don't even know how you think you can believe anything Jamie says, after what she wrote in that note about Dane."

I roll my eyes. This is tiresome. I wish Jenny would come back from rehab or whatever. I take out my headphones and stick them in my ears, but my music won't play. Stupid battery is dead. Oh well. I leave the headphones in because I'm too lazy to take them out.

"It doesn't matter. You can't tell anyone," says Britney, her voice low but still audible. "Promise me."

"I promise! Duh! About Jillian?"

"Her dad *molested* her!"

"OMG! No way!"

"I'm serious. And she's going to stay with her grandma, who's making her go to the Catholic school. She has a therapist and everything!"

"That is so sick!" Annika squeals, then slaps her hand over her mouth. "I know I shouldn't laugh, but ewwww! I totally knew something was weird about her, too!"

"Shhhhh!" I can feel Britney's wide, vacant eyes on the back of my head. "You can't tell *anyone.*"

Annika laughs, but more softly. "She can't hear us. She's got her music on." She raises her voice a notch. "Right, Cassie?"

I don't react. I continue deliberately linking text boxes from the front page of the paper to their continuations on later pages. It's not that I want to keep listening to their stupid conversation, but I can't handle them knowing I've been listening, either. It feels wrong, hearing them talk about people like this, and I wish my music were playing right now, so loudly I could truly claim ignorance of these awful gossip sessions.

"See?" Annika giggles. "Besides, Cassie doesn't care about

Jillian screwing her daddy. *She's* only got eyes for that Neanderthal comic book girl. Kayla with the weird dinosaur."

"Do you really think?" Britney sounds uncertain.

"Oh, she's totally a lesbian. Look at the way she dresses."

They're talking about *me*. I have to fight to stay focused on the screen, which is now blurry. I will not cry in front of these stupid, shallow mean girls. *Will not.* My hands want to curl up into fists, but I keep them on the keyboard, thumbing shortcuts to place a new ad into the space at the bottom of page four. There's an empty spot. I'm supposed to fill it with an image of the Gordon Golden Gophers or maybe a reminder about the upcoming Winter Carnival. Instead, I blink back tears and type in the url for my new blog.

I make it look like one of those plain little business card ads, with my name in the center—*Divinia Starr*. I pause. *Mystic and Medium.* Silly, a little, but I don't have a lot of time here to think. I tap my fingers on the keyboard, thinking of a slogan, but my head isn't in the best place, so I type *You know you're curious!* below the web address and save the ad. Ha. It sounds like porn.

Glancing over my shoulder at Annika and Britney, whose heads are still bent close together sharing scandals in fake-shock stereo, I open the browser and click over to my site so I can add a few details to my post—a fake reading about a boy who wants to know if the girl who sits next to him in English class would go out with him—before it goes live. I wish I could make my answers kind of clever and cryptic, like little riddles, but I'm afraid I'm not a good enough writer for that. And I'm not nearly a good enough tarot reader. I read through the draft, adding a few details from my memory of the cards and a few from my imagination. What does it matter if I embellish a little? The boy doesn't really exist. I plug in a card from Eric's reading—Temperance, the winged angel figure with the triangle. It's visually interesting, and the meaning fits my advice to go for the girl. *A perfect union*, said my guidebook.

I'm adding tags to my post when Britney says his name: Eric Randall. I keep my head from snapping around. They have to realize he's my brother, right? We have the same last name, the same high forehead, the same unruly brown hair.

" . . . gave Eric a black eye, you know." Britney's voice is so soft I have a hard time catching the words.

"What's their problem?" Annika says, slightly louder.

"I don't know, but there's going to be trouble."

"That's so disgusting, though, you know? Nasty."

"I know. I can't even believe they're telling people. They're so freaking gross." Britney laughs with that awful wind-up laughter that all of the mechanical girls use around Annika.

My face burns. The computer screen in front of me grows dim and swims in front of my eyes. I can't believe they're talking about my brother like this. Okay, so I guess it's not so surprising—it's not like I've never heard gay bashing before, but, like, I thought we were beyond this at my school. I mean, did they really call my brother and Gavin *nasty*? They're the ones who are nasty.

I punch my index finger against the mouse button, publishing my post, and then close the browser and send the newspaper file to pdf. I want to get out of here, away from these vacuous backstabbers.

"That's the worst part," says Annika. "The fact that they're actually *bragging* about *urinating* on Gavin's car. Like, grow up, losers. *Obviously* they have a deep-seated feeling of inadequacy to be overcompensating like that."

"Right?" Britney laughs again.

Wait. Okay, so Britney and Annika think the *other guys* are the disgusting ones? And they know who they are? I pull my headphones out of my ears.

"Hey." They both look up, startled by my presence. "The file's ready for the printer. We're right on schedule to distribute tomorrow."

Twin fake smiles, as the two girls wonder how much I heard. Do they realize that they are, like, exactly the same kind of people as the "overcompensating losers" that they're making fun of? Do they not even see the comparison between the kind of gossipy meanness they excel at and the cowardice of whoever attacked Eric and vandalized Gavin's car? More importantly, though, can I get them to tell me who it was? I search their eyes for any hint, but the two sets of bright blue eyes are equally empty. Robot Bitches, activated to "saccharine-sweet."

"Cassie, we looooooove you!" gushes Britney, using her best baby-voice.

"You saaaaaaved us!" Annika adds her own nauseating squeal.

"So you know who punched my brother in the eye."

Instant uncomfortable silence. The two girls look at each

other and shrug. "Blake Peters," says Britney, at the same time as Annika blurts out, "Ronnie Fischer."

Blake and Ronnie. Of course. Lead guitarist and drummer for the Youth Group Praise Band. No wonder Eric doesn't want to go to church. Looks like tomorrow night just got more interesting.

"Don't tell them we told you, though," says Britney, her voice once more a breathy hush.

Annika laces her fingers into her blond hair. "Yeah, they'd kill us," she says.

20. If you were a fictional character…

Darin fixes me with a piercing look. "Shut up. Don't tell me you couldn't get a single line of your poem written, Cassandra. I'm the laziest one in this whole class, and even I have something to turn in today." He turns his paper over, but I catch a glimpse of stars, an inky galaxy with a tiny stick figure at the bottom, gazing up into a giant telescope.

"I got something," I say, closing my notebook quickly. "I'm not quite done yet."

"You got two lines, both of which were written by Whitman." He shakes his head. "Why is this so hard? Just write something."

"I will. I just…haven't yet."

"I bet I could write a song about you."

My heart. It feels like someone just scrubbed my entire chest over an old wooden washboard: *thumpa thumpa thump.* "Yeah, right. There's nothing to write about me," I say.

"I'm pretty sick of you saying that." He picks up his black pen and takes my notebook.

"Hey, that's mine."

"Just a sec," he says, pulling a blank sheet of paper out of the middle. "I celebrate Cassandra and sing Cassandra." He writes quickly, in tiny block letters. His hands are sheathed in the cuffs of his sweatshirt, holes cut in the seams for his thumbs. "The quirk of her eyebrow as she debates whether or not to smack me." His look is baiting; he returns to the page in a furious scribble, narrating as he writes: "The spikes... of her dark hair... like a... a... hedgehog halo... above her increasingly... annoyed countenance."

I reach for the page, which he guards with his arm, still scribbling. "Her charming lack... of self-awareness. The futile blows... of her fist... against my shoulder. The long, wavering gust... of her... angry... sigh. *Ouch!*"

I punch him again for good measure. "Okay. I get it. I'll write something."

"Maybe you should ask this chick for some help." He pulls a rolled newspaper out of his back pocket and spreads it out on the table. "Here. Divinia Starr." He taps the small ad I placed yesterday.

Am I blushing? I hope not. "A fortune-teller? How is that going to help me?"

"A mystic and medium," he says. "Come on, don't you think it could be fun?"

"I don't believe in mystics and mediums." It's the first copy of this edition of *The Gordon High Gazette* I've seen today, and I get a little thrill from seeing my ad there, even if nobody knows it's mine.

Darin grows serious. "Oh, right. I'm sorry, Cass. That was insensitive, I guess."

"What?" What happened? How did this conversation go so fast from flirty and funny to awkward and weird?

He shrugs, looking down. He doodles a little crystal ball in the middle of the ad, and then he shrugs again and looks up at me. "Well. You go to Joyful News, right?"

Oh, *that*. I shake my head quickly. "I'm not ... I don't ... "

"It's cool." He smiles, peering up at me again through his bangs with those incredible eyes. "I shouldn't have brought it up."

My mouth is dry, but it forms the words, "I'm on my way to becoming an atheist." Something about this kid pulls the truth out of me.

I don't expect the laugh that explodes out of him. "Well, write about *that*, Cassandra. I mean, being an atheist in a family of fundamentalists has got to count for something of interest, doesn't it?"

Does it? "It's not something I can write about," I say. I can only imagine what that poem would stir up, if anyone in my family read it.

He nods. "Ah. Gotcha. Well, maybe you can figure out a metaphor?"

"I think I'm allergic to metaphors. I get hives." Okay, so metaphors aren't so bad once someone explains them to me, gives me detailed notes to spit out on the exam, but please don't expect me to interpret them on my own. And dream on if you think I can write one.

Mr. Dawkins taps the edge of my desk. "So did you make something up?" His voice is gentle, but the set of his mouth means business.

"I'm still working on it." I work on shrinking down to a size so insignificant he'll forget I exist and pass on to the next slacker, but he doesn't budge.

"Let's see what you have so far." Mr. D's persistence is admirable for a veteran teacher. Most of the faculty at Gordon have already settled into their pre-retirement mode of half-hearted, long-memorized lectures and prolonged sessions of busywork. Mr. D insists on being one of the ones who still pushes, relentlessly, against the tide of student apathy. Today I hate him for it.

"It's too rough," I say, keeping my hand flat on top of the cover of my closed notebook. "I'll show you when I get it polished."

"Show me, and I can help give some revision ideas."

Panic. "It's on my computer at home." The old stand-by excuse.

"Recreate it here," he says, and he officially becomes the second person to pick up my notebook without my permission, sliding it out from under my resisting hand. He opens it up to a blank sheet of paper. "*Now*, Cass. I'll be back to check in ten minutes."

"Now you're screwed," says Darin out of the side of his mouth.

"Sure." I draw geometric shapes in the top margin. "I celebrate myself, and sing myself, for I am screwed."

"Write it," says Darin.

"Write that?"

"Write your song. Write Cassandra." He's drawing, too, on the silly poem he wrote about me. A spiky-haired girl with manga eyes glares up from the faint blue lines. In her hand she wields a crystal ball.

"I can't..." I don't know how to finish my sentence. Why is he drawing me as a fortune-teller? Once again, I feel like he somehow *knows*.

"Can I tell you something?" Darin keeps drawing, adding to his picture. I can see now that he's drawing the Cassandra myth... and her brother, Hector, dead on his shield. Lovely. "It's weird."

"*You're* weird," I say, but I smile. Somehow I'm always smiling around him.

A little pause, and I can feel him sort of gathering up his words. I feel bad for teasing him—it's obvious he's being completely serious here. I open my mouth to apologize, but he holds up his hand.

"I can remember the first moment I realized you existed." He clears his throat, but not nervously—like a storyteller, maybe. "It was in the underground mine, back in eighth grade."

"The field trip." Of course I remember the underground mine. There's this awesome elevator that takes you a mile under the earth's surface, and they turn out the lights when you're under and it's perfectly dark. "You remember *me*?" I add. From eighth grade? I try to remember him, but the best I can do is a faint recollection of a Spider-Man lunchbox. And that could have been any of the middle school boys, really, with their fuzzy little buzz cuts and their pant legs always too short.

"I remember your face. During the tour. There was this lady talking about that underground physics lab, you know? She was talking about dark matter and, like, neutrinos whizzing around the earth through solid bedrock, and I looked up at your face—I remember I'd just finished reading *A Wrinkle in Time*—and you were so enthralled. You reminded me..." He trails off, ducking his head closer to his drawing.

"Of what?" *A Wrinkle in Time* is the last book I truly loved. Ms. Privett in the fifth grade read it out loud to us, and she had the most amazing Mrs. Whatsit voice. I asked my mom for a Bunsen burner that Christmas, but she thought I was kidding.

"Write something." He taps my paper, which is still empty. "You reminded me of Meg Murry," he says, and he shrugs. "I thought you'd be a cool person to travel through time and space with."

I laugh. "I am pretty good at math," I say. "Much better than poetry."

21. Describe the kind of student you are ...

Mr. D keeps me after class to discuss my midterm grade, which he will be "forced to mark as an incomplete" if I don't finish this stupid poem. And if he does that, my parents will get a stupid automatic email alerting them that I have to turn in the missing work within two weeks or I'll get an F.

"So you'd best get that amazing creation off your computer this evening and bring it in to me before homeroom Monday. My grade book needs to be finalized by noon, and I'd hoped to get everything for this half of the term marked over the weekend."

Ack, it's like I'm right back in middle school. Okay, so I'll write the damn poem, right? I'll do it tonight. I will. Except I have youth group tonight. And then I have to babysit for Mrs. Rennan's twins all day Saturday. And Kayla and I have talked like five times this week about how we're going to the movies Saturday night ... so she'll probably call, for real this time.

"I will, Mr. D. It's practically done on my computer, I promise."

"Cass?" He's doing it again—those bony teacher fingers gripping my shoulder in a clutch of concern. I take a step back, wrenching free of his worry.

"Have a good weekend!" I force a smile and head toward the door of the nearly empty classroom.

"Cass, is everything okay?" He doesn't move to follow me, but his hands sort of float around in midair like he's lost something important and is trying to put his finger on where he left it.

I feel bad about taking off so abruptly when he clearly would like me to confide in him. Mr. D is a genuinely nice guy, and it's not really his fault he's a teacher. I mean, how many jobs can there possibly be for guys who wear corduroy blazers and get all jittery over the words of some dead guy's poetry?

"Everything's great, Mr. D. See you Monday!" And I'm out, merging into the slipstream of hallway traffic before he can say anything else, anything that would change even the slightest fiber of my existence.

22. Your typical
Saturday night...

"You are so completely transparent, Cassandra Randall." Kayla slides her lunch tray along the metal runners as she expresses her disdain.

"And you are so completely...the opposite of transparent." I crash my tray into hers, just because. Because she's here for once, with me, eating lunch. Like a best friend. Okay, so I had to beg her to get her to come, but still.

"*Enigmatic. Obscure. Ambiguous.*" She ignores my bumper-car move.

"*Arrogant. Patronizing.*" I pause, searching my brain for a vocabulary word. "*Pontificating.*"

"Uh, *no*," she says, rolling her eyes. "And I'm talking about Divinia Starr."

"Shhh." Does she not get the concept of a pen name?

"It was in the newspaper, Cass. Everyone's talking about Divinia Starr and her ridiculous tarot reading."

I have to learn how to control my facial capillaries. "Already?" My voice is barely above a whisper.

"The paper came out while we were in the lab for social studies, so of course half the class checked out the blog."

"And?"

Kayla sniffs. "I suppose most people were reasonably intrigued. But really, Cass. The boy who has a crush on the girl who sits next to him in English class? Could you *be* more obvious?"

Damn it, I'm blushing again. "He won't know it's me," I say. "Will he?"

"Maybe I'll tell him."

"You wouldn't." I should never have told her about that. Also, what was I thinking with that entry? Okay, so it was difficult to come up with a question out of the blue. I may have borrowed from real life, or at least from wishful-thinking life. My cheeks burn.

"Do you really think he has a crush on you?" We sit at our old table and I glance around to make sure nobody else is listening.

Emily Friar looks at me over her peanut butter sandwich. "Who? Who's got a crush on you?" She grins and elbows Cordelia, who looks up from her sheet music or whatever she's studying and squints at me as though she can't remember who I am, even though I eat here almost every day.

"Nobody. Nothing," I say quickly, shooting a nasty look at Kayla. "No. I don't know. It wasn't him."

Kayla takes a bite out of her droopy slice of cafeteria pizza. "Uh huh."

"It wasn't." *Uh huh.*

"Are you talking about that boy from the fortune-teller blog?" Emily leans forward, but Kayla shoots her a scathing look and changes the subject.

"You gonna be busy tonight? Speaking in tongues, I suppose," she says to me.

"Shut up." It's not like that. Okay, so sometimes people at church do actually speak in tongues, like every once in a while. Very rarely. I mean, I can remember, like, three times. "I don't make fun of your religion."

"You couldn't. It's too boring." She shrugs. "Anyway, I thought I'd see if by some miracle, or anti-miracle I guess, you weren't busy tonight so we could do something, but whatever."

"Aren't we going to a movie tomorrow?" She promised. Saturdays used to be our regular movie and sleepover nights, but ever since Kayla's dad married Rhonda and bought Kayla that old hearse to make up for it, she's been running to the Twin Cities to stay with her sister every weekend, leaving me all alone. But this weekend, she promised. My stomach lurches a little at the evasive look on her face and I can't believe she's ditching me again.

"Yeah, well. I might have … I might have a sort of date-type thing." A bit of color creeps over Kayla's pale cheeks.

"A date?" Emily squeals, determined to get some gossip one way or another. "Tell all!"

"I'm not at liberty to say." Kayla clams up, and once she's gone broody there's no way of getting her to talk again, so we spend the rest of the lunch period mostly in silence. Even

Emily gives up after Kayla puts her headphones on and takes out her sketchpad.

I poke at my food with a spork. I can't believe she's going on a date instead of having a movie night. I know who it is—that weird Gary kid from her art class who's always hanging around our locker at the end of the day, being awkward. Kayla's no stranger to boys, but her type is usually the (much older) musicians who play at the all-age shows she's always going to down in Minneapolis. From her brief reports, those guys are mostly hook-ups involving varying degrees of sobriety and nakedness. And then there's Gary. He's so *weird*. I imagine them sitting next to each other for hours without talking, both of them immersed in their own sketches. At the end of the night, Kayla would unload him from the hearse with the same disinterested wave she gives me, and that would be that.

In any case, my Saturday night now stretches ahead of me wide open and empty, with nothing to distract me from my stupid poetry assignment. My eyes slide over to Emily and I listen to her talk about how she's going to the roller rink Saturday night with her cousin and her cousin's boyfriend, but I can't manage to invite myself.

"We barely ever do anything together anymore." I pull Kayla's headphones out of her left ear to whine like a jealous girlfriend. This is pathetic, but I don't care. She may not be perfect, but she's my best friend, and I want something to remind me why. And this ... this is not doing it.

She shrugs and looks away. "Maybe ... "

"Maybe what?" What is she saying?

Kayla pulls the headphones out of her other ear and sighs,

closing her eyes for a second. The sound of her music spills out and I remember the summer the two of us decided to be in a heavy metal band, despite the fact that neither of us played a musical instrument or knew how to sing. I wonder if my guitar is still in the basement, waiting for a new set of strings. I should go and look. When did I become such a shadow of myself? No wonder Kayla's dumping me.

"I don't know, Cass. I guess it's ... well? I don't know." She picks at her nail polish, little flecks of black drifting down on top of her creamed corn in slow motion.

"Talk to me, Kayla. What the hell does that mean?" I can't believe this. I've been her best friend since second grade. I stuck with her through that awful pixie cut when she was nine, and the slouching when she grew to be six feet tall overnight, and her parents' divorce, and her dad's remarriage, and the black makeup and the boyfriends and the obscure comics and the disdainful hatred of everything related to Sterling Creek. And all this without expecting anything from her.

Her shoulders bob up and down again, and she stares down at her fingers. "It means nothing, Cass. It means I have a date, that's all."

"So ... it's nothing ... with us?" Oh god. Did I really just say *us*, like we're going out? Maybe I *am* a lesbian.

"Look." Kayla grips the edge of her tray with both hands and makes eye contact. "We're fine. But you're always busy with church, and ... well, I don't know. I feel like we're ... growing apart, a little."

Growing apart, what the hell? "I can't help the church stuff, Kayla. You know that. But this ... "

She stands up, holding the tray in front of her. She towers over me. "It's fine, Cass. It's only a date. But . . . well, memories from middle school aren't always enough to have in common with someone." And then she's gone, headed down to the basement art grotto, probably, and I'm alone.

23. When you look in the mirror…

Dicey leans on me in the pew, her head on my shoulder. It may sound sweet, but she's totally doing it to annoy me.

"Get off me." My voice is a low hiss, but of course Mom hears me and glares.

"But I looooove you, sissy!" Her whisper is right in my ear as she leans, leans, leans. I fight the urge to shove her, because that will piss everyone off and give her what she wants, besides—to get me into trouble.

"Lean this way, Dice," says Eric. I keep staring at his profile, looking for some sign of his discomfort, but he looks happy to be here, his face serene and attentive. He puts his arm around Dicey's shoulders and pulls her off me. Pastor Fordham spits and sputters, and I busy my fingers with braiding the ribbons hanging out of the Bible in the rack on the pew ahead of me. I'm so focused on my braiding that I miss the actual landing of the projectile, but I certainly can't miss my dad's reaction.

"Young man, *what* in heaven's name do you think you are doing?" This is the first time I've ever witnessed my father speaking *out loud* in church when it is not his turn to do so.

My brother shakes his head. "I didn't..." He bends to retrieve the tiny, folded-paper wedge that bounced off the side of his left temple and landed on the floor in front of my father. Eric's face is red as he ducks down into the space between Dad's knee and the back of the pew in front of us. I can't see the place where the paper "wasp" hit him, but I would bet there's a welt forming at this moment. I've only been hit by one of those things once, in the middle of my back where my bra clasp is, and it hurt like crazy for days.

I turn in my seat. I can't believe this. Who shoots a freaking paper wasp in church? Who shoots a paper wasp outside of seventh grade?

The faces behind me are uniform, factory-molded into identical expressions as they wait for the sermon to conclude. Several sets of eyes narrow at me, making small judgments about the type of girl who turns around in the middle of service and cranes her head about, staring at people. Didn't they see the paper wad come sailing through? I search for a face that looks different—a guilty face. A face that looks almost painfully interested in Pastor Fordham. The pale, freckle-smattered face of Blake Peters.

"It was Blake," I hiss to Dicey, who tells Eric, who shakes his bowed head a fraction and keeps his eyes on his hands, folded in his lap. I think about that stinging bit of paper he's folded his fingers around, the way it must feel to hold that piece of someone's hatred, to know yourself a target. The bruise is fading around his eye. His huddled shoulders are narrow beneath his neatly pressed polo.

Dicey gives me a look, and I shrug. What can I tell her? What can I tell anyone? Dad's eyes keep moving along the row of us, trying to figure out what's going on, but all that really matters to him is that there is order. After a while, he places one of his heavy hands on Eric's knee for a moment—a benediction or a dismissal—and then he focuses his attention back on Pastor Fordham, who is winding up into the part of his sermon where he ties all his scattered points together and binds them up in the reedy cord of his passionate voice. It's the part that draws murmurs and head nods from the members of the congregation; the ones who especially want to prove they were paying close attention throughout the sermon may add in an exclamation of "Praise the Lord" here and there, in a moderately reserved, Minnesota kind of way.

Friday night isn't real church; it's a "brief message" followed by Bible study for the adults and youth group for those of us who are still clawing our way through our adolescence. Most of the time, our discussions on Friday are pretty laid back, and often they're combined with or followed by a social activity, such as bowling or a movie/game in the church basement. Tonight, though, Terry looks absolutely dead serious as he leads us downstairs to our meeting. We gather around, pushing the two battered serving tables together and sliding into our habitual spots.

Eric hasn't said a word about what happened upstairs, and he keeps his head down, though I see Blake trying to catch his attention by snapping a rubber band around his wrist. Bile rises in my throat. My hands itch to rip him to shreds.

"Hey, Cass." Drew scoots in beside me and offers a shy smile. "What's up Terry's butt tonight, do you think?"

I laugh before I remember that this is Drew the Shrew, and I'm not supposed to be encouraging her. "Clearly something very sharp and ugly," I say.

"Wow, you've got your Bible for once."

"Yeah, you know me. I wouldn't want to make waves."

Beside me, Eric snorts. The breathy girl across the table listens, her mouth turned down in a little bow.

Drew nods, and I think about the little ripples she makes, the ways she challenges the thinking of this group in small ways. "I'm lucky," she says. "I'm not here for my parents."

Drew's parents aren't members of Joyful News; I've never even seen them. She comes here all on her own, week after week, though nobody ever talks to her. Okay, so I talk to her a little bit, but only because I can't handle being blatantly cruel to someone that weak. Still, why does she come? I don't understand, I guess, what would draw a person here without some connection. I'm not saying I think you'd have to be forced, like I am, but it's not like she started coming with a friend or something. She showed up all on her own.

"I would never be here if it *weren't* for my parents," I say. It's perfectly true, but at the same time it's false, a statement like that. You can't really tell the truth about never and always. Who would I be, without my parents? Without my brother, without my friends? All along, I've been trying to answer this, but I'm all snarled up in everyone else's truth, in everyone else's lies.

Around the table, eyes flicker up to mine and then away. They start to talk about their beliefs, about why they're here. Everyone who speaks up claims to be here out of faith, out of belief. They look at me, judging.

"What? I'm here, aren't I?" I want them to stop staring at me. It's not like I chose to be this person—this rational person who can't accept their truth without some actual evidence. I didn't look for reasons to doubt, and it's not like their disapproving scowls are going to convince me of divinity, either.

Ronnie and Blake have positioned themselves exactly opposite Eric and me. They elbow each other. "If you hate it so much, maybe you should leave," says Ronnie.

"Yeah, maybe you should." Blake snaps the rubber band against the inside of his wrist and I look at Eric, at the red mark above his left eye.

Terry clears his throat. "Everyone is welcome here," he says. "And anyway, this isn't the topic I wanted to discuss this evening, so if you could just..."

"Everyone's welcome?" Ronnie isn't ready to let it go yet. "What if I don't feel *welcome* here knowing that some of our members don't believe."

"And what if I don't feel welcoming toward people who are deliberately defying the teachings of Christ?" adds Blake. I hate the way his freckles give him that cute, innocent-kid look. I'd like to scour his face with steel wool. "You're always telling us that we should keep away from evil influences," he adds, staring at me.

"Yes!" says Terry, pouncing on the words. "That's what I want to discuss!" He's breathless, desperate to get the discussion back on track. "Evil influences are all around us. The images we are fed every day from our televisions, from movies and music videos—these images don't support a healthy spiritual connection with God." He pauses for a moment to consult his notes, and I feel a little bad for the guy. I can picture him sitting alone in some efficiency apartment, his nervous preparations.

"Yeah, like all the gay-rights people who try to convince us to turn away from God's path," says Ronnie. His greasy gaze slides over me and lands on Eric, whose head is bent over his Bible, one finger resting on the page. I know without looking that he's pointing to John 3:17, the verse about God sending Jesus here to save us, not to condemn us. Eric keeps these words on an index card taped to his bedroom wall; he letters the passage neatly onto the covers of his notebooks, recites it as a mantra. These are the words that allow him to exist without being torn in half by his faith.

"Uh…" Terry always hates it when the discussion wanders into sex. Usually he chooses this moment to suggest a group prayer, but instead he pulls a newspaper out of the canvas tote bag near his feet and opens it to a page that looks very familiar to me. "This is more what I wanted to talk about, actually." He points at the ad for Divinia Starr.

I smother my laughter. It's all so ridiculous, you know—to go from a rather uncomfortable public examination of my lack of faith, to an implied attack against my brother's sexuality, and now this. They're fast, I have to give them credit for that. It's funny, right? So funny.

"What is it?" It's the breathy, earnest girl. She reaches for the newspaper and reads the ad with her lips moving.

"It's evil," says Terry simply. "Insidious evil. In your school newspaper."

I can't breathe. I push my chair back and mumble an apology—I have the hiccups, a scratchy throat, my contact fell out—whatever, I don't even know what I'm saying, but I need to get out of here before I lose it to the tsunami of laughter inside me. I run into the bathroom and stare into the mirror above the sink, trying to get a grip, to stare down the mirth inside me. A yellow beam of light from the ceiling fixture falls across the glass, making it hard to see. I lean in closer—for whatever reason I feel like I need to see myself clearly.

Okay, so I'm not crazy, but really, this is what happens. Have you ever done this? Have you locked eyes with yourself in a strange mirror and wondered about the spaces between the spinning motes of dust? There is the Cassandra in the mirror, and here is the Cassandra standing on pale pink tile, leaning over a sink that is decorated with a crocheted yellow soap dispenser cover and a little wicker basket filled with slightly dusty potpourri. And which one am I? The Cassandra in the mirror is clearly the crazy one. I can't take my eyes off her eyes (or can she not take her eyes off mine?), and I watch as two round tears well up and hang on her lower lashes, water molecules desperately clinging together against the force of gravity. I don't understand. Why is she—am I—crying? I feel a drop on my hand. I reach up to touch the surface of the mirror with the tip of my finger, forcing myself out of the dissociative moment and into reality. The teardrop slides across my wrist, leaving a trail.

This is reality. I have no faith and my brother is gay and my youth group leader thinks I'm insidious evil. And I can't tell the difference between myself and a reflection.

"Cassandra?" Drew whispers from the doorway of the bathroom. Her voice doesn't surprise me; I heard her turning the knob. I knew it would be her, yet I didn't do anything to hide this mess. Neither Cass tries to fix herself up, to look a little less crazy.

"Are you ... okay?"

I mean, it's obvious I'm not. But I nod because ... well, what else am I going to say to Drew freaking Godfrey? It's not like she's going to somehow help me, when she can't even help herself. I tear my eyes away from my eyes in the mirror.

"I'm fine." Haha.

"Is it what Ronnie said?" Drew chews a little on the end of her ponytail. "You know. About the gay thing?"

The gay thing? I study her face, trying to read the intentions behind the question. "No." I wipe the back of my hand across my eyes. "It's not that. It's ..." And what is it?

She hands me a tissue and smiles. "Well, they were being stupid, you know. Not like that's a big challenge for Ronnie and Blake."

I take the tissue, squeeze it in my fist, brave a quick glimpse at Mirror Cass to see if she's less crazy now or what. "I'm failing my English class."

Wait. I didn't say that, did I? Really? Why would I tell Drew Godfrey about my stupid English grade?

"I saw him talking to you after class," she says, and then she blushes. "I mean, I'm not stalking you or anything, you know. I've got Dawkins' class after you. The regular American Lit class. Not honors."

Oh, right. I remember her now, slipping past us with her lumbering tread. "Yeah, it's this poem thing," I say. "I can't write poetry."

Mirror Cassandra catches my eye, but she looks okay now. She looks relieved, like she's actually glad I told someone about this stupid poem. Like she's glad I told Drew.

"I … I could help you?"

I hate it when people uptalk. "I … I don't really think it's the kind of thing someone could help me with." Unless she wanted to write it for me. But I've seen her poetry, and it pretty much sucks. Though, does it suck as much as me not turning in a poem at all? But okay. So I need a poem. But … I think of Annika, the way her nose scrunched up, the way she said she was looking out for me. I know—I'm not dumb. I know Annika's awful, and the way she treated Drew wasn't right. But … if I start letting Drew think that I'm her friend, won't it be worse for her? She's going to come up to me more often in the halls, and Annika and Britney will be even meaner. Or maybe they'll drop me, too. Like Kayla did. The empty hole of my weekend stretches out ahead of me, and for a second I'm afraid the stupid tears will come back.

Drew's face turns a dark plum color. "Maybe you could come over after group ends, and we could work on it together?

I mean, it's Friday, you could...well, I suppose you have week-end plans already."

I tear the tissue in my fist into shreds. The only plan I thought I had has evaporated. I look up, but Mirror Cassandra looks as uncertain as I feel. I need an excuse, a reasonable excuse, and fast, why I can't go over to Drew's house. An excuse that doesn't involve me telling her she's gross or stinky or that she has this pathetic habit of being unable to recognize the end of a conversation.

"It's okay," she says, shaking her head and smiling. "Really, I get it, Cass. You're so nice to me here that sometimes I forget we're not actually friends." She shrugs and goes back to playing with her hair. "Do you remember that time in sixth grade? What you said to Gunnar Nelson during the rehearsal for the Christmas concert?"

"I think that would be great," I say. Wait, what concert is she talking about? "If you could help me on my poem, I mean. I don't have any other plans." Gunnar Nelson was an incredibly stupid kid with white-blond hair and a turned-up nose who used to go to this church. I'd forgotten about him entirely.

"Really? You'd come to my house?" Drew's voice rises almost a whole octave in her excitement. "My mom will be so excited!"

Her mom? I give Mirror Cassandra a stern frown, but her returning frown looks sort of...I don't know. Satisfied, some-how.

"What did I say to Gunnar Nelson?" I can't believe I agreed to this.

She giggles. "He was flicking my neck, you know? He

used to do that all the time, and you turned to him—you know how you raise that one eyebrow like you do? You did that, and you said, 'Do you think it impresses people when you act like that? Because, frankly, it makes you seem like the biggest moron.'" She moves one hand to the nape of her neck, her fingers tracing over old memories. "He stopped flicking me then, and he never did it again."

24. Your inspiration . . .

It takes about five minutes for Drew to decide that I'm hopeless.

"I can't help it," I say, my voice laced with whining. "The words don't line up for me, not like this. There's nothing to sing about myself."

She stares at me. "I don't believe you."

"What?"

"I can't believe that someone as perfect as you could have trouble finding things to celebrate about her life." She doesn't blush, doesn't chew on her hair. Drew is surprisingly confident about herself here in her own bedroom.

I don't really know what I expected Drew Godfrey's bedroom to look like. Pathetic, I guess. Pink, maybe? Filled with cross-stitched Bible verses and photos of babies in flowers or something? I don't know. Instead, it's pretty and sophisticated like the rest of the house, with framed photographs on the wall—black and white prints of a bunch of women singers I don't recognize. She has a beautiful dark wood desk that matches the dresser and bed frame, and there's a tall vase full of some kind of creamy white flowers on the desk. It's nothing at all like any teenager's bedroom I've ever seen—more like a magazine photo—and it's nothing like the baggy-sweatshirt, dirty-hair mess that is Drew.

"Right, I'm perfect." I roll my eyes, because what else is there to do? There's no way to convince someone who thinks your life is perfect that, in fact, it's really not.

"There has to be *something* you enjoy doing, that you're good at." She waits, like Mr. Dawkins waited, like Darin waited, like Kayla has apparently been waiting for the duration of our friendship. Waiting for me to do something interesting.

"I don't know." My mouth opens, and there's an instant where I actually think about telling her about Divinia Starr. But that would be so dumb.

"What do you think about that fortune-telling blog?" Drew's question startles me. It's like she's reading my mind.

"What?"

"That ad Terry was talking about, right before you left youth group? It was for this fortune-teller, I guess. A blog. Her site asks people to email her questions and then she'll read some kind of fortune-telling cards or something and give you an answer. I think Terry's overreacting. I mean, it seems like a game, not pure evil or whatever." Here in her bedroom, Drew has opinions. She waits for mine.

"I don't know." I can't tell her. "I don't really believe in evil." Once I've said it, though, I'm not sure. It's one of those absolutes, those truths I have a hard time pinning down.

"Not at all? Like...you don't believe in hell?" She raises her eyebrows, but she's curious, not shocked.

I don't know. Hell isn't very logical. Where *is* it, for starters? And sin. It's so absolute. How can someone draw a line down the center of life and say these things are okay and these things will cause eternal damnation, with the fires and the demons and the pain. And heaven too, for that matter. When I was a little kid, I used to believe in God, used to imagine him holding me at night when I was scared or sad or having a hard time falling asleep. I used to believe he would put his arms around me and rock me like a little baby, like a mother would hold her baby. But now?

"I don't believe in anything," I say. Is it the truth? Yes and no, I guess, like everything else. I expect Drew to be upset, to argue with me, maybe. To ask more questions. Instead, she sort of frowns like she's deep in concentration and takes a battered spiral notebook out of a small desk drawer. She writes something without looking at me. I feel so awkward.

"Drew?"

She doesn't look up, her pen moving fast, until finally she brings her pen up to her mouth and bites the end. "I celebrate Cassandra and sing Cassandra," she says. "The girl who disbelieves. Free of heaven, free of hell, free like grass and leaves." She laughs. "I was trying to make a reference to the *Leaves of Grass* thing, you know? But I'm ridiculous about rhyming, and I don't think Whitman would appreciate that at all." She tears out the page and crumples it into a ball. "But you could...play with that idea, maybe?"

Her stupid uptalking again. I scowl. "What idea?"

She chews her pen, speaking around it. "The freedom of not believing in stuff."

I look down at my own page, which is still empty aside from those two lines of Whitman: *I celebrate myself, and sing myself, and what I assume you shall assume.* So I assume nothing. And this is enviable for Drew? "But you don't *have* to believe anything," I tell her. "You choose to come to church all on your own."

"Oh, I know. I have freedom, too." Drew shifts a little, looking her usual uneasy self for the first time since we got to her house. "Especially with my mom gone all the time. She's a textiles buyer. Travels all over the place. She used to let me come with her sometimes, but..." She tugs at her sleeves. "My skin doesn't react well to lots of different kinds of water and soaps and things. Also, the textiles. It's all kind of bad for my eczema."

I remember the red patches on her arms when she came to the nurse's office, and I don't know what to say. The rosy blotches she sometimes has on her face—the way Annika and Britney are always teasing her about having acne. *Stop.* I am not going to start feeling sorry for Drew Godfrey. I'm not so desperate for a friend that as soon as Kayla dumps me I go running to the lowest common denominator. I'm only here for some help with this stupid poem. With my stupid English class.

"So, this shouldn't rhyme?" I ask. See Cassandra panic. See Cassandra change the subject. See Cassandra fail Basic Conversation Skills.

Drew rubs her arms through the fabric of her shirt—two

brisk movements—and then she straightens up, composing her face into a businesslike mask. "Walt Whitman was free verse."

"That's so … free." I yearn for my five paragraph essay. For thesis statements and parenthetical notations. "I need guidelines."

"I know. I'm hopeless about rhyme." She looks thoughtful for a moment and then flips back a couple of pages in her notebook. There are pages and pages of poems, all with those little hearts dotting the letter i's. "Did you ever show my poem to Annika and Britney?" She keeps her eyes on the words in front of her, one thumb folding up the bottom corner of the pages and then smoothing it out—folding and smoothing, folding and smoothing.

I can't lie to her, even though I don't really like her. Or … well, it's not that I don't like her. I can't quite make sense of her, the pungent scent of her in the middle of this perfect room, her bad poetry in the middle of her kindness. "Not yet," I say, which is another one of those part-truths that keep me here in the middle.

"Oh, good," she says. Her fingers twitch and then a whole sheaf of pages is torn loose from the spiral binding, stray bits of paper raining on the perfect carpet. "That one was no good. Can you give these instead? I mean, I don't know exactly which ones, but maybe you could read them and pick a couple that you think are best?" Her hand trembles a little as she holds out the pages.

I take them. What else can I do? I hold them in front of me, staring at the verses on the first page in the same way I stare at the script font on sappy birthday cards, pretending to read with an appreciative smile and a nod. "Aw, that's really beautiful." What is? The imagery? The sentiment? The handwriting? I hope she doesn't ask me to elaborate. There's no way I'm going to read these. I'm not going to get to know the secret pain of Drew Godfrey so I can feel like even more of a complete asshole when I won't wear her BFF necklace and make Annika and Britney be nice to her at school.

"Maybe they'll inspire you a little when you're working on your song," says Drew. "I know you've inspired me." She looks up at me, her eyes all shiny and stupid.

"Um, really?" Oh god, this awkward moment needs to end.

Her face goes pink. "Well, you know."

I don't know. But, *oh god*, she's going to tell me.

"Like...well, like with Gunnar, you know? You stick up for people, Cass. You're *nice*. And like at church, I like the fact that you think about stuff instead of just accepting what Terry or Pastor says."

"No, I don't." Okay, so I do, but I never say anything. I don't speak up—I roll my eyes and maybe send a sarcastic text to Kayla. I don't do anything...*inspirational*. And I guess I'll believe her, that I stood up to that idiot Gunnar a long time ago, but how hard is it to tell some annoying boy to stop acting like a moron? "I'm not nice."

She smiles. "Well, you're nice to me."

"I'm not nice." Right now here I am, pretending to read her poetry, breathing shallowly so as not to gag on her stench, calling her a Shrew behind her back. Walking away from her with Annika, not defending her.

"You are *so* nice."

Okay, so we could do this all evening, but it doesn't matter. None of it matters, and my poem is still not getting written, so I still have an F in English and I'm still the most uninteresting person on the face of the earth, except, on top of being boring, now I'm also a mean girl who somehow has fooled this slightly nauseating girl into thinking I like her and that I'm nice and really, all I am is a fraud who believes in nothing.

And I start to cry. Again.

Stupid, just like that, to start crying in Drew Godfrey's bedroom. What, do I want her to feel sorry for *me*? Oh god, and what if she *hugs* me? I'll throw up, I swear. I drag the sleeve of my fleece jacket across my eyes and scoot backwards a few inches across her bedroom carpet so she'll get the idea.

"Cass?" She doesn't try to get any closer, thank god.

"I'm okay." I'm okay. Perfect. What the hell, Cassandra? You're okay.

"Do you want to bake cookies?"

"What?"

"Cookies. I always bake when I'm stuck."

"Stuck?"

"Stuck, like, emotionally, I guess." Drew laughs. "Like when you're feeling something and you don't want to be feeling it anymore, but you're not sure what to do to get rid of it? I get stuck a lot. And I eat too many cookies, according to my mom." Her smile is sad, and I think about this, about what Drew's mom might be like, about how she might be as disgusted with her daughter as everyone else.

"I'm not stuck. I'm fine." I speak too quickly. Maybe my own mom is disgusted with me. I think of the way her face falls every morning during prayer. It's bad enough that my best friend doesn't like me anymore, but what if my own mom couldn't love me? Surely I don't fit into her life any more seamlessly than Drew fits into this polished, magazine-photo home.

"It's okay," says Drew, just as quickly. "I know I don't need to eat any more cookies. I know it's not good for my complexion, and it's definitely not good for my stupid diet." She leans back against the side of her bed, the notebook falling off her lap to the floor.

"No!" My voice is so loud, and this is so stupid. "No, that's not what I meant. See? I'm trying to be nice, and I'm such a failure."

"You? You're not a failure."

"I'm failing English."

"You'll pass English. You just have to write that poem about yourself."

"Okay, but I'm stuck."

"I know." She giggles. "So let's bake some cookies."

25. If you were a tree...

I walk into the kitchen after spending the whole day chasing six-year-old twins, and the last thing I want to do is take a family shopping trip, but Mom's trying to pile everyone into the van for new shoes. "I've got homework," I say. Which is true, of course, although I have no energy for poetry right now.

My dad frowns. "You never showed us the project that kept you from youth group on Wednesday."

"I turned that one in." Liar, liar. "They're really piling it up for midterm," I say, and then I curse myself. *Don't remind them about midterm.*

Mom's gaze is unreadable. "Didn't you say that you and Kayla were finally going to see a movie tonight?"

"She has a date."

Her eyes widen, as if I've told her that Kayla can't go to the movies because she's busy getting an abortion.

"It happens, Mom. I mean, to other people." I try not to think about the fact that I spent my Friday night baking snickerdoodles with the stinkiest girl in the school. Worse, that I had fun doing it.

"Are you sure you don't need new shoes?"

"Yeah, I'm sure." I roll my eyes and retreat to the safety of my room, where I wait to hear the front door lock before I reach into the back of the closet and pull out the cards.

I wait an extra ten minutes before logging onto the computer, enough to allow for them to remember something they forgot and come back for it. My hand sweats on the mouse as I log into my new email. It's the first time I've managed to log in since the ad appeared in the paper.

Divinia Starr has forty-seven emails in her inbox. Forty-seven. One is from the email service. Twenty-three are comments on the blog. As I read them, it kind of amazes me how much it means to me, that people read my post and took the time to comment. Some of the comments are stupid, and a couple are predictably religious—evil tarot, blah blah blah—but a good number of the comments are people actually complimenting me on the advice I gave to the kid with the crush, asking me how I learned to read the cards so well, and one says I'm an awesome writer. Flattery or whatever be damned—it feels *good* to be recognized. It feels good to know that this is all mine, and that people like it. They like me.

The other twenty-three emails are questions from *Gordon Gazette* readers, questions ranging from the skeptical—*Tell me what I had for breakfast yesterday*—to the heartbreaking—*Can you help me find where my dad went because my baby sister and I really miss him?*

I skim through the subject lines, looking for one that would make an interesting tarot reading, and open one that says, *Complicated new beginnings—please help!*

I'm starting a new school, and things are really complicated right now in my home. You could even say dangerous. So ... I have to leave, to start over, and I'm afraid I might never make the kind of friends I had at my old school. I'm worried everyone will hate me, and I'm even more afraid that my secrets will follow me there, that no new beginning is possible at this point. Are my fears going to come true, Divinia?

Sterling Creek is a small town. I think of the girl Annika and Britney were gossiping about. The girl who was starting a new school because of a complicated, even dangerous, family secret. Jillian. I shuffle, reading through her question. *Are my fears going to come true?*

I spread the cards out on the kitchen table in one long snake of blue diamonds, fanning out in a perfect line, the repeating parallel lines of their white borders blurring into a staircase up to the stars. A new school, a complicated home.

The first card. An Ace of Wands. The beginning of everything—of life, of adventures. A forest, an invention. Something alive or with the order of life. I think of the girl they talked about, molested by her father. Even if this is not her, I imagine her. Jillian. Her new school.

I turn the next card. Eight of Cups, crossing her. This is shyness, the girl's shame, impeding her progress along the path.

Two of the next four cards are also cups, played upside down, empty. In her recent past, the knight—a swindler. Clearly the girl's father. In the immediate future, a period of stationary life, a sort of feeling of being stalled out. Then there's the Justice card, and the Four of Wands, which shows a picture of a joyful wedding. The reading is totally hopeful. *Hang in there, Jillian. It's going to get better.*

I flip the final four, all big cards. The Page of Wands. The Page of Swords. The Star. And finally, up at the top, the Nine of Swords, looking grim and nightmarish in the "final results" spot. There's got to be another reading for that card, something that doesn't look as grim as the card looks, with all those swords hanging in the background, the woman seated and weeping. I spend a few minutes reading through my guidebook, puzzling out the possibilities. *Death, despair, shame, miscarriage.* Yikes.

I titled my first reading "Starr-y Eyed," with a play on Divinia Starr's name, so this entry is called "Starr-Strong," which is not as clever as the last time, but whatever. I guess if I were a brilliant writer I wouldn't be failing English, right? So instead of worrying about how it sounds or looking at my notes, I set everything aside—especially the picture of that final card and the swords so heavy—and I write to this girl as though I'm writing her a note and slipping it into the slots of her locker. A warning and a tiny sliver of hope.

Dear Complicated:

Okay, so the best thing about what I'm going to tell you is that I'm going to begin and end with talking about how strong you are. This is a good thing. I know you've had to be way too strong already—what with this complicated at-home stuff and the cards in

*your recent and distant past, which suggest betrayals
and a swindler of the worst kind, the most damaging
kind ever—but your strength is far from gone.*

*This is a beginning for you, like a seedling sprouting
up from the fallen log of your old self, the self that
has been hollowed out by your circumstances.*

*When you first start your new school, it may feel for
a while like you are not making any progress, like
you would have moved forward from everything a lot
faster at your old school, even with the complications,
even with the secrets. Even with who might know
about them, and what they might say. But this reading
also tells me that the people who call themselves your
friends now are not true to you; they aren't the right
kind of friends. They couldn't possibly stick with you
through it all, and they certainly wouldn't stand beside
you and block the wind or fight off enemies to give
your seedling self a chance to grow and change.*

*They would try to keep you the same, to define you
by your past, to keep you from sprouting new leaves.
They would block out the sun to feed their own need
of feeling big and tall and powerful.*

*There's someone coming into your life, a new best friend,
maybe. This person is strong, too, but in a different way.
Not like a tree, but sharp like a sword. She will be able
to cut through most of your crap, and I mean that in*

a nice way, you know. You are so steady, so enduring;
nobody knows what you're going through. But this
person will see right through that, and while it may be
difficult to let her in, remember that she will be a friend
unlike the ones you had before.

The hardest part about what I have to tell you is that
the final cards are pretty bleak. You worry about being
disappointed, or about being a disappointment, and
this tendency puts you in danger of becoming a self-
fulfilling prophesy. The ending card shows uncertainty,
anxiety, even loss. It's not all sunshine and rainbows.
But I told you the best part of this reading was found
in your strength, and so I want to remind you of the
fact that your seedling strength is sinewy and alive.
Good luck, Complicated, and you're making the right
choice in your move!

26. When you're alone...

The weekend passes, I am incapable of writing my poem, and Kayla doesn't call. By Sunday night I'm determined; I'm not going to follow her down to her basement lair tomorrow to drag the details of the date out of her. I'm not going to chase this friendship. If she wants to be friends, she can make an effort. And if she doesn't, well, I'll deal with it. I'm more than a Kayla-appendage.

Okay, so now it's Monday and my bus is inexplicably early, and the halls are filled with people clumping up in knots comparing hangovers or whatever people do when they do things over the weekend that do not involve making crazy-eyes at the mirror or crying into cookie batter with the school loser. I'm alone. I make a half-hearted attempt to clean the locker, but it's really not all that messy, so it only takes like two minutes. Kayla's coat hangs there, its thin black wool exuding a faint odor of cigarettes and secondhand store, so I know she's down there in the art room waiting for me to come and find her, like I always do. Or worse. Maybe she's not waiting for me at all. Maybe she's actually hoping that I'll take her brush-off to heart and stop hanging on her. I slam the locker door on her stupid stinky coat. I guess I should be glad she hasn't kicked me out of our locker yet.

I look around for Emily Friar, but she drives to school now, which means she can get here whenever she wants. My stupid parents and their stupid rules. Even hanging out with Cordelia would be an improvement over standing here all alone, clutching my books to my chest like a big loser. I wonder, for a second, where Darin goes in the morning, but I dismiss the thought quickly. He barely knows who I am outside of English class, probably. Maybe I should go down to the art room after all. Maybe she couldn't call me because she got in trouble or something. Maybe.

I suppose I could go to homeroom early, but that would be so out of character that Ms. Franklin would probably try to talk to me. Maybe she'd call a guidance counselor or something. I'd tell her I have homework, but that would mean I'd have to actually work on some homework. I could finish my stupid poem, since I'm probably going to fail the class for real if I don't finish it by noon today. And by finish I guess I mean start. But I don't feel creative, not right now. Not yet. Maybe I'll write it during English class. Or lunch, I guess, if I'm desperate. Noon. I can do this.

I could go down with the orchestra geeks and practice my violin or whatever, but I can't imagine. I haven't brought it home to practice since, like, November. I'm not sure I could play a scale, to be honest. I open my locker again and take my backpack off the hook, dropping it onto the floor. Maybe it needs some organizing. I crouch down and unzip the top, peering doubtfully into its chaotic depths. Okay, so. Will this be less painful than being a loser?

"She's here! OMG, Cassieeeeeeee! The newspaper looked so awesome!" A barrage of squeals, and I turn to see Annika and Britney leading their posse of wind-up girls, who are all cooing and making a fuss, though their eyes are on Annika, not me.

I smile. "I didn't do much. Plugged stuff into the holes, that's all."

"Oh, you're too modest," says Annika, grabbing my arm. "Come on, Cassie, what are you doing here in the loser hall? We've been *waiting* for you. Let's go."

"Go?" She pulls me to my feet, but my backpack tips over in the process; all my junk spills out across the floor.

She tosses her hair. "The Commons, duh. Where else?"

"I'll throw this away for you," says Britney, picking up a tube of lip gloss that rolls away from me. "Wrong color."

"No, I—" I like that color. Whatever. I smile and wave my hand. "I guess you can toss it."

The Commons. Duh. I don't go there if I can help it. It's where the jocks leer and make comments and give ratings to girls' asses while the girls toss their bright, shiny hair over their shoulders and laugh so loudly I'm sure they're laughing at me. The school made a big fuss about it at the beginning of the year, made us all discuss how we feel in homeroom; the outcome of the whole deal was that they put teachers in the Commons to supervise, so now, instead of having a number or a letter grade shouted out and laughed over and forgotten, you get this prolonged murmuring game of disgusting telephone. Gross.

"What's this?" Annika bends to pick up a packet of folded pages that has fallen out of my pack—gray, lined pages with pink writing.

"Give it to me!" Of course, that's the wrong thing to say. The wrong tone, too urgent. Let me go back in time a couple seconds and I'll get it right. "Oh, I dunno," I'll say, totally nonchalant. "Something from my little sister, maybe."

"It's *poetry*!" Shrieks of laughter, as Annika hands the pages around to the group.

Okay, so no big deal. It's not my poetry, anyway. Besides, most of these girls can't even read. I fold my arms over my chest and sigh. "Give it back, Annika."

"Oh, this is so adorable," says Britney. "So *precious*, Cassie, really."

"The kindness in your *eyes*, is my greatest *prize*," says a girl whose name I don't know, exaggerating the rhyme. She makes an equally exaggerated gagging sound.

"No, no, don't make fun," says Annika. "This is Cassie's heart on the page, guys. Don't tease her. Her 'heart is squeezed like it's in a *vise*, waiting for your words to be *nice*.'" She covers her mouth with her free hand, making a show of her struggle to keep a straight face.

"Give them back, you guys. Please?" I try to stop myself from pleading, try to take away this power they think they have over me, but I don't know what to do. I don't know how to diffuse this.

"Tell us who you wrote these for, and we'll stop." Britney's eyes gleam greedily.

"Yeah, tell us, Cassie!"

"We'll tell him for you. We'll totally make this happen!"

"Is it Flynn? It's got to be Flynn. Everyone loves Flynn."

"No, it's that weird Darin kid. I've seen you talking to him." A hand, shoving me. They're surrounding me, waving the pages in front of my face.

"No, please…" I hope Darin's locker isn't nearby.

"Him?" Cruel laughter. "Don't you mean *her*?"

"Yeah, everyone knows Cassie's got the hots for Giant Goth Girl!"

"Who? That girl with the eyeliner?"

"Cassie's a lesbian?"

"The girl who draws that weird comic that *nobody* understands."

"Cassie's a lesbian!" Sing-song taunting.

"Listen to this one, you guys, it's *darling*."

"*Stop it!*" I tear the poem out of the girl's hand. "They're not mine, okay? They're not my poems." If I could go back in time, I'd stop here. "They're not mine! They're Drew Godfrey's. She wanted me to submit them for her, to the newspaper." I hate myself. *I hate myself.*

Oh no. The blondes all go quiet at once, awaiting further orders. "Oh, that is so awesome," says Annika, and she collects the pages, each girl handing them over without a word. She takes a poem out of my hand, and I'm too disoriented to react until it's too late.

"Wait—what are you doing with them?" I hold out my hand for the poems, but Annika only smiles.

"You said she wanted to submit them," she says. "So consider them submitted."

The girls giggle in unison, the clucking, automatic sound of a robotic army of chickens.

"Yeah, but I don't think she wanted..." I don't know why I feel like such a betrayer here. I mean, Drew did want me to submit them. "She wanted them to remain anonymous, you know?"

"Oh, sure," says Annika, with those wide eyes. "We'll make sure nobody knows they're hers." She turns to the rest of the girls. "We could sign them Stinkygirl. The Stench Wench? Dirty Hairy?" More clucking responses from the mechanical girls.

"She..." I'd like to be the one who defends her. The one who stands up to the mean girls. The one who puts them in their place. But that's just the thing. They already know their place. All their wide eyes narrow at once as I face them, a strangling in my throat made up of words unspoken and tears unshed.

"She can't know it was me who told you." My voice is a squeak, a squawk, the cluck of a chicken, and I merge into the circle of hens, Annika's hand tight on my elbow as she steers me toward the Commons.

27. Something you regret saying ...

"Sign this." Kayla slaps a paper down on my desk and turns on her heel, heading over to her seat. Mr. Dawkins claps his hands to signal the start of class. It's the first time Kayla's spoken to me all day, and now she's all "sign this." What the hell? I try to catch her eye across the room, but she's doing that thing where she pretends she's paying attention to the teacher.

"Whoa. What's her issue?" Darin reaches for the paper, but stops when Mr. D clears his throat and shoots us his patented *shut up for the love of god* look.

I sneak a peek at the page. It's a petition to save the Winter Carnival. A petition to save Martin Shaddox and his sculpture contest from the God Squad. I sign and slide the page over to Darin. "Pass it on," I whisper. He does.

Did you check out that tarot card blog from the newspaper? Darin writes on a piece of scratch paper with his neat block letters.

No. Is it cool? Lies.

Really interesting. And there were metaphors. "You should totally try it," he whispers. He underlines *metaphors* twice.

"Try what?" I raise my eyebrows in what I hope is an innocent way, but wow, he's right. There was totally a tree metaphor. Trees are pretty clichéd. Still, even a cliché is better than an F...

Try asking Divinia for help with English class.

I laugh. "It's not a homework help line," I whisper. "Besides, it's due in like an hour."

"Well, it's too bad about the assignment, but what she says about you could spark some creativity, maybe. For life beyond this class." He draws a little stick-Cassandra having a lightbulb moment.

"Ha." I draw a big X over the bulb. "I don't think creativity and I exist in the same universe."

"Cass? Darin?" Mr. Dawkins stops his lecture and turns to us. "I hate to be that guy who stands up here and asks you if you'd like to share whatever's so interesting with the class, but I seem to be lacking attention from the two of you, and I'm about to give some instructions, so if you could..." Mr. D trails off and then turns to the white board, where he's pulled up a William Carlos Williams poem off the Internet. The plum poem, the confession. "This is Just to Say."

"So, as I was going on about in what I believe to be a very captivating manner, we've been studying the transcendentalists, and *most* of us have tried our hands at writing a little transcendentalist poetry of our own." Here he pauses to give me what feels like a very pointed look.

I will kill myself if he makes us write another poem. I scrawl my suicide note with Darin's pen.

"Today we're going to try our hand at a very different type of poem, one based on this well-known WCW poem..."

Darin draws a comic of a stick girl poised on the roof of a skyscraper.

"...But before you all freak out about having to write poetry, please understand that William Carlos Williams is all about simple language and straightforward imagery. All you need to write is a confession, or an apology."

Darin scribbles a thought bubble above the girl's head. *This is Just to Say / I have been melodramatic in English class! / WOE IS ME.*

I roll my eyes. Okay, so he's right. The plum poem isn't nearly as bad as "Song of Myself," that's for sure. I can write an apology, right? A confession?

"Go to it," says Mr. D, and I realize I've missed the specific directions for the assignment. "Ten minutes."

"What? What does he mean, ten minutes?"

Darin shrugs. "We have to read our confessions in ten minutes." To my surprise, he's already filled several lines, which he hides with a casual motion of his hand.

"Out loud? To the whole class?"

"Yeah, he said that's sort of the point. Confessing."

"What is this, church?" I can't write a confession, an apology —not for the whole class. Seriously, Mr. D, are you trying to kill me? What is with all this ridiculous poetry writing?

"Cass. Don't think about it. Pick something you want to apologize about and write it down. Put it into three stanzas if you can, like that poem, and maybe use some of the same words. Don't think about it."

Don't think about it. That has to be the most useless phrase in the entire language. Okay, so what can I confess? I don't know why, but Drew Godfrey jumps to mind. I push the thought away. I haven't done anything to her. I've been *nice* to her. At least... I've been nice enough. Right?

"Thanks for passing the petition around." Kayla is suddenly standing beside my desk, holding it out to show me all the signatures. "We got the whole class. I mean, really, this is so stupid. Now they're trying to make a big deal about supervision, saying that last winter there was some kind of bullying going on or something. They've been going on and on about teens thinking about sex when they see comic book characters, and dancing for Satan around the bonfire, but when that didn't work, now they're saying it's about violence. Well... all I can say is if they cancel my snow sculpture contest, there may be some violence."

I tear out a sheet of paper. *Don't think about it.* I pick up Darin's pen and tap it against my bottom lip. And then I write. My confession.

> *This is Just to Say*
> *that I have*
> *been trying*
> *to be more*
> *interesting*

which you
have probably
been wishing for
all these years

forgive me
I am so dull
and I suck
at poetry

"This is for you." I hand the poem to Kayla, who reads it and laughs.

"That's the lamest WCW knockoff I've ever read," she says, though her smile softens the words. "But I forgive you."

She forgives me. For writing a bad poem, or for being a boring human? "How was your date?" I'm asking more about our friendship than about Gary's conversational skills, but she only shrugs and hands back my poem.

"What are you doing next weekend?" she asks.

There's something so guarded about her right now, something that tells me that while the petition and the poem may have broken the ice, our friendship isn't back to all good again. Or back to all normal, which might not be the same thing.

"I . . . nothing." As long as I'm not trading makeovers with Drew.

"Yeah, so you should come to Minneapolis with me for once. I mean it. Bryan's band is playing at First Ave on Saturday night. You remember Bryan, right? It's an all-age show. You know my sister won't care if you stay over."

It's a test. There's no way my parents will let me go, and she knows this. So it comes down to the same thing it always comes down to with us: my parents. And my reluctance to defy them. Well, things are not the same with us anymore.

"All right," I say. "Sounds like fun."

"Are you talking about Bryan Crypt?" asks Darin. "From Categorical Denial?"

"No way, you've heard of Bryan?" Kayla seems to notice Darin for the first time. "He's my boyfriend, pretty much."

Okay, so I'm guessing things didn't go all that well on her date with Gary if Kayla's calling this old drummer dude she hooked up with one weekend her boyfriend.

"I've already got tickets for that show," Darin says. "I'm totally going." He shakes me by the shoulder. "Cass, if you go too, that will be so freaking awesome!"

Wow. He's that excited about me going? Words leave my mouth. "Yeah, I'm going for sure." Okay, so I'm panicking now. My parents are seriously never, ever going to let me do this. It's highly probable that they would actually lock me in my room to prevent me from going. What am I going to tell them?

"And Kayla's *going*, too," says a voice behind me. I turn to see Mr. Dawkins, smiling that patient-yet-exasperated smile of his. "Right back to her seat." He raises his voice to the rest of the class. "Four minutes, folks, and then we're sharing these confessions."

"Awesome, Cass," says Kayla as she walks back to her spot. I guess I passed the first test. Or, knowing Kayla, that was only the first question on the first test.

Mr. D picks up my poem. "You only suck at poetry because you think you should," he says mildly. "Dare I ask about your song?"

I make a face. "Can't I write, like, three extra essays on transcendentalism or something?"

"Give me seventeen lines," he says. "One for each year of your life."

"But…"

"Grade reports go today, you know."

"Please." I'll never see the light of day again, much less get to go to Minneapolis with Kayla and Darin, if they get an email about an incomplete.

"I'll hold yours. End of the day, Cass." He walks away, but then turns back, once, and says, "Seventeen lines."

"I'm sorry," whispers Darin. He sketches a pile of weird little shapes underneath his drawing of the girl on the skyscraper.

"What are those? Rocks?"

He tosses his hair, looking shy. "Marshmallows," he says.

28. When you grow up …

Seventh-period study hall is basically my last chance, so of course I'm not making any progress on my poem. It's not really my fault; Eric won't stop talking to me.

"Everyone's going on and on about this Divinia Starr thing," he says, and then he lowers his voice. "People are commenting."

"Yeah." When we went to the computer lab for social studies, I saw new comments even from the last time I checked. I didn't have time to read them all. I'd like to do another reading tonight, and I'm quiet for a second, thinking about how to get on the computer without Mom and Dad finding out.

Eric shifts in his chair. "They'll be upset if they catch you. Like, crazy upset." He knows what I'm thinking, like always.

I sigh. "Kayla wants me to go down to the Cities this weekend with her. I really want to go, but I have no clue how I'm going to get that one past them."

"For what?"

"Her boyfriend's band is playing."

"Oh, no way. They won't let you go."

"Also, I'm failing English."

"What? Cassandra, what's going on?"

"I—" I glance up at the study hall monitor, who's giving us a dirty look. I lower my voice. "Nothing's going on, Eric. I can't write this stupid poem Dawkins is making us write. I can't do it. It's due in like twenty minutes and I've got exactly nothing."

"Cass, just write something."

"Yeah, that's what everyone says."

"You should listen, then. Cass, seriously, Mom and Dad will kill you if you fail English class. What about college?" Eric's already applied, like, everywhere. I haven't even finished getting my exams scheduled.

"I'll go to the community college. Or I'll take a year off." I have no idea what I want to do, anyway. Why spend a bunch of money and go into debt when I don't know what I want to do with my life? Sometimes I think I'd like to be a scientist, but what is that, even? All I have in my head are these vague images of lab coats and sketchy details from a biography of Marie Curie. What *kind* of scientist? What would I study? Where would I go to work?

"Listen, do you . . . " Eric pauses, his hands sliding over his jeans absently. "Cass, do you think there's anything, actually, to this whole tarot thing? I mean, do you think you're really doing some kind of fortune-telling?"

"I *knew* you were going to want a reading. I think it's a great idea."

"No, it's not that, sissy. It's just … I'm worried, you know?"

"Worried? About what?"

His eyes slide down to the empty page in front of me. "Well, don't you think it might be wrong? I know you hate to believe what the church says, but what if sometimes they're right? Don't you think there could be things in the world that are actually evil? Powers of darkness, that kind of thing?"

"It's a bunch of cards, Eric. Cards with pictures on them and a little book that tells me what they mean. It's not like I'm inviting demons into my soul or something." I press the end of my pencil against the page until the lead snaps.

"How would you know?"

I look at him. He's truly concerned for me, for my soul. I click the end of my pencil to get more lead. He should stick with being concerned for my English grade.

"What do you mean, how would I know? Are you saying the devil writes my blog posts?" I stare at the page. *One line for every year I've been alive.* When I was born, I had a fuzzy black mohawk and gave my mom some kind of stupid depression that made her cry all the time. Should I write that?

When I was one, I had an allergic reaction to Eric's birthday cake and ended up in the hospital. Exciting, but it really doesn't tell anything about me, except that for about a year I was allergic to eggs. If it was Eric's poem, we would learn that even as a toddler he was such a nice kid that he didn't cry once about his birthday getting ruined, and he gave me one of his stuffed animals to cheer me up.

"Not the devil, not exactly." Eric presses his finger against my paper, picks up the little chunk of lead and examines it. He drags it across the page, making a faint gray line in the margin. "I don't know. Probably I'm being stupid. I just... I can't help it that those cards give me a bad feeling, somehow. Like you're messing with something that shouldn't be messed with." He keeps his eyes on the page and I take a long look at his profile; the skin around his eye is still a bit swollen, a little yellow. He looks older, somehow, like he's already left us all and moved on.

"What was I like when I was a little kid?" I ask.

"You used to suck my thumb."

"What? Gross."

"No, like... I actually remember this. You were little, just a baby, and you had that huge pacifier thing. It was purple, and it had a big button on it."

I nod. "Yeah, I've seen it in pictures. It had Winnie the Pooh on it."

"Yeah." He brushes the lead off my paper. "I don't know. It fell out, when we were napping or something. We had one crib for a while, and I can remember you fussing, and I reached over and gave you my thumb." He holds his left hand in his right for a moment, a thoughtful look on his face. "This one," he says, giving me a thumbs-up.

"You couldn't remember that. You were only a baby too."

"Well, but I do remember. You were all right, as a kid. You're the one with a good head on her shoulders. You've always been the one asking questions, like why is the sky blue, or where does this meat come from and why is it called chicken when that cute little birdie is also called chicken."

I laugh. I remember that one, how uncomfortable it made my mom to explain that the two chickens were one and the same. "You stopped eating meat after that," I say, remembering Eric's big eyes, all full of sympathy for the poor animals.

"Yeah. I jumped into that plan without thinking things through, though." He smiles, both dimples creasing his cheeks. "I didn't actually like vegetables, you know."

I stare at my paper, wondering if I can put this into a poem. The One Who Asked Questions. Questions that made my brother have an ethical dilemma and nearly starve to death. Questions that made it impossible to believe in God? I shake my head. "It didn't bother me, eating the chicken," I say. "I wanted to understand how it all worked."

Eric nods. "You always want to understand things, Cass. At least, that's how you used to be. Methodical, I guess. It's like Dicey's this flurry of silliness, and you know me, I'm the moody one, daydreaming all the time. You're the solid one, Cass. You're reasonable. You're our anchor."

"Oh, hey, it's a metaphor: I celebrate and sing myself, an emotionless anchor in the riptide of my family, dragging everybody down." I stick out my tongue at Eric.

"Yeah, that's the kind of thing you've never had patience for, I guess."

"What?"

"Metaphors. You know. You like things to make sense

right away, logically, no pieces left over. No messy feelings left out in the open."

It makes me sound like a robot, unfeeling. "That's not true." Is it? Am I so rational I lose track of feelings? "I just don't like contradictions."

"So write about that."

"Like, how? How is that poetry?" I remember what Drew wrote, those few lines about Cassandra believing in nothing. How come everyone else thinks they could write a song of me when I can't?

"I think you need to think about it differently, Cass. Poetry isn't just pretty words. You're so insistent on logic, but sometimes a contradiction can be true, you know?"

No, I *don't* know. "You're as bad as Mr. Dawkins."

"I don't mean to be." Eric brushes his hands lightly across the legs of his jeans. "I'm nervous, Cass. About this class you're failing, but especially about that blog. It's not like you. You're not using your head." He looks behind me, over my shoulder, and I know he's looking at Drew. "People are sort of like poems," he says.

"They don't make sense?"

"Not all the time."

"Or never, if they're like you." I sigh. "Now go away. I've got to turn this in before the end of the day. I'll never get to go to the Cities for the weekend if Mr. Dawkins gives me an incomplete in English."

"Cass. You wouldn't be going if all the teachers got together and wrote sonnets about what an awesome person you are. Skipping church? Going to a concert alone? Riding in a hearse with a girl who won't come into the house during prayer circle?" He laughs. "You're not going."

And it's official. Now I *have* to go.

29. When you were a kid …

Mr. Dawkins isn't impressed by the page I finally hand in, seventeen lame lines about each year of my life. I point out my use of metaphor—*I'm a heavy anchor dragging everyone down*—but he only rolls his eyes and gives me that wry teacher-face that says he thinks I could do so much better. He makes a deal with me, "because I know you have it in you." He's putting in enough points to keep my grade at a C for midterm, which is still going to make things interesting at home, but if I don't revise and turn in a "worthwhile effort" within the two-week grade adjustment period, he'll let the grade revert to an F. He also reminds me that people with a failing grade at midterm won't be able to attend the Winter Carnival. I don't care. It buys me some time.

"So … this means you're really going to the concert with Kayla, right?" Darin falls into step with me outside the English room as I'm heading back for the last few minutes of study hall.

"What class are *you* supposed to be in?" Okay, so I'm not sure at what point I became a freaking hall monitor. What am

I doing? "I mean..." What do I mean? My brain is nothing but an endless stutter of stupid.

"You mean, why am I stalking you?" He grins, shaking a set of car keys. "I saw you walk past on your way to Dawkins' room, so I left French on a bathroom pass. I was wondering if you wanted a ride home."

"You *are* stalking me. Creeper." My cheeks tingle, and I hope they're not turning pink. I can't even stand here like a normal person right now; I keep rocking up on my toes, all ridiculous. Everything about this moment feels strange and new, like the junior hall is a foreign country or something. I'm spending most of my conscious brainpower trying to keep myself from giggling, honestly.

"So I shouldn't tell you all about the adorable puppies in my white van?" he asks.

So much for not giggling. "My mom will probably freak if I'm not on the bus." Oh *god*, Cassandra, Empress of the Lame. What happened to growing a spine when it comes to my parents? "But I mean, I'm seventeen years old. I'm old enough to get into any strange white van I want, right?" I'll cross my fingers she's at the church again this afternoon. She doesn't care so much about me being on the bus, but if I come home in some boy's car she's going to want to meet him, and that's just awkward.

Darin smiles. "I'll meet you at the doors by the junior lot. But, uh... I actually drive a ten-year-old compact car with a bad muffler, so don't get your hopes up about the puppies, okay?"

Fifteen minutes later and I'm sitting in the passenger seat

of Darin's car, wishing I had some kind of witty banter planned out for this occasion. Instead, I clutch my backpack in my lap and come up with, "Your car is clean."

Darin nods, both hands on the wheel, eyes straight ahead. "Yeah, I guess. I like to have things in order, you know?" I wonder if he's as nervous as I am. He's doing this sort of adorable thing where he's almost biting his lower lip, grazing it against his eye tooth.

"I live over by the mall. Well, just past it, on Aspen Circle." Otherwise known as God's Armpit.

"Do you want to go straight home, or..." Darin steals a glance in my direction, and I look away quickly, aware that I've been staring at him—at his *lips*—like some kind of weirdo. *Straight home or...* my cheeks tingle again.

"I don't know." Okay, so I hate this. All this energy I've spent trying to be more decisive, more *myself*, and here I am shrugging and blushing like I don't have a single original thought in my head. "Wait." I push my backpack away and sit up straight. "Let's go to the playground by the old water tower."

Darin turns left instead of right at the stoplight and finds a parking spot beside the chain-link fence that surrounds the playground. "I haven't been here in years," he says, reaching into the back seat for a warm hat. "Are you dressed warm enough? Got a hat? Scarf?"

"I'm a Minnesota girl." I wrap my scarf up tight and button my wool coat up under my chin. "Besides, it's above zero today."

"Barely."

I lead the way to the swing set and wedge my butt into one of the cold plastic seats. "Do you ever lean way back on your swing and look at the world upside down?" I don't wait for him to respond; I pump my arms and legs hard and feel the cold wind rush against my face as my swing flies through the air. I remember when we were younger, Kayla and I used to have races to see who could get the highest the fastest, here on these very swings. She had the advantage because her arms and legs were so much longer than mine, but I loved the feeling of flying through the air more than she did.

"Honestly, swinging makes me a little queasy," says Darin. He sits on the next swing over and twists gently from side to side.

I lean back farther on the way up, tipping back in the seat so I can see him rushing away from me, upside down, and I stick my tongue out at him. *Queasy*, ha! This is amazing. I flip back upright, pulling at the chains, gaining speed and height. I feel myself lifting up, out of the swing, so light and free. My arms ache and I'm smiling so wide that my face actually hurts, and *why* has it been so long since I've done this? The freezing cold air on my face makes my eyes water, or I might even be crying, but it's good—so good—and at the top of the next arc, I wiggle up to the edge of the seat and let myself follow the momentum off the swing, flying off it through the air, so high and fast that my stomach plummets and adrenaline rushes to my arms and legs in a tingle of fear and excitement. The ground is hard—frozen solid—but I land on my feet and only skid a little bit on the ice. I throw my arms in the air, victory-style, and Darin cheers.

"That was entirely made of awesome," he says, and he jumps up from his swing and runs right over. For a second I think he might hug me, but we both get shy at the same time and look down at our feet. "You were seriously flying. Like I was afraid you'd just...take off, zoom up to the sun or whatever." He makes this adorable little airplane motion with his hand.

"I landed kind of hard, but it was worth it," I say. "Those three seconds I was up in the air were, like, the first time in forever I haven't been all anxious about who I am and what makes me special and what things are all mine and..." I trail off, aware that I'm talking too much to this kid I barely know, that I have something that's sort of like tears in my eyes, and that maybe I look a little bit crazy. "Hey." I point up the hill, toward the rocket-ship slide. "You afraid of heights?"

He nods. "Yeah, but what the hell. I'm always up for an opportunity to face my fears." We hike across the snow toward the giant metal structure. "Anyway," he says as we climb the final rungs and squeeze into the cone of the rocket, which sways in the wind far above the frozen playground, "if I get too scared, you'll hold my hand, won't you?"

I smile. My hands are sweating, even in my warm mittens, and I clasp them around my knees, feeling the chill of the metal slide seeping through the seat of my jeans. "So. Did you dream of being an astronaut when you were a kid?"

Darin tips his head to one side, thoughtful. "Not an astronaut, exactly," he says after a pause, "but I did want to be the kind of person who was able to identify all of the constellations. I had a telescope and a couple of star maps. I had a hard time locating the actual constellations, though, so I used to make my own and draw pictures of them in my sketch pad. I remember I drew Chuck the Chicken and the Juggling Jackalope and a whole bunch of other ones I can't remember." A particularly strong gust of wind makes the rocket ship groan and shudder, and he scoots a tiny bit closer to me. "How about you? You seem like the type who would be up for a spacewalk."

I shake my head. "Yeah, not a spacewalk, so much." Despite my habit of jumping off swings, I'm not really a risk-taker. "But you know that song, from like the sixties, the one about us being stardust? When I was a kid, I read a science book about how all the carbon and whatever it is that makes up life on earth came from supernovas, how the atoms that make up all of us were once a part of stars that exploded a billion years ago in outer space. Ever since then, I just…I can't get enough of looking at the stars."

It's true, and it warms a spot in my chest to think that this is mine—this is something all my own, even if I only realized it by sharing it with Darin.

"So both of us were kids who spent their nights gazing up at the heavens, imagining," Darin says, and we look up right now, through the rust-colored metal slats of the creaky old rocket-ship slide. The sky appears—to our eyes, like usual, the flat white color of winter. But underneath that color—or beyond it—we know the stars are there.

30. To save your friendship, you would …

I haven't said anything yet to my parents about going with Kayla, even though I've had two somewhat promising opportunities to speak with Mom about it—once while I helped her carry in groceries, and once while the two of us made the dessert we're bringing to Wednesday-night church. It's just that "promising" is not quite the word for my chances here. There's no way they're going to let me skip church on Sunday for an unsupervised overnight trip to a rock concert.

But what if they thought I wasn't missing church? Could I convince them that I'm going to services in the Cities? Not with Kayla. She's nominally a Lutheran, but she and her dad don't attend church outside of Easter and sometimes Christmas. Mom and Dad wouldn't believe me for an instant.

But as long as I've already crossed the mental barrier between honesty and dishonesty, why do I have to tell them I'm there with Kayla? Who else would they believe? I come up empty.

"Cassandra, are you getting into the van? Because you should be."

"Getting my Bible," I call, and then I have to actually get it. What can I tell them? And then I do the stupidest thing on the face of the earth. "Drew Godfrey asked me to come to the Cities with her this weekend for her cousin's kid's baptism," I say, climbing into the waiting van.

My father's eyes focus on me for a moment in surprise, and then he nods. "Drew from youth group? She's a sweet girl."

"She sings beautifully," says my mom. "I wish she'd sign up for the choir. I hear her singing the hymns, and I think it's such a shame she won't join."

For a second I puzzle that out, as if it really matters that Drew Godfrey can sing, as if it really matters that it's something I haven't noticed about her, something I don't think I've even contemplated. Her singing voice. I spend a moment trying to recall the last time I heard her sing, but then my brother jabs his knee into the back of my seat and it hits me: Oh *god*. What have I done?

And what am I going to do? I have to take it back, retract this crazy lie that tumbled out of my mouth. I have to fix it. We're on our way to church. We'll be walking in there, and Drew will be there, and . . . wait. Just wait. What if . . . what if it *works*? What if I can convince my parents that I'm going to church in Minneapolis with Drew Godfrey? What if I can convince Drew to lie to my parents and cover for me? Okay, so this is too much. I can't make Drew lie for me.

"Yeah," I say, my chance to turn back rapidly fading, "Drew from youth group."

I'm not going to say I never lie to my parents—it's probably more accurate to say that I'm rarely one hundred percent honest with either of them—but this is a big deal. And not only for me.

Dad turns to Mom. "That seems reasonable, if we could meet her parents," he says. "Doesn't it?"

She taps her fingertips together. "Well, I don't—" She twists around in her seat belt and studies my face. "What about church on Sunday?"

I can't do this. I can't ask Drew to do this for me. But... *Darin.* I curl my fingers into my hands, remembering the little smiley-face fingertips. He was so excited to hear I was going to the concert, and especially after our rocket-ship moment, I feel like he's more excited about seeing *me* than seeing the Crypt People or whatever. And Kayla. Okay, so I realize our friendship has strayed a long way from where it used to be, but it's not hopeless, is it? I don't want to lose her, to lose our history together. I don't want to *be lost.* She's my best friend. And if I don't go...

But Drew. I can picture her hopeful face, looking for me, catching my eye. I'd be asking a lot of her. What would she want in return? For me to come over again and bake more cookies? That wasn't so bad, if I'm going to be honest with myself here. Okay, so it was awkward at first, but the cookies were delicious. And now that I think about it, of course my mother's right about the singing thing—how could I have forgotten? When we were baking, Drew sang the whole time, belting out all these classic musicals that I've never heard of. It was kind of cool, to see her surrounded by such confidence.

I wonder. Should I … should I ask her to come along to the concert in the Cities? The thing is, I could see it working maybe a year ago, when Kayla and I were on more solid ground. Maybe we would have looked at a weekend with Drew as a fun challenge—a makeover, a project. But this weekend *I'm* the project. It's the Cassandra Makeover Challenge —transforming me into someone interesting enough to keep my best friend. So, bringing Drew along is not going to bring success in that arena.

But maybe later. Maybe, once I get all this stuff figured out with Kayla, I'll be able to widen our circle.

"We'll be going to her cousin's church," I tell Mom. "For the baptism." I have no freaking clue if Drew even has any cousins, or if her cousins have any kids. What if my parents say something to her before I have a chance to fill her in? What if she *won't* lie for me?

"We'll see." It's an answer far more positive than I ever hoped.

Eric sits directly behind me, in the last row of seats. He won't stop poking me in the back, but I don't turn around. I know he'll try to talk me out of this, give me some stupid warning about how angry Mom and Dad would be if they found out. But you know what? It's time I did something dangerous, took a little risk. Maybe next time, I'll have something to write on that stupid survey. Maybe I could write the stupid Song of Myself.

At church, I see Drew before anyone else does, and I run over to say hi. Very uncharacteristic, of course, but she doesn't seem surprised. Probably now that I've baked cookies with her, she thinks I'm her best friend.

"Hey, Drew. I have a huge favor to ask." I go right in for the kill because there's no time for circling.

"Hey, Cass. What is it?"

Ooh, she's sharp, doesn't agree before hearing the favor. Possibly I've underestimated her. Or overestimated her desperation.

"I . . . I know this sounds ridiculous, but I need you to cover me to my parents about where I'm going to be this weekend. I'm super, super sorry to ask you to do this, but it's important. It's pretty much an emergency." I mean, really. It's a friendship in crisis. And Darin. Just the thought of him makes me feel a little giddy. And it *will* be a legit emergency if she won't lie to my parents for me.

"Oh." Her face is expectant. She doesn't look appalled or horrified or judgmental or anything. "What's the emergency?"

Oh, crap. What is the persuasive version of the emergency? I haven't thought much about convincing her. I sort of thought she'd be thrilled to do anything to help me out, and I guess I feel a little bit rotten about that, like it never seriously occurred to me that she'd turn me down. "It's . . . well, it's kind of a little bit about a boy, but listen. My parents are going to walk over here and ask you about this in like thirty seconds, and I swear, I'll . . . " I'm about to say I'll be her best friend forever —not for real, but, like, that's just what people say when they're asking for a favor. But Drew's probably not the kind of person people say that to. "If you could tell them that I'm going with you to the Cities this weekend for your cousin's baby's baptism?"

Oh god, she made me uptalk. It's freaking contagious. I wait, searching her face, but she still has that weird, expectant look, like she's waiting for the punch line. For the April Fools? For me to tell her I'll be her best friend forever? I can't say that. "Could you tell them we'll be going to church on Sunday morning, and then be back here by supper time? Please? And..." Okay, so am I seriously asking her this? "And, uh... then would you be willing to stay home from church on Sunday so that it looks like you're at the baptism?"

She isn't going to say yes to that. Out loud, it sounds as ridiculous as it is. I'm asking her not only to lie to my parents, but then to stay home from church and hide while I go down to the Cities to have fun. And I'm not even inviting her to come along.

Her face flickers with indecision, but I give her my best pathetic pleading face and she nods faintly, her mouth settling into a small, downward-tilting smile. "I guess so," she says. "But I don't know. Won't they want to talk to my mom or something?"

"Tell them something. She can't talk to them. Tell them..."

"Well, my mom can't talk to them anyway. Or she won't. She's out of town this whole week for business." Drew shrugs. "She's in Italy, buying fabric or something."

"That's okay. Tell them that. Your mom's out of the country, so she wants you to stay with your aunt and uncle in

Minneapolis for the weekend, and she wanted you to be able to bring a friend for company."

"And my cousin's baby is getting baptized?"

"I guess so. That's what I told them."

"So what's my fake cousin's fake baby's name?" She laughs, but it's an uncomfortable sound. It's the kind of laugh that's hard to forget when it's gone.

31. What worries you …

I have another reading that I want to do, and I'm contemplating if I dare try it on my bedroom floor again, sitting against the door. Mom and Dad are in bed, and Dicey's sleeping too. I might even be able to sneak onto the computer and type up my answer tonight.

Eric knocks.

Good. He can help me keep watch. I open the door.

"Hey, Cass." He's slouching in the hall.

"Sit right there," I say, pulling him inside the room and closing the door behind him. "Give me as much warning as you can if anyone comes."

He sits, his face in the shadow of my dresser, his back against the door. "What did Dawkins say about the poem you turned in?"

"He said it was enough to get me up to a C, anyway."

"Cass, this thing with Drew has been bugging me all day. It's going too far."

"Don't worry so much, Eric." Inside the closet, my voice echoes, fills my head with its own certainty. I crawl out backwards, the box of tarot in my hand, and then I spread them out on the carpet in front of me, face down, and swirl them around in circles. "Should I do a reading for you?"

He frowns. "I'm serious, Cass. This...it isn't *you*, any of this. You're getting more and more into these cards. You're making Drew lie for you. The blog...I know it seems like innocent fun, and I admit, I was a little excited to see how much attention it was getting at school. I even thought maybe..." He stops. "I'm worried about this coming back to hurt you, sissy."

I pull the cards together and shuffle. "I'm offering comfort and advice to people in trouble. How could that be a bad idea? How can a deck of cards be good or evil?"

"I've got a bad feeling," he insists. "Someone at school will find out it's you. I know it." He gets up and leans over the cage to give a treat to Pumpkin and Nut.

"Nobody will find out unless you tell. You're being insufferable, Eric. I'm helping people make sense of their futures."

I flip the cards down, arrange them into the cross formation that now seems so familiar to me, and concentrate on my next questioner, a girl who wants to know if she should give her boyfriend a promise ring at the Winter Carnival. She writes:

Dear Divinia,

I can't decide if it's a good idea to write to you. I'm pretty sure it's not a good idea, but I'm looking for advice and it's hard to ask anyone in person,

*for reasons I'd rather not get into. I want to do
something really special for my boyfriend at the
Winter Carnival, since it's our last one before we
both go off to different colleges. I bought him a
ring—not an engagement ring, but like a promise
ring, I guess. I'm nervous about people's reactions,
and about how he'll feel about getting the ring,
especially in public. I need your advice. Will you
please ask the cards if this is a good idea?*

—Nervous Nellie

Eric leans back against my door, Pumpkin tucked into his
arms. "I'm not going to tell," he says. "But I don't think you're
on the right track in this whole 'finding yourself' business. I
don't for one second like what's going on with Drew."

"Drew is awesome," I say. "She didn't mind at all." It's
not entirely true, and I still feel sick when I think about what
happened to her poems, what still *might* happen to them,
but I push that out of my mind and take a long look at the
cards lying in front of me. This isn't a bad thing. I'm *helping*
people with these cards, like this nervous girl who wants to
give her boyfriend the promise of her heart. I wonder about
the "reactions" she says she's worried about. Jealousy? Maybe
her friends think she shouldn't tie herself into a relationship
so early. I admit, I'm not one who can really believe in that
Romeo and Juliet love-at-first-sight kind of thing, but just
because someone is a teenager doesn't mean she can't fall in
love for real, forever. Maybe this girl has a boyfriend like that.

I turn over a card, and there's Death staring at me, all skull-faced, kings lying prone on the earth beneath his horse's hooves. Eek. Okay, so maybe she's making a mistake.

I flip quickly through the guidebook, taking notes in my English notebook, which is still empty of poetry. Death, as a card in the Major Arcana, isn't actually as terrible as its name implies, according to the little book, but there's still something muddled about these cards, something hard to read.

"That poor girl," says Eric.

"What about her?" I frown at the cards I've flipped over, wondering what he sees when I can't even make sense of it all using the book. This reading is making me almost as nervous as Nellie herself. There's something dramatic and unexpected about the ending, and I hope I can understand it enough to spin my response to be true and helpful while not altogether devastating.

For a second it occurs to me—a sense of my own power in all this. If a questioner believes Divinia Starr, the reading becomes a sort of prophecy. Something to believe in. Something to guide the person's actions. I think about that other Cassandra, the one Darin told me about, in the doomed city of Troy. Her knowledge of the future was a burden that would have been heavy even without the curse of doubt on all sides, but would her predictions have remained true if people had believed her?

"*What about her?*" Eric repeats. "Well, we can start with the fact that you're forcing her to lie for you. You know, Drew Godfrey? The girl you're *using* so you can sneak out to a stupid concert?"

Oh, *her*. I look away.

We're both quiet, and the awkwardness is so thick I can't look at him. I can't bear the accusation that I know will be in his eyes. That I know I deserve. But...Drew didn't really seem to mind. Besides, I'm not *using* her. She's doing me a favor, that's all. A favor I'll repay someday. Whatever. It's not like I've never done anything nice for Drew.

I shake my head to clear it and tap my pen on the notebook page, looking for a way to start my post to this nervous girl with the complicated ending. Should she give her boyfriend a promise ring? Should she make a big deal out of it or do it somewhere quietly? Slowly, the words come to me— words that comfort at the same time as they caution. Words that encourage Nervous Nellie to give the ring, to face the fear, to have hope in the power of love even in the certainty of an uncertain future, full of changes and growth and difficulties and joys.

I survey the cards with a strange assurance. Their bright surfaces seem to speak to me, almost in full sentences. I scribble away, making the side of my hand dark with ink—the black ink of Darin's pen, which I seem to have stolen. *No matter the outcome, the cards show that your ring will be received with joy.* Forget about everything; this is the truth, even if it won't stay true for always.

I barely look at the guidebook. The words flow up to me, into me. Suddenly I stop—how do I know this? Where is it coming from? *How would you know?* Eric had asked. How would I know if I were possessed?

I look up to find Eric studying me closely. "I have a bad

feeling, sis. A greasy, no-good feeling, like a black splotch in the future. And I'm worried about you." He tilts Pumpkin gently back into her cage, turning his attention away from me.

What if Eric is the prophet instead of me, speaking truth? What if I'm the idiot who doesn't believe? Whatever. It's ridiculous that he's worried about me instead of the other way around. I'm not the one who's been threatened via hate-urination.

I tuck my cards back into their hiding place and tap my notebook, where my reading is now ready to be typed up tomorrow morning in homeroom. Everything's under control. "I'm fine," I say. "Really." Except maybe for English class.

32. You don't believe in ...

By Friday-night youth group, Drew has warmed up to the lie and tells my mother charmingly humorous anecdotes about her fake cousin Lainey's fake baby, Simon, who will be baptized on Sunday morning. She tosses her head back and stops fiddling with her ponytail as she gets more comfortable. I've honestly never seen her more confident; it's like telling stories about a fictional cousin is easier for her than being herself.

"We looked up, and there he was, covered in ... " She fills in some disgusting thing, and that's how the stories end, the stories about the baby. Gross.

Mom laughs in her own charming way, playing the role she loves so much—the mother with the perfect family. It occurs to me again, watching her, how I might be a disappointment to her, how she might have wished for a different daughter altogether. Maybe one who sings beautifully. Maybe one who builds houses for the homeless or plays first-chair violin. "How lucky for your mother to have people close by to look out for you when she has to go away on business," says my mother. "You should come to dinner at our place whenever you're home alone. It gets so lonely, all by oneself." She sips her cup of hot apple cider and smiles, but her eyes are pensive.

"Mom, don't embarrass her." What was that about? My mom isn't lonely. She has things she does, things that keep her busy during the day. Church things, mostly. I follow her eyes as she gazes at the people smiling and talking, laughing and sipping coffee—complimenting each other, teasing, flattering, gossiping—all around the basement of the church. These people are the reason my mom was able to keep her smile. They make up her system of care and nourishment, and the faith they all share makes up her system of hope. Why don't I feel that connection, that community? She probably wishes for a daughter who could enjoy being here with her instead of grimly enduring each minute or lying to get out of it.

"Oh, but she's right," says Drew, a shade too eager. "I would love to come for dinner sometime, Mrs. Randall. And I'm sure my mother would love to have you all over sometime, too."

I shake my head a little. There is no way my parents can meet her mom. No way. Doesn't she realize that the first thing they'll want to talk about will be her aunt and uncle and Lainey and Baby Simon with his adorably disgusting anecdotes? Doesn't she realize that we can't actually be friends?

Oh god. I'm a horrible person. My throat seems to swell.

Then Drew winks at me, a tiny twitch of her right eye as she's looking away, so I know it's all a part of the pretending. Good. But it's too late, because I've already started seeing beyond what I thought I knew about Drew Godfrey. I've already realized the selfishness behind my request, what this will cost her. And it's occurred to me, though I push the difficult thought aside, that despite her bad skin and her social inadequacies, Drew is a more interesting person than I am.

At last we slip free of my parents and step outside to wait for them in front of the church. Our breath makes frosty clouds in the night, and I shiver even inside my down jacket and thick wool hat. The street is dark and empty, a light glaze of ice glinting in the streetlights.

"Did you see they're having a special session for parents this Sunday after church?" Drew doesn't wear a ski jacket or a regular dress coat like everyone else; instead, she has these flowing, velvety, cape-type things, several of them. She stands perfectly still, like a mountain emerging from the base of the church steps. "They're talking about that tarot card blog again, warning parents about the dangers of sorcery."

I'm three steps above her, and I can see the fuzzy line of her part. I wish she would wash her hair. It's not like she couldn't be presentable if she would make a few changes. I see her house, the sleek sophistication of her bedroom. Maybe she's this way on purpose. Maybe it's some kind of pretending, like everyone else. Pretending she's in control of who she is.

"What's the big deal with this blog, anyway?" I ask. It makes me nervous to think of the church getting involved. But really, what are they going to do about it? It's the Internet. They don't own the Internet. And, okay, so they could convince the school not to let the newspaper advertise the blog, but it wouldn't matter because everyone's already heard of it, and nobody at the *Gazette* knows where that ad came from. Kayla and Eric know, but they're not going to turn me in.

I'm certain of that. Except, as soon as I think about it, I'm less certain. Kayla could tell because she's mad at me or bored with me, or because she's having a bad day. And Eric could tell because he's worried about me.

"Have you seen it? I think it's fantastic," Drew says, ducking her head and looking over her shoulder. "But to hear Pastor talk, it's a sin to even read it."

Even though I just got done thinking about the people who know betraying me, I have this almost undeniable urge to tell Drew that it's me. It's like somehow I want to make it up to her, for all of it—that I'm "using" her, that we can't ever be real friends now, that I haven't stood up for her at school. It's like a part of me wants to give her this power over me—and over the Vomit Vixens, a little bit—but of course I don't tell her the truth. Or anyway, not much of the truth.

"I saw the first one," I tell her, which is not a lie.

"You don't think it's a sin, do you, Cass?" She reaches around to tug her hair toward her mouth. "Like, do you think it would be unforgivable to ask her a question?"

"Ask who a question?"

"Divinia Starr."

"I told you before, I don't really believe in sin. It doesn't make sense, eternal punishment." I'm not completely certain on this, but it feels good to say it, like I'm confessing a crime. "I don't believe in hell, either." See, if I believe in one thing—like God, or Heaven—then I have to believe in all these other things too. Angels, demons, saints, miracles, eternal reward or eternal punishment. And it's not logical. People are so complicated—how could you ever decide which eternity they deserve?

"But then, what would keep people from murdering each other?"

"I mean, murder is pretty messy," I say.

She turns around and tips her head up to look me right in the face, and for a second I think she's offended, that I've been too flip about her beliefs, but then she laughs, and I laugh, and it only takes a second before we're both giggling like we're goofy. Like we're friends.

"Hey," she says when the wave of giggles subsides, "do you want to come over for a while? You could sleep over, and Kayla could pick you up from my house tomorrow." Her hair is back in her mouth, and the easy confidence she had earlier when telling stories about her cousin's baby is overtaken by her usual awkward self.

Eric waves at me as he exits the church. "I'm bringing the van around," he says. "You want to come with?" It's his version of a truce—saving me from Drew the Shrew, even though he still thinks I'm a big meanie.

I jump down the three steps to the sidewalk. "Yeah, coming!" I look back at Drew standing there, solid as a mountain in her heavy cape, her face stoic, prepared for the worst. I think of my mom, talking about loneliness. I could leave Drew here, make up some lame excuse, and things could go on like they have. It's what she expects me to do, probably. Or I could say yes, go to her house for the second time, and then what? She'll want to talk to me at school. She'll hang around, and I'll be forced to choose between being mean to her again, which I cannot stand to do, or defending her to Annika and Britney. And maybe that wouldn't be so bad. It's not like I really want to be friends with them, but it's not that simple either. I can't go back to being an unknown, flying below their radar. I think of the gossip, the way they turned on Kayla. I think of how they took Drew's poems, and my face heats up with the knowledge of my own cowardice. I know the truth, and it sucks: I'm too chicken to stand up to them. I'm despicable.

I stare up a Drew, a lame excuse cued up in my mouth, but she smiles and shakes her head. "Oh, you know what? I just remembered, my mom told me I couldn't have anyone over while she was away. Maybe when she gets back in the country?"

I nod, too quickly, and tell her thanks one more time for everything, and then I almost trip over my own feet as I run to catch up with Eric. "I'll call you later!" I say, glancing back over my shoulder as I hurry away.

Her face is wistful, and when we come back with the van, she's gone.

33. Your ideal future ...

I manage to get a quick peek at the blog while my parents are in their bedroom changing out of their church clothes and having some kind of serious discussion. It could be anything, but the low murmur of concern I can feel rumbling down the hall makes me think it must be about me. They might be talking about my C in English, which already has them in a tizzy even though they're unaware it's dangerously close to turning into an F if I don't rewrite my poem. They could be worrying about my trip to Minneapolis tomorrow. Or maybe they're talking about the tarot blog, judging by what Drew said about that parent concern meeting or whatever.

I log into my Divinia Starr account, and there are *one hundred sixty-two* messages. Again, about half of those are comments on the blog and about half are people wanting me to read for them. It's weird. I never knew it would feel like this, to get so many responses—it's like my entire body feels lighter, somehow, like I'm having trouble staying seated in my chair. People are reading my posts. They're interested in my blog, interested in *me*. Granted, they don't know that it's me, but still.

It feels too disjointed to read the comments in my email window, so I click over to the blog itself, where I can see the whole conversation, everyone talking to each other in the little window. It's surreal, all these people who never speak to me at school, people who don't know I exist, commenting on something I wrote. Some people use their own names or something similar, and a few have a photo of themselves as their icon. A lot of the comments are anonymous, though, or the user accounts have weird names and icons with their favorite TV show character or singer or whatever.

I only get a chance to skim over a few comments before I hear a sound down the hall, like the scrape of a door against the bedroom carpeting, and I use my quick keyboard-shortcut skills to flip over to an open document, my fingers automatically typing up the opening line of Whitman's poem—the words that keep running through my brain now, though nothing will come after them. *I celebrate myself, and sing myself, and what I assume you shall assume...* I celebrate myself. I am Divinia Starr, and I have a hundred and sixty-two messages in my inbox.

My pulse races and I hold my breath for a second, listening. I can still hear their low voices, trading off. I can hear Dicey's music playing, farther down the hall. I flip back to the blog and keep reading.

The comments start out supportive—people congratulating Nervous Nellie on her relationship or writing things like *Awwww! So sweeeeet!*—but my smile falters a little as I go farther down the thread. It starts when someone called sk8r-grrl writes, *What the hell is the point of a promise ring?* Instantly, a string of people start agreeing with her, and their comments range from calling the ring *the desperate act of a controlling bitch who can't bear the thought of all the hot chicks her boyfriend is going to bang in college* to illiterate and lewd suggestions about sexual favors that would be more welcome to the boyfriend than *some stupid girly ring*.

I flip over to the open document again, my heart pounding. This... it's not what I wanted. I've only skimmed through half the comments, but it makes me uncomfortable that people are saying these things after all the work I went through to make my post balanced and hopeful. I feel like I should post, too, to say something to these trolls, but maybe that ruins the whole thing, you know? Divinia Starr in her own comments begging for people to play nice doesn't seem very mystical.

Besides. Okay, so the people are getting a little out of hand, but it's not like anyone's being any worse than other places on the Internet. Significantly better than other places on the Internet, in fact. It's not my fault. It's the Internet. People will say anything online, hiding behind their anonymity. Okay, so I'm doing the same thing with my anonymous blog, but I'm not being mean about it, even though Kayla wanted me to.

Still, I've got to admit some of the comments are kind of funny. Of course I'd never say them myself, and if someone said them in real life, I'd like to think I'd be the kind of person to speak up and say they're being rude. Should I delete the comments?

My ears are trained on the sound of my mom and dad. Their voices seem a little louder now, and tense. Almost like they're arguing, but that doesn't happen. Sure, they have an occasional disagreement, but never anything ongoing. Mom and Dad are a united front.

After reassuring myself that they're still occupied, I flip back over to the blog. A few jerks starting a little drama, that's all. Welcome to the Internet. A couple of commenters bring the conversation back on track by saying that the promise ring is a sweet gesture, and a bunch more people jump in to agree, once again. It's funny how people do that, the way they hang back, waiting for someone to say what they're thinking, letting someone else be the first one to go against the main sentiment, and then they'll jump in. How many people are there, looking on, waiting for someone brave? The trolls are mostly forgotten, an ugly blip in the comment stream. In my head, I picture them as Ronnie and Blake. I'm glad I didn't have to get in the middle of it, to be honest.

I finish skimming and flip back to Divinia's inbox to find an interesting problem for my next reading. *Is my boyfriend cheating on me? Will I get into any of my top choice colleges? Will anyone ask me to Prom? Will my mom's cancer stay in remission?* Yikes. I'm definitely not going to tackle that one. Again, I think about the power of my words here, if people look at this as something to actually believe in. They don't, right? They realize it's just an advice column and not magic? If it were magic, I'd write my own question. *How do I get my best friend back?*

When Kayla and I were younger, before her family got

all complicated and she got all difficult, we'd always beg and plead with our moms to let us have sleepovers. Eventually we'd win, even though everyone knew we'd be cranky and tired all weekend long. We'd sit and giggle over Kayla's Magic 8-Ball toy, asking it a million questions and trying to get it to tell us what we wanted to hear by rephrasing our questions a million different ways. Okay, so most of our questions involved when we would finally get our first kiss, and who it would be with when it happened. Come to think of it, it was soon after K's first kiss that the sleepovers tapered off, which was right around the time her mom moved out and Rhonda moved in. And Kayla started doing everything she could to get out of that house.

Maybe if I had found someone to kiss, too, it might have helped us to stay close. Maybe we would have kept giggling about the boys, about how far we'd gone, what it was like. But after Kayla started skipping her Friday classes with a forged note and driving down to the Cities, I don't think even that could have saved us, especially once she started hooking up with all these guys. Guys who were nothing like the boys in our yearbook, those names we would ask the Magic 8-Ball about, over and over. Her new guys were scary and fast, and no matter what she said, I couldn't believe that they actually *liked* her.

And okay. So is it totally lame if I still haven't had that first kiss? I guess so, but the boys Kayla hooks up with, it's like they're breaking her somehow, making her into a stranger, someone who's really good at hiding the part of her that used to be more like me. They use her and then leave her full of this strange angst that I don't know anything about.

I sigh, clicking to the next message. Come on, I need a good question. *I think I'm pregnant. What should I do?* Can I even begin to tackle this one? I find Eric's words coming back to me, how some things are too important to leave to a silly deck of cards to decide. But then, here's this girl in crisis, writing to my blog. Should I answer her in private or something, tell her I think this decision goes beyond me as a fortune-teller? Should I ignore it? What happens if I do, and then she feels all lost and desperate? I wonder who she is. Even wondering makes me feel guilty, like I'm as much of a gossip as Annika and Britney. But still. Who is she? I click past the message; something to deal with later.

The next one has an interesting subject line, just one word: *Quitter?* I read.

Dear Divinia Starr (or whoever you really are),

Are you someone at our school? If you are, it feels weird writing to you, but here's the deal. I play… a sport. I don't want to say which sport because, well, that would make it so much easier to figure out who I am, and I can't let anyone know who I am. I play this sport and I'm okay at it, maybe better then okay. My parents think I'm good enough to get a scholarship or whatever to a college and that's pretty much the only way I'm getting into college, so they are really gung-ho about me playing, you know? And I used to like playing but I had this

thing happen, well, I guess it's called an epiphany, right?
Like this moment where I saw myself playing this sport
and getting into college on a scholarship and having
to keep on playing this sport and having everything get
more and more competitive and difficult and dangerous
and then I thought hey, I don't want that kind of
pressure. Maybe it's lame of me but I want an easy-
going life. I want to stop this path but if I quit, like I
said, I'll have no chance at going to college really. And
everyone's counting on me to do this, to go to college, and
I guess in my family it's sort of a big deal since I'd be the
first one. Everyone else has grown up and worked at the
mines and married and had kids or whatever and I sort
of wish that could be my life too, you know? Why do I
have to be something special? Anyway, I've never said
any of this to anyone at all so I hope nobody will guess
that it's me. I just want to know what your cards say
about my future and if there's any way to make it work
out all right.

Thanks Divinia and if you publish this, will you
go through it and change anything you think might
help people guess who I am? I appreciate it.

—Quitter

I read through the email twice, and it's sort of stupid of
me, but my throat gets all tight and scratchy like I'm going to
cry. I can't really explain why, but I *get* this feeling he has. Or
she has. I understand it. Okay, so my parents don't have my

future all planned out, and obviously I don't play any sports or have any pressure on me to be the first in my family to go to college or anything. So what is it about this letter? Why do I feel like this kid is speaking a truth about me?

Footsteps. My parents' voices grow louder down the hall, and though some of the strain is gone from their interactions, it still sounds different than normal. I clear my browsing history and get off the Internet, and by the time they enter the kitchen, I'm staring at the Whitman words, tapping my fingers lightly on the keys.

"You'll drink some tea if I make it?" says my mom, digging in the cabinet above the stove. She's clearly speaking to my father, and she's just as clearly trying to reconcile some disagreement, since tea is my mother's main peacekeeping weapon.

"I suppose I will," he says. I can feel him peering over my shoulder at the screen, but he doesn't say anything. Even without looking back, I can picture him adjusting his glasses, searching for any minimized windows. I'm glad I cleared the history.

I celebrate myself, and sing myself. Seventeen years, seventeen lines. I know Mr. Dawkins wants something better for my revision, something new, but how can I start? A baby with wild black hair. A one-year-old with food allergies. A two-year-old sucking my brother's thumb. I type up the lines from memory, more or less like the first draft I handed in, but none of it is poetry. A three-year-old...

"What was I like when I was three?"

My mom gives me a startled glance. "Messy," says my

dad, at the same time as my mom comes up with "sweet." They laugh at their own descriptions.

A sweet, messy three-year-old. What a boring poem. I type the line anyway.

"What are you working on, honey?" Mom leans in closer, wafting along the smell of some flowery tea.

I close the document, not bothering to save it. "It's nothing." I shut the computer down as fast as I can and escape to my room.

34. When you
look at the stars…

Kayla makes me go shopping with her in the Cities before the concert, shows me what to buy and how to wear it. For a while it's like old times.

"Hold still." She's putting eyeliner on me in the mall bathroom, pinning my eyes open under her thumb. She bites the edge of her upper lip as she works. "And…ta-da! You officially have a face."

"I didn't have a face without these lines?" I lean over the sink and examine myself in the mirror. Kayla has drawn in huge, smoky black lids above my eyes, and she's teased my hair up so it's dark and spiky. It's dramatic, halfway dangerous. I can't help staring.

"You don't mind if we split up after the concert, right?" she says, adding more eyeliner to her own eyes in the mirror above me. "You know, me and Bryan, you and Darin? Text him and see."

"I…" I don't have Darin's number. I never asked, he

never offered, and now my stomach starts to twist because I see how it is. I thought Kayla and I were going to do this together, to be best friends again, but that was never her intention. She's here to see this guy, and now that she has me here, her plan is to set me up with a different guy so we can meet up to swap stories later. Is that what friendship is now?

"Oh, forget it, Cass, *god*." She sighs to let me know she thinks I'm being a baby.

And I don't believe her. She's totally going to abandon me when we get there, and honestly, I don't even blame her. This whole weekend—I can't believe all the shit I went through to make it happen, all the shit I put *other* people through, and it's not going to change anything because Kayla's the same Kayla and I'm the same Cassandra. It's like I'm a wax dummy—she dressed me up and painted my face, and now she'll ditch me for Bryan even so.

I look up, keeping the tears from streaking down my face in big black lines, and I try to enjoy being with her, try to rummage around inside the dummy to find someone that she'll enjoy being with, too.

So we're driving and we have eyeliner and Kayla's blasting the debut album of her boyfriend's band (okay, so Bryan's not exactly her boyfriend but they've hooked up a couple of times after his shows), and I'm laughing too loudly at everything, trying to match her squeal for squeal. It's not me, not exactly, but we seem to be having fun until she passes me a joint, which I take and then panic when I realize what it is. "Kayla, *jesus*." I'm surrounded by windows and cars and even people walking right there, in big crowds along the street. We're in a purple freaking *hearse*. "What am I supposed to do with this?"

"What are you afraid of?"

"All this traffic. Getting arrested. Dying in a fiery crash under the influence." I bend down and shove the burning thing into my coffee cup. "I can't believe you handed me that right in the middle of all these people." My hands shake. Kayla laughs.

At the door there are two lines spilling out onto the sidewalk, and Kayla herds me into one. I trip over the chunky heels of my new boots, and a girl I accidentally push up against turns to give me a tough look.

"Sorry." My voice is raspy and a few layers down; it doesn't work until the second syllable, and by then the girl has turned away again as though I don't exist, as though her eyes passed through empty space. Music emanates from inside the building, bass vibrating into my belly, and I wish for a second that I had smoked that joint, that I could be a step outside of myself, outside of normal.

Beside me, Kayla is beaming, her cheeks flushed and sort of shiny, and I suspect she's more than one step away from normal. Pills, probably. For a second I wish she'd offered some to me. Okay, so I probably would have said no, but just the fact that she didn't offer means she assumes I'd say no, which makes me think I should actually say yes, which…makes me sad that she didn't ask. If only we hadn't been in the middle of all that traffic.

In any case, I am completely sober and wearing too much makeup and dressed very unlike myself. Also I'm invisible.

We pay, get our hands stamped with ultraviolet ink, and enter the club. Kayla grips my upper arm and steers me toward the stage via her approved course. She pushes me through the crowd where I don't even see a gap, using me as a battering ram—I'm left to mutter apologies to the people parting along each side, and she keeps grinning, nodding her head in time to the electronic pulse of this weird trance music.

In the flickering blue strobe light, people are dancing. Their bodies gyrate slowly in frozen frames. I feel queasy. I bend my knees a little, to make sure I don't fall over, and scan the gathering crowd, looking for a familiar face. Looking for Darin, I admit to myself. I don't see him.

The opening band is rowdy, with pyrotechnics and loud, loud instruments. My ears are already ringing, even before I get to hear Bryan's band.

"Let's walk around," Kayla shouts, toward the end of their set. "We can get back up front once Categorical gets onstage."

I follow her through the crowd this time, which is easier since we're moving away from the stage, toward the edges, where there's a walkway that goes around the back. The sound once we're back here is much more tolerable, and the ringing in my ears settles into a dull buzz. I should have brought earplugs, but that's such an old-person move. The rush of people around me blurs into a kind of whirling pattern, a kaleidoscope spinning. The lights shift from red to blue to purple to strobe again, and I blink, dizzy and unsteady in my heels. Nobody makes eye contact with me. Kayla slips farther and farther ahead—a sliver of her shoulder disappears behind a chaos of elbows; a flash of her shiny, velvet-black bob glimmers above the horizon of hair. She doesn't look back.

When she's gone—when I can't identify any relic of her in the press of bodies around me—I panic, a little. What should I do? Should I keep moving, or stay still and hope she remembers to look for me? Around me, kids are swarming all over. I can see the stage, and it looks like the band is getting ready to play. I don't see Kayla or Darin anywhere, but this isn't such a bad spot to watch the show, so I stay where I am. I try to enjoy myself, whispering Kayla's sister's address under my breath so I don't forget. This is what I wanted, after all. Something exciting. Something interesting. I force myself to smile, and the kid next to me smiles back. The music is loud. I close my eyes for the smallest of moments.

"I've been looking for you!" A voice next to me, shouting, breath on my ear. A tingle traces down my spine, and I open my eyes to see Darin, incredibly close to me. "Where's your friend?" he asks.

I shake my head, my smile immediate and spontaneous. "No idea." I have to shout to be heard over the bass and the drums as the band starts into a long musical intro to their set. A long, *loud* musical intro.

"You want to hang with me?" Darin shouts it in my direction, but he keeps his eyes on the stage, nonchalant.

I nod and take a half step closer to him.

"Awesome," he says, and he holds something out to me.

I look down. "What?" It's a pad of Post-it notes, the classic light yellow. Two stick people are standing, a bit off-center, on the first sticky note.

"Watch," he says, but I have to read his lips, and then with his other hand he flips through the sticky notes in rapid succession, and I watch his little stop-motion animation. In Darin's stick-figure world, the stars come out one by one while the two little stick people watch and point at each one and draw constellations in the darkening sky. In the last picture, the two stick people are holding hands.

It's the perfect film of a stick person romance. Darin flips through the book only that one time, and then he turns, stuffs the sticky notes into the side pocket of my backpack, and focuses on the stage, his cheeks a little pink.

The music pushes against my pulse, quickening, and I'm thinking about the rocket ship and Darin's made-up constellations as I take hold of his sleeve, to keep us together in the crush as Kayla's boyfriend takes the stage.

35. Something worth saving...

The club is not large; we'll see Kayla again before the show is over. We actually see her twice before she finally disappears, messed up on whatever she's been messing up with and draped over the arm of the drummer, giggling. (Okay, so this drummer. Bryan. He's hot, yes, but it's in that... dangerous older guy kind of way that's hotter when it's unattainable. The way he curls his arm so tightly around her waist, like he owns her—I can't stand him. I can't even recognize the girl I used to play Magic 8-Ball with.)

"So should I... like, save you?" I say. I raise my eyebrows at her, and she waggles her own, which are penciled in thin and dark above her dramatic eyes. I wonder if I could have saved her if I had paid more attention, months ago.

"You can come with us," she says, still with that high-pitched giggle. "We're going... for a drive."

I'm torn. I don't want to let her go with this creep, but... I look back, over my shoulder. "Darin—" He's leaning against the wall, holding my sweatshirt for me. He tosses his hair a little and gives me an encouraging wave. Very dorky. I sort of love it.

"I mean ... don't come if you're not into ... *joining in.*"

This is not my best friend. Her face is pink, her eyes glassy. Still, she holds my gaze while she's all sleazy and shit.

"*What?* K, I'll call your sister."

Her eyes narrow, the dark black rings ominous and mean. "Don't touch that phone." Her grip is tight on my wrist.

"Easy, easy," Bryan mumbles, his eyes flitting back and forth between us with mild interest. "No need to fight over me, ladies."

"*Leave me alone*, Cass, I'm serious. God ... you need to get a clue about partying. This is ... this is what my world is like, baby girl. You call my sister ... and we are *through.* You and me, Cassandra. Don't fuck it up."

Okay. So I turn around, you know? What else am I going to do? It's not like I can stop her. I cross half the distance that separates me from Darin, my ears full of her slurred laughter, before I look back. She has her arms around him and they're facing away from me. Her right hand in his back pocket. But she looks for me, over her shoulder sort of, and her one hand snakes out of his slimy pocket and gives me the finger. *Fuck off, Cass.*

And it's so stupid, I know. It's stupid, but I've lost my best friend, and I can see now that this was all a mistake coming here, lying to my parents, using Drew—all of it was useless because Kayla's been like a shadow to me for so long, and I had myself convinced that if I met her challenge and found a way to go with her, I'd really be *with* her. But this...this isn't me. This is me chasing after her all over again.

My eyes get all soupy and the whole world blurs. The stupid crowd is barely a crowd anymore—everyone's filtering out and crowding into their stupid cars. Into their stupid purple hearses. What's even more stupid is what comes bubbling up to my lips, these stupid words. "Dear God," I find myself whispering, "please don't let Kayla die because I didn't stop her." A stupid prayer.

"You tried," says Darin, putting a plastic cup in my hand.

I look down. Ice and brown liquid. Bubbles. "Look, I'm not saying I don't ever drink, but..." But not like this, abandoned at a weird concert and my former best friend gone off the deep end.

"It's an energy drink," he says. "Thought you might be getting thirsty."

"Okay. So it's an energy drink?"

He smiles, his steady gray eyes on mine. "Of course."

"I don't...she was my ride."

"We'll figure it out," he says. *We.* It's a good word.

"Did you drive?" Maybe he'll give me a ride to Kayla's sister's apartment, except how am I supposed to go there now? I mean, maybe she's used to K going MIA, but it's still so awkward. I wish...it's lame of me to want this, I guess, but I wish I were back at home right now, snuggling the piggies and talking with Eric. I'd work out a reading for that kid who doesn't want to play sports anymore and sneak onto the computer to post it. And since I'm being lame, right now I'd even rather be hanging out at Drew's house.

"I..." Darin looks around, shrugging his narrow shoulders. The DJ is playing the music loud, and Darin is practically whispering. "My car isn't really reliable enough to make it here and back, so I took the bus down. I didn't really know...I didn't know if I'd see you, or what to plan for after...but I mean...there's a bus...tonight...going back up north." He tugs the bottom of his T-shirt, which has that Internet comic strip on it, the one with the stick people.

"I thought you planned this out a while ago." I take a gulp of my drink, wincing a bit as a sliver of ice slides down my throat.

Darin is quiet for a second, and his face turns pink. "Well, you weren't supposed to find out," he says, shaking his hair into his eyes.

"Find out what?"

"Find out that...I never had tickets to Categorical Denial like I said. I bought them after I heard you and Kayla were going. I just...wanted a chance to see you again. Outside of English class, you know?"

"Like..." Like a *date*? There's no way I can say that out loud.

"Yeah, I guess." He raises his index finger and wiggles it at me, the inky smiley face making me grin, and then, so quickly I think I could have imagined it, he brushes the finger lightly across my dimple, and then my lips. "Gotcha," he says, and ducks back beneath his hair.

"Well, as far as my parents know, I'm here with Drew Godfrey at a baptism until tomorrow afternoon, and I have no idea where I should stay now, or..." My smile fades.

Darin twists a ring around his middle finger as he thinks. "This is going to sound so dumb," he says at last.

I cross my arms and give him the stare-down.

He smiles, and when he does, he could be a little boy for an instant. And then I'm pretty sure I have a close-call moment where I almost lean in and kiss him. But I don't, and we don't, and at last he shrugs and says, "I have a ... well, it's sort of a tree house. In the woods." He laughs. "I mean, it's my studio, and it's in my backyard, but that's like, the woods. We could sleep there."

"Until tomorrow?" Is that even possible? Won't we freeze to death?

"Until whenever," he says, and for a moment I allow myself to imagine that—to imagine living with this boy in a tree house in the woods *until whenever*. "I stay out there all the time," he adds. "There's a woodstove."

"In your *tree* house?" I raise my eyebrows.

"Mostly house, I guess," he says. "There's a ladder up to its roof, and from there, stairs go up to a platform in the tree. My sister and I basically grew up in it."

I laugh. "You are so weird." It could have been the wrong thing to say. But Darin grins.

"I'll take that as a compliment," he says.

I take another sip of my drink, which is sweet and heavy on my tongue. "So there's really a bus going back home this late?" I'm glad I grabbed my backpack from the hearse when we got here. I can't believe Kayla really took off and left me with no one. Well, that isn't true. I have Darin, and a tree house, until whenever.

An image rises, in my head, of Drew. Not as I usually think of her, but as she was the other night when we baked cookies at her house. Drew, gospel-singing, out of place in the perfect kitchen yet thoroughly in place at the same time, a splash of white flour across the front of her sweatshirt. What if I really had come with Drew for the weekend to attend her cousin's baby's baptism? What if I would actually rather be her friend than Kayla's? Or Annika and Britney's, for that matter. But it's too late for that now, unless I want to come clean to my parents, and as Kayla knows, I've always been too chicken to face them with any kind of conflict, any kind of truth.

"This used to be the bus station," says Darin, helping me into my sweatshirt. We walk toward the door, tossing our empty plastic cups in the garbage as we pass. "Now it's a couple blocks that way."

"Perfect." We walk, our hands swinging free. Darin's shoes are silent, but my boots make a clop-clopping sound on the sidewalk, and the rhythm of my steps forms a little pattern in my head, soothing me. I can almost believe that everything is going to be okay—that Kayla will be fine and we'll still be friends and my parents won't catch on and I'll stop feeling bad about using Drew, and Darin won't find out how boring I am and Eric will find a way to be happy and what the hell, maybe I'll find a cure for babies dying and be a hero and get the Nobel Prize or some shit.

"Did you see the latest Divinia Starr reading? Because you should have." Darin breaks the pattern with this question, and it surprises me.

"What? No, I've only read the first one." Nice, Cass. Call

his attention to the fake reading about the English class crush whose origin is suspiciously close to home.

"Oh, that one."

Is he blushing?

"I thought it was cute," I say. Blurt.

Darin clears his throat, and there's a brief awkward silence. Then he clears his throat again. "No, uh...this one was for someone who wants to give a boy a promise ring at the Winter Carnival, and I thought maybe you'd read it because...well, I'm pretty sure it's your brother."

"Some girl wants to give my *brother* a ring?" I don't understand.

"No, like, I think your brother is the person. I think...I think Eric wants to give his boyfriend a ring. You know. In front of his sculpture of Northstar." Darin pulls his wallet out of his pocket, trailing one of those long chains from his pants.

"What? Eric would never..."

Darin buys our bus tickets, and we shuffle off to one side of the door to wait. I think back. It all falls into place. Nervous Nellie, the reactions "she" was worried about. I remember the ending—dramatic and possibly devastating?

Darin hands me my ticket and I stare at it, but I can't read any of the information in front of me. "How do you even know about Eric?"

Darin shrugs. "Your brother came to talk to me about something, and I..."

I swear Darin's face goes red again. I'm so confused.

"I offered to help him with his snow sculpture." He looks

back down at the ticket in his hand. "We've got a little time before this bus leaves."

"Wait—what did my brother come to talk to you about?" The heel of my left boot digs into my foot. I'm going to have a blister, and worse, I'm going to ignore the blister as it forms to avoid looking like a dork in front of a boy. It really is the apocalypse.

"Well, that's also going to sound a little stupid," Darin says. He ducks his head, hiding under his hair once again. "He heard I was talking to you in English, and, well, maybe he heard that I was asking around about you. A little."

"*What*? Did he make you get a background check or maybe fingerprint you while he was at it?" Wait. He was asking around about me? "And you *are* a stalker, aren't you?"

Darin smiles. "Eric's a cool guy. He just wanted to know, you know. Who I am. And then he told me about the sculpture, and I started helping him after school, and, well..." He shrugs. "You should come and help us. Monday after school, at the carnival grounds."

I nod. "I will, yeah." I fiddle with my gloves, pulling them loose from the ends of my freezing fingers, wondering what it would feel like to take a risk, to take his hand.

36. A time you got caught...

The sway of the bus lulls me—not all the way into sleep, but into a sort of semi-conscious state. I keep my head from drifting over onto Darin's shoulder, but I dream, in a way, of tree house adventures. In my dreams, questions about keeping warm don't matter, and I don't fret over who will sleep where and wearing what. I imagine peering down at the woods through a rustic window, hanging out in a tree all day and all night. I float in the space between waking and sleep, my head full of images of rope ladders and pirate swords and signs that say *No Girls Allowed*.

When my phone rings, I jump, practically out of my seat. I can't figure out what that sound is. *Kayla*. I slide my finger across the screen. Wait, what? It's my mom. Oh god. I pick up.

"Hello!" I make my voice seem like the voice of a girl who's spent the last few hours playing board games with Drew's aunt and uncle. Miss Scarlett in the conservatory with a candlestick. For a minute I forget that it's almost two in the morning and I've been sleeping on a bus on my way to running away or something.

"Cassandra, good heavens! Where are you?" Mom's voice is near panic. Near panic, over me.

"Mom, I'm fine. What's going on?"

"When did you last see Kayla?"

Oh god. Kayla. The truth is my only option. "About an hour and a half ago," I say. "Tell me."

"She was arrested. She was drinking and driving, and … some other things. She told the cops your name, said they had to find you and make sure you got to her sister's all right. She was a mess, but they pulled her over before she got into an accident and got herself killed or something." Her voice crumples into a sob. "Cassandra, where are you? Why aren't you with Drew? What the … *heck* did you think you were doing?"

"I'm on a bus, Mom. I'm on my way home. But my battery's dying. I—" I switch off the phone. "Damn."

"What's up?" Darin looks like he has to crawl up out of a few layers of sleep. He straightens his spine and tips his head back and forth a few times.

"Kayla got picked up by the cops and told them about me, so that was my mother on the phone." The words describing the situation emerge calmly, matter-of-factly, but none of it has penetrated my sense of unreality. The dream images of tree forts and risky freedom begin to dissolve.

"Frantic, enraged, or murderous?" The corner of his mouth curls up, but his eyes are kind, that same steady concern.

"A mix of all three, I think, rolled together in a dusting of prayer." I turn my phone over and over in my hands, wondering about my eventual homecoming. "I think I should prepare some last words, in any case."

"You could read your Song of Myself."

"You *would* have to bring it back to that stupid poem."

"I'm kidding," he says, but it's okay. I mean, he's not really kidding. I do have to write this freaking poem. And judging by the depth of the shit I'm in right now, passing English may be an actual life-or-death situation.

37. A warning you should have heeded…

My mom is so angry she can't even speak to me. That's got to be it. When I walked through the front door early this morning, she hugged me silently but didn't speak. Not even a prayer crossed her lips. My dad was nothing but a shadow looming in the hall, an angry presence that receded as I slipped into my room. I stayed in bed as long as I could, waiting for them to order me to get up and go to church, and now I've really got to pee, except that involves leaving my bedroom and facing her wrath. I listen at the door, shifting positions, trying to figure out the locations of my family members, but the house is silent, inscrutable.

At last I run for it, on tiptoe—I accidentally catch the tie of my robe in my bedroom door, but I make it to the bathroom without encountering anyone. It's late, though, and they never miss church. Is it possible they left me home? I twist the lock on the door and take full advantage of my position of safety, treating this moment as a sort of Last Toilet. I take a hot bath, exfoliate, and even paint my toenails a sparkly purple. I moisturize my face carefully, staring into the mirror while my fingertips make tiny circles on my cheeks, concentrating deeply as though I could occupy my entire brain with lotion. I'm waiting for her voice, for my mother to call me out of the bathroom and in for my sentencing.

Will I have time to eat first? Do I dare hope for a Last Breakfast as well? I stand with my hand on the doorknob, steeling myself, and then I stride down the hall toward the kitchen, dead girl walking.

"Isn't this a new tactic?" says Eric. The sound of his voice startles me; my heart lurches into a faster rhythm, then slams on the brakes when I see my brother, alone, perched on the edge of one of the tall stools at the counter, leaning over a plate of cheese and crackers. "They're gone, Cass. They left, Dicey too, in the van."

"Did they ask you to come?" This makes no sense.

Eric makes a triple-decker sandwich and holds it up close to his eye. I can see his focus change as he looks at me past the sandwich. "Not a word," he says. "They're gone."

Gone. Certainly not what I expected to happen, but maybe it's all in their master plan—leaving me in suspense until I beg them to punish me. Some parental torture device my dad picked up while reading a child psychology magazine.

"They were mad?" I ask this because I need to make conversation, not because I need to know the answer. Of course my parents are mad. But I'm not ready to come right out and say what's really on my mind: Was it him who wrote to Divinia Starr about giving the boy he loves a ring?

And if he answered "yes"? Would I change Divinia's response? For some unknown girl, I was supportive yet cautionary, but when I think about that pee in the snow, about the black eye that Eric still won't admit came from some asshole's fist, I worry about that complicated ending I glimpsed in the cards. What if something bad will happen if Eric professes his love for Gavin in public? Something really bad? And then what about all those jerks who wrote the nasty comments on the blog—when I didn't know they might be talking about my brother, it seemed almost amusing, but now I'm angry. They had no right to talk about him like that, like he's some desperate and manipulative person just because he's in love. I wonder if I should tell him, if I could explain the cards and why I didn't tell the whole story in my post. I think once again about that other Cassandra, whose true prophesies were disbelieved. What if he won't believe me?

Or what if he does believe me, and then it's the *change* he makes that's actually the cause of the cards being wrong. If you listen to a warning and avoid the danger, then the warning becomes false, right? And maybe I could see all of this, untangle the web of cause and effect, if I were better at reading these stupid cards, but I'm only a beginner. Maybe I shouldn't be reading them at all. Maybe I'm going to do damage, like Eric said, not because the cards themselves are tools of the devil, but because my own ignorance is.

"Everybody's talking about that tarot card blog," Eric says. Is he reading my mind now, too? "I mean, everybody. Even Mom knew about it."

"It's the stupid church," I say. "They're up to something."

And then I remember. "That's right. Drew said they were having a meeting today after church, and she said it was at least partly about the blog." The voices, my parents murmuring in their bedroom, must have something to do with my blog. "They're going to pull some kind of power play with the school, some kind of stupid protest like they're trying to do with the Winter Carnival, and once word gets out about what happened with Kayla... they're going to cancel the carnival."

Eric looks up from his last piece of cheese. "What?"

"Well, for starters, Kayla got *arrested*."

He nods, to show he's heard this, but his face registers some shock even as he does. It's still fresh, this news.

"She's the carnival organizer, and the church has been trying to shut it down for months now. Either this whole blog thing will divert their attention, or it will fuel their heavenly duty to rid the entire world of anything resembling fun."

Still. My brain seizes on a wisp of a thought. If they cancel the carnival, they cancel the snow sculpture contest. And if they cancel that, Eric won't be giving Gavin a ring, and if he doesn't give Gavin a ring, Blake and Ronnie will leave him alone, and... crisis averted!

"I'm starting to change my mind about it," says Eric.

"About the Winter Carnival?" Wait—if he changes his mind now, does that negate the reading? Or is it a *part* of the reading? True, or False? Destiny, or Free Will? Sometimes, Never, Always? Maybe I should look at the cards again, do another reading. Maybe I should *stop* doing readings.

"No. About the blog," Eric says. "I think maybe I overreacted. They're just cards, right? It's an advice column, and advice is meant to help." He stands up, meticulously brushing every crumb into his hand and into the sink. "I mean, those cards, you know, the church is...well, I've been talking with someone about things like that. Things I believe and things I thought I had to believe. Allowing a few contradictions, you know?" He grins—two dimples—because he knows how crazy faith makes me.

"Yeah?" I wonder if I can ask him who that someone is, whether his change of heart has anything to do with the reading I did. Whether those contradictions have anything to do with Gavin. "I've got a few readings I'm working on," I tell him. "I guess, since everyone's gone...do you mind if I work on them now, in case Mom and Dad kick me off the computer forever?"

Eric looks thoughtful. "You know I'm only looking out for you, sis."

Again with the big brother protector act. Which *reminds* me: "I can't believe you interrogated Darin." I swat his shoulder, but I can't keep the smile from my face. "He's just this kid. In my English class."

"He's a cool kid." Eric tips his head toward the computer. "Do your thing, Cass. I'll let you know the second I see their car." He takes a can of vegetable juice out of the fridge.

"He's a weird kid," I say, but Eric's leaving the room and I don't know if he hears me. "I was going to live in his tree house," I say. I log into Divinia's email.

There are two hundred and seventeen messages. Comments, questions, condemnations.

I'll never even have time to even skim these, not if I want

to get any readings done. I let my eyes wander down the subject listings. And stop.

Youth group "friend" only using me? Pls help!
I double-click.

38. A time you had good intentions...

I tried to help her when she was struggling. I even shared some of my personal poetry with her. It seemed like we were becoming friends, but in the end it was more of the same—I'm used and abandoned. I'm not going to get into details because they're too depressing, but I'm tired of it, Divinia. I'm tired of being alone.

Youth group friend. It has to be from Drew.

I can't stop thinking about it.

"This is your fault, Cassie." Annika shoves her chair away from the work station and spins toward me. "It's your church attacking the carnival."

"I'm not in charge of my entire church." I try to sound like none of this is bothering me, but I'm sure it's all right there on my face.

"You should be," she says, obviously annoyed but trying

to act like she's joking around. "What else are we paying you for?" She turns back to her computer.

My parents came home yesterday completely riled up about the blog. My dad stomped in and the first thing he did was check our browsing history to be sure none of his family members had logged into Divinia Starr. Then he put us all through the third degree.

It should have been harder, lying to them. If I were a truly good person, my voice would have trembled; my eyes would have fallen to one side out of shame. Instead, I found the words tumbling off my tongue easily as I feigned innocence. It didn't matter—even though their indignation was momentarily derailed, both of my parents left me to understand that they were *not* happy about my weekend escapades and there would be *severe consequences* as soon as they agreed on what they would be.

It's weird, though. For the first time in my life, I'm not really concerned about anyone's approval. This blog is all mine, and I don't care what kind of histrionics my stupid church throws out into the universe. The Internet is free, and my blog is staying put. It's helping people, and if giving advice is the devil's work, then there are an awful lot of busybodies in the church who had better say a double dose of prayers each night.

As far as the concert goes, I'll take the punishment they dole out, and I really do feel bad about all of it. I feel bad about Drew, and I feel bad about lying to everyone, and I even feel bad about Kayla. I sort of wish she hadn't told the police to track me down, but getting caught was probably the best thing for everyone, in the end. Now that the truth is out, Drew won't have to lie to my parents anymore—which also makes me feel a little bit better about her email to Divinia Starr. Except then I feel worse, because obviously Eric was right and Drew really did mind having to cover for me.

God, this whole thing got so complicated—and all for nothing, really. The whole reason I said I'd go was to prove something to Kayla, and of course that shouldn't be the way best friends work, and I can't figure out where along the way everything got broken. The only good part was Darin showing up.

Darin. Okay, so I have to admit, hanging out with Darin was amazing, even without the tree house. Amazing enough to endure all this trouble? Am I a terrible person if I think so? I take a breath to steady myself and try to drag my focus back to the article I'm formatting.

I should fill out that stupid Internet survey now. More interesting things have happened to me in the last month than all last year combined. I check over my shoulder, where Annika and Britney are gossiping, Britney sitting on Annika's desk like usual. I sort of want to click over to the blog right now, to prove to myself that this part of me exists—and to check the comments on the post I put up for the sports kid on Sunday—but I don't want Annika to see me.

As if summoned by my thoughts, Annika rolls her chair in my direction, frowning. "*You* placed the ad for that stupid Divinia Starr blog. Where did it come from, anyway?" She taps her pen against the frames of her fake glasses.

Oh god. "From the email, I think? I don't really remember."

It's harder than it should be to get a full breath of air into my lungs. "So should I get your approval on the ads from now on?" I jot this down on my pad of sticky notes, nodding seriously. "I can do that." The stick figures on the corner of the Post-it make me smile, and I take a second to riffle through them with my thumb. The kid is good at this sweet, goofy stuff.

"Not *every* ad," says Britney, peering over the divider between her computer and mine. "Just the ones that are going to cause a shitstorm of protests about the fundamentally immoral nature of this school, this newspaper, and the Winter Carnival."

"Right. Shitstorm." I scribble on the Post-it. "Is that one word or two?"

"What did you do with the email?" Annika is still tapping her pencil on those stupid glasses. "Whatever. I'm sure we can track it down through accounts receivable."

Accounts receivable? Oh god. All the ads are paid for, and accounts receivable will not have a record of the Divinia Starr ad. Will they drop it at that dead end, or will they keep on looking, trying to get to the source? Can they trace stuff on my computer? I tap my fingers gently on the keyboard, wondering if every keystroke is being recorded on some school usage report, waiting for the IT guys to follow my tracks. I spin my chair away from the computer and change the subject. "Are they really going to cancel the carnival?"

"That church is only attacking the blog so they can get more leverage against the carnival," says Annika. "They think they can get the school to cave just to get the heat off them." She makes a scoffing sound. "The Giant Goth Girl didn't make matters any better by getting arrested or whatever. Good thing she's still underage."

"You know what I heard?" Britney's head pops up over the divider again. "I heard she wasn't actually driving when she was pulled over. I heard she was…otherwise occupied with a dude from one of the bands she went to see." She giggles, her tone sharp.

"Go, Giant Goth Girl!" says Annika, laughing too. "And we all thought you were a lesbian." She turns quickly to me and puts her hand over her mouth, acting the part. "Oh, *so* sorry, Cassie! I forgot the two of you *used* to be friends. Or was she…you know…your *girlfriend*?"

I make a face. "Whatever." The stupid barb about Kayla being my girlfriend doesn't hurt like the part about how we *used to be* friends. Is it true? She's not in school today and she hasn't answered my texts, but it makes sense she'd be grounded from her phone.

"Well, I hope you dump her," says Britney. "I mean, it's a bitch move to give your name to the cops like she did."

I wish they would leave. I need some time to figure out what to do with my next blog entry, in which I'm going to tackle that awful email from Drew—writing about me, the mean girl from her youth group.

I'm not going to get into details because they're too depressing, but I'm tired of it, Divinia. I'm tired of being alone.

The email expressed Drew's loneliness with a painful honesty that's lost in the rhyme scheme of her dreadful poems. I have to answer; only an unfeeling monster could ignore her.

But her cards... I did a reading for her yesterday, with Eric standing guard. Sitting there with his back against my bedroom door, he watched me shuffle with a little frown on his face, and then he blurted out, "You remember Pastor Jake, right?" His words tripped out right in a row, as though he'd been holding them in his mouth for quite some time. Sometimes, even now, it takes him a while to break a silence, especially with something hard to say.

I nodded. I'd been thinking about Pastor Jake when I pulled that card for Eric's reading—the supportive man in his recent past.

"Well, we've been running together on the treadmills at the Y, and he's looking somewhat human again," Eric told me, smiling. "He's been through a lot, you know? His wife dying, and he had some trouble finding his faith after that. Did you know his daughter is gay? She's living out in California or something right now, and... I don't know. It's been good talking to him."

I studied his face. "And?"

"And... it's helping." Eric kept his eyes on his fingertips as he raked them through the carpeting, making spiral patterns. I turned my attention back to the reading for Drew, jotting down notes so I could type up some kind of a reading the next time I was at a computer.

Which would be right now, if the mechanical girls would finally disappear. I've been dawdling over these fonts for almost an hour, waiting for my chance to write up my post. I keep my notebook out of the sight of Annika and Britney, trying to figure out what I could possibly say to Drew that would make up for what a jerk I've been.

Okay, so maybe what the blog really needs to be doing is not related to the cards. Maybe what people need is just a helpful advice column. Maybe that's what Drew needs. And maybe, even though she won't know it's me, maybe somehow Divinia Starr's reading could try to make amends, ask her to look beyond my initial failings. I don't want to be Drew Godfrey's best friend, don't get me wrong. But I would like to be able to speak to her without making her face collapse.

The cards I pulled for her last night were…disastrous. I mean, seriously, how can I write to Drew—or, as she signed herself, *Alone and Betrayed*—and tell her that basically, this is as good as it gets? That her future involves something symbolized by a bound and blindfolded person among a bunch of swords? No. Drew needs some hope. And if Annika and Britney will leave me alone long enough to write this post, that's what Divinia Starr will give her.

"Cassie." Annika snaps her fingers in front of my face. "I said, are you coming to the carnival?"

"My brother's doing a snow sculpture."

Oh. I remember, I told Darin I'd help out with that. I could go now. I could forget about the blog and being Divinia and go help someone in real life, as myself, with my own two hands and a shovel.

Annika sighs as though I'm being difficult on purpose.

"Cassie. We do a kissing booth at the carnival every year. Didn't anyone tell you this?"

"A kissing booth?" Oh, no *way*.

Britney giggles and reappears over the divider. "It's a fundraiser, Cassie. There's a prize for the person who raises the most money."

"And it's going to be me," says Annika. She takes off the silly glasses and bats her eyelashes at me.

"I'm going to be grounded." That came out too fast.

"Cassie! Are you a kiss virgin?" Annika's laughter is the screechy kind that carries across a room.

"No!" My face burns. I totally am.

"You *are* a kiss virgin, OMG!" Britney adds her own horse-laugh at my expense.

"Shut up, you guys." Lamest comeback ever. God, why won't they leave?

"*Shut up, you guys!*" Both Annika and Britney parrot me in a taunting sing-song chorus and then continue their dueling squeals of laughter.

"Seriously, my mom is super pissed at me because of the shit that went down this weekend, so ... " It's true, one hundred percent. My dad has done nothing but glower at me and my mom keeps doing this long, wavering sigh-thing to make sure I'm aware of how deeply my actions have hurt her. "I *trusted* you," she whispers, tragically.

"What really did go down?" Annika leans in for some gossip, done mocking me.

"Goth Girl did, from what I heard." Britney's still laughing.

I grit my teeth and turn back to my computer. "Okay, so . . . I guess I'll get started on the ads for this week."

Annika smiles. "Brit and I are heading out. Text me if something goes wrong."

"And remember," says Britney, and I hear their computer shutting down, "call us if there are any *weird* ads, you know?"

"A shitstorm of protests, gotcha." *Just get the hell out of here.*

Britney smiles. "Exactly."

Annika waves. "Bye, Kiss Virgin!" I stick out my tongue.

At last, I'm alone with the computer. I take out my notes and type, my fingers moving across the keys with a decisive clatter. Switch a few cards. Fudge a few meanings. Create a little hope for *Alone and Betrayed.*

39. When you get nervous...

"What do you think?" Darin smiles, his face flushed from the cold and the shoveling.

"It's a nice pile of snow." It's more than a pile, really. They've made a box thing out of wooden pallets wired together and shoveled the snow into the form so that it's packed in solid.

Eric stands on top of the huge snow cube and points a spray bottle at me. "We start carving tomorrow," he says.

I pick up a shovel lying in the snow. "So do you need me to do something?"

"What took you so long getting here?"

"I...uh...had some stuff to do on the computer."

He raises his eyebrows, and I nod. Yeah, that stuff.

Darin gives me a hopeful look, but he doesn't nag me about my damn Song of Myself, which is a good thing because I may take a swing at him with this shovel if he does.

"Hey, did you guys know the newspaper staff has to run a freaking kissing booth at the carnival?" I demand.

Eric laughs. "You know how many guys live the entire

245

school year dreaming of the day they get to pay Annika Nielson for a kiss?"

"Are *you* going to do the booth?" asks Darin.

Does he sound concerned about that? A giddy wave of hope crashes over me, and for a moment I can't answer. I shrug, to gain time. "I...I told them I was going to be grounded, but I dunno." I have absolutely no intention of being a part of this kissing booth, but I kind of want to see what Darin has to say about it. Will he try to stop me?

"No way," says Eric. He jumps down and lands beside me. "My little sis is *not* going to be mauled for money by a bunch of horny teenage boys."

I punch him in the arm, a little too hard. "I can take care of myself, thank you very much." It's sort of funny and a little sweet, this protective streak he has. But I'm still going to give him a hard time about it. "Bad enough trying to intimidate Darin the instant he speaks three words to me in English class."

Darin smiles. "It was more than three words," he says.

"How much more?" Eric pretends to be threatening and suspicious, but it's clear that they like each other.

"She *should* do the kissing booth," says Darin.

The giddiness fades. "What?" I try to keep my tone light.

"What?" Eric doesn't try.

"Yeah, I mean, it's a great fundraiser. And, you know..." Darin shuffles his feet, examining the pattern his boots make in the snow. "I've got a little savings. It's supposed to be for college or something, but I could part with it for a good cause."

Did he just awkwardly tell me he wants to kiss me? I feel a blush creep over my face, even in the chill. "Oh."

Brilliant, Cass. Speaking of awkward.

"I get the feeling you won't have to break out your piggy bank," says Eric. He's the only one who seems to be at ease with this conversation. In fact, he seems to be finding it highly amusing, judging by the look on his face. My face burns. Cassandra the Kiss Virgin, dying of humiliation.

"No, I . . . I'm not doing the kissing booth," I say. *But I do want to kiss you.* It's silly, the way these words almost escape my mouth. Do I really want to kiss Darin? I like him. But do I—to use a middle schoolism—do I *like* him like him? I watch him toss his hair, watch the way his mouth twists into a shy grin. Certainly I like him enough to kiss him, right? I don't want to be a kiss virgin forever.

"Well," he says, and this time he meets my eyes with his steady gaze. "I guess I'll have to keep waiting for my chance."

It's his eyes that do it. They seem to suck all the air out of my lungs, but in a good way, if that makes sense. If anything can make sense at this moment. "I . . . I guess you will," I say, and then, perfectly delirious, I turn and run all the way back to school, gulping cold air through my grin.

40. When there's drama, you...

I left my bag in the newspaper office, but luckily the school is still unlocked, waiting for the custodian to make his final rounds. I'm pretty sure Darin would have given both me and Eric a ride home, but it's not that far to walk. As I open the door to the newspaper office, I'm lost in thought—and okay, so most of my thoughts are about Darin. Does he like me? My stomach wobbles a little when I think of him, but is that love? Or *like*? Or... anxiety? All of the above?

There's only one bank of lights on in the office, which is plenty for me to sneak in and grab my bag. I loop the strap off the spinny chair and onto my shoulder, and in the process, I bump the mouse. The computer screen comes alive.

I'm tempted to check the blog to see if there are any comments yet, since I'm probably never again getting on the computer at home. My post to Drew has been up for about an hour. I hope she sees it; what I wrote reflects a far more hopeful outlook than her dire reading did. The comments on my post to Quitter were positive, and I'm hoping people will give Drew some support too. Maybe then she'll give me another chance to be a good person, if not a friend.

It would just take a second to check if anyone has commented yet. I log in, my rapid fingers tapping lightly on the keys.

"Cassie?" Britney pops up from behind the divider.

"Britney!" Heart. Lurching. What the...? "I didn't know you were here."

"Yeah." She giggles. "Hey, have you seen this? This pathetic chick went emo on that weird blog your church is protesting, and they're commenting."

I walk around the divider so I can see her screen. "My church?" I can almost feel my pulse in my eyeballs.

"They've made like a million comments condemning everyone on earth to hell," says Britney, giggling again. "The sad part is that every time your church makes a big deal over something like this, the whole town starts passing it around, sharing it, waging their little wars. Getting noticed by the church was the best thing to ever happen to this stupid blogger." She reads from the post in a breathy, pitiful tone. "*Dear Alone and Betrayed*," she says. She tries to get ahold of her laughter. "*Sometimes it can seem like everyone is against you, as though there is no one on earth who cares one bit. I know most of us have felt like this. But when I look at the cards before me, I see evidence of hope, even as I feel your pain, stuck there as you are with the eight of swords crossing you. I know you're feeling trapped and hopeless.*" Britney points at the screen. "Look at that picture. It doesn't look good for this chick."

The figure is bound and blindfolded in a river, surrounded by swords. "Those cards freak me out a little," I say. "Do you think they're magic?"

Britney makes a dismissive face. "I don't care if they are or not," she says. "They're like those little paper fortune-tellers we all made in middle school. The ones that would tell you what boy likes you and what kind of house you'll live in, how many kids, all happily ever after."

"But those were silly."

Britney shrugs. "Didn't keep us from making new ones all day long." She nods at the computer. "I'm sure Divinia's losing her audience, though, when she tries to make it all happy ending for this loser." She reads more from the post. "*That 'friend' from youth group is here in the cards, and yes, her heart is false. Right now she's like a camera lens focused on herself, and the rest of the world is a little blurry. It doesn't mean she can't learn how to be a friend.*"

Tossing her ponytail, Britney looks up at me. "See? Way too nice. *Bo-ring.* More drama equals more readers. Divinia Starr should write to *me* with her self-promotion questions," she says.

I laugh, and it isn't a stretch to make it real. There's a new kind of confidence in Britney right now.

She scrolls down the page. "Look at all these crazy comments."

I read the first few, all of which seemed to do the same thing: condemn Divinia Starr to hell for her sorcery and warn the reader of the dangers of reading such filth. "They had a special meeting about this blog," I say. I can't believe how many comments there are already.

"Let's hope they'll be so distracted by it that they'll leave the Winter Carnival alone," Britney says. "Anyway, why are you here so late?"

"I was helping Eric and Darin work on their snow sculpture, but I forgot my bag, so I came back to get it." It's the truth, though I still feel my face heat up with a guilty blush. I'm not brave enough to ask her why *she's* here so late.

Britney nods slowly, but she furrows her brow slightly, staring at the screen. "Not all these comments are from the church people," she says. "Some of them are from plain old assholes."

I cringe when I see the mean ones she points out. Okay, so a girl wrote in with a problem, and some of these comments are super rude, like the one that says Drew is *a huge loser and u should be thankful enyone will even talk to u!!!* Another nasty person writes, *u r prolly a lesbian and u shd take a hint... shes not into u!!!!!!* Like last time, once the gate is open on the mean comments, people flood in with all their cruelty. I don't want Drew to see these. I need to delete the comments, but I can't with Britney here.

I chew on the edge of my bottom lip. I wonder how soon I can sneak onto the computer at home. Given the Minneapolis fiasco, it really could be never. I might come home and find the computer packed up in a box. My mind races, weighing possibilities. What if I tell Britney about Divinia Starr, that it's me? She seems different tonight, away from Annika. I could almost like her.

"These comments are disgusting," I say.

"Speaking of disgusting, OMG, what about Annika's stupid fake glasses?" Britney closes down the browser.

But I can't trust her. I smile. "They were all right, I guess." I'm trying to be noncommittal, avoid getting pulled into some gossip, but Britney narrows her eyes when I don't immediately support her.

"Hey," she says after a moment. "Didn't that girl in *your* youth group give you a bunch of poems?"

Shit. "Uhhh, no." Why does Britney leave out the part where Annika stole all of the poems from me? "Well, yeah. I mean, actually, a girl did give me some poems, but they were for the newspaper, you know." I should stop there, but my panic makes me babble. "But it's probably not her. I mean, I barely know her."

Britney only nods. "I'm locking up tonight," she says. "So if you'd grab your bag…" She smiles sweetly, that fakey, saccharine glaze returning to her words and actions.

"Yeah, it's cool." My voice shakes. "See ya tomorrow."

But Britney doesn't return my farewell. As I let myself out of the office, I look over my shoulder to see her swivel to the screen and open up the browser.

41. Your biggest mistake . . .

I step outside and instantly regret my decision to walk home—it's cold and dark, and it started to snow while I was in the school. There's no way I'm calling my mom to come and get me. Walking, even if it results in frostbite, is better than spending a mile alone in a car with Mom right now. But after about four blocks I can't feel my toes anymore, and my cheeks are so cold they burn. The wind pulls tears from my eyes, and they basically freeze in their tracks down my face. I wrap my arms around myself and huddle on the corner of Franklin and 2nd. Maybe I should text Eric to see if there's any way that he could get Gavin or someone to pick me up.

I'm trying to decide if my frozen fingers can even operate a phone when a car stops by the curb, the window rolling down. I lean my head over and squint through my slushy eyes.

"You look like a snow zombie, shambling along out there." Darin quirks an eyebrow at me. "Can I give you a ride?"

"At least you're not Mrs. Johnson, my old Sunday School

teacher," I say as I climb into the passenger seat of his car. It's a clunker, and I have to admit not exactly toasty warm, but it's better than walking. Plus. You know.

"I feel loved," he says.

"So you're determined to be my stalker, then? Because just for the record, contrary to what you might have picked up from the media about what girls want, some creepy dude watching me sleep is *not* a turn-on." Oh my god, did I really say turn-on? Thawing ice drips off my burning face.

"If I was stalking you, don't you think I would've at least picked you up before you got to the freezer-burned stage?" He laughs. "I'm coming from your house now, actually. I drove Eric home, and he invited me to stay for dinner."

"Dinner?"

"We were waiting on you, but with this snow, I got worried."

He pulls into what I assume is my driveway. I can't see— my eyes are open, but my vision is swimming. He's coming to dinner? He was worried about me? I blink. He's holding my hand.

"What kind of Minnesota girl is too cool for mittens?" he asks, giving my fingers a brief squeeze with his gloved hand and then pulling away like it's nothing. Was it nothing?

"I'm not too cool. They're … " I pull my heavy mittens from my coat pockets. "Soaked."

We make an entrance. A snow zombie, a strange boy, and a flurry of flakes swirling in through the kitchen door.

"Is this the boy?"

"Dad, this is Darin. Darin, my dad. Uh, Price Randall."
I shrug.

"Mr. Randall, please," he says, extending his hand to Darin. "I'm an old-fashioned guy, Darin, especially when it comes to my daughters." *Ouch*, he's revoking the first-name rights.

"He's here with *Eric*." I push at my dad's arm playfully, trying to lighten up this moment, but he barely moves.

"Thank you for making sure Cassandra got home safely," he says. "Twice now."

"Yes, sir. It was no problem."

"Not to *you*, anyway," says my father.

"Dad!" Why is he being such a jerk?

"I don't have a thing to say to you, Cassandra Jean. Not a single thing." And he turns away, his arm on Darin's back, leading him away toward the dining room. I drip on the linoleum —melting snow and a humiliating rush of sudden tears.

My father hates me. No, worse than that. He doesn't have a thing to say to me. I wipe a sodden mitten across my eyes, across my nose.

"Cass?" It's Eric, sock-skidding into the kitchen like we all do when we come in from the long hall with our speed up— even Mom does it. He whispers, "You saw it, didn't you?"

I look up. A trickle of cold snow slides down my back; my spine shivers. "Saw what?"

"The blog?" His face trades one look of dismay for another. "Oh. You *didn't* see it." He pulls my hat off my head and throws it toward the heater behind the kitchen door. "Come on, hurry. I'll show you. Get that wet stuff off."

Quickly, with one eye on the dining room where my (disappointed-in-me) father is holding my (wishful-thinking) boyfriend hostage, I strip off the snowy outerwear and drape it across the kitchen chairs. "You mean the comments," I say.

"I mean the catastrophe." Eric opens the browser. "This is a shitstorm, Cass."

I run my fingers through my hair. "That's like, the word of the day." I scoot the chair closer and check the damage.

At first, nothing seems any different. I skim through the comments—praise Jesus, bad sorcery, evil filth, stay away. The mean comments are still there, anonymous of course, although I can imagine the likes of Blake and Ronnie with their sweaty hands and halitosis, hunting and pecking for the keys to inflict their stupid insults. And then I see it. The catastrophe.

"Where did these poems come from, Cass?" Eric looks down at me. "You didn't really write these hateful things..."

"No!" I can't believe he'd ask me that. "God, no. Of course not. I don't know..." This is bad. So bad. "It was Britney. Or Annika, since I think she has the poems..." I can't believe this.

Okay. So. The situation. I take a breath to steady myself. After I left the newspaper office, someone posted a series of comments, addressed to Drew, pretending to be me—Cass Randall. *You're completely disgusting, Drew Godfrey, and your poetry stinks almost as bad as your hair. The thought of us as friends is so ridiculous! Honestly, I'd KILL MYSELF if I had to be your friend, and not to be mean, but I think I'd kill myself if*

I wrote this kind of lame poetry, too! Just kidding, but seriously, what am I supposed to think when a GIRL gives me poems like these? GROSS!

"How did they get the poems, Cass?" Eric scrolls down, points at the screen. "They've plastered them all over the place."

"Annika stole them from me a while ago. I tried to get them back. I didn't…" My eyes are drawn back to the screen. It doesn't matter. They're using the poems as weapons, and apparently the whole school is online, looking for a reason to ridicule Drew.

"You have to fix this," Eric says, shaking his head. "Delete the comments and turn comments off. I can't believe you let people post anonymously without moderating. What the hell were you thinking, Cass?"

My mind is empty. I was thinking… that people would be nicer? That nobody would really read it? "I didn't think I'd be able to get on the computer much to moderate," I say. "I didn't think it would matter much because the whole blog is anonymous."

"You didn't think," says Eric. "You didn't think this could get real."

Is it real? I mean, is it that bad? It's still just one post on a silly blog. I'll delete the comments and only a handful of people will have seen them, and really, who's going to believe it was actually me who commented? Why would I have given my name when nobody else did?

"Look, Eric, my name is there, too, okay? I'm deleting them."

257

"Dinner!" Mom calls from the dining room, and I remember poor Darin, in there with my dad. "I'll finish as soon as we're done eating," I say.

"No. Do it now." Eric stands guard, and I hastily change my blog settings to full comment moderation.

"Damn it, there are already eight more comments." All anonymous, all making mean comments about Drew, and a few about me as well. Drew's dirty hair is mentioned in five of them, and the other three are much worse, full of disgusting speculation about her hygiene and sexual health. "Oh god, they're horrible." I begin to delete the comments, but I can only delete one at a time, so the going is slow. At least the new comments land only in my Divinia Starr email account now, instead of going straight up. Still. Is everyone from school reading the blog at this exact instant?

"Hurry."

"That's not helpful."

"Helpful was when I warned you ages ago not to play this game."

"Look, I'm going as fast as I can, okay? You can go on about how you told me so once I'm done, but right now I've got"—I check the total—"sixty-six more comments to attend to."

"Eric and Cassandra, we're waiting." My dad. There's no arguing with this summoning.

"I got the worst of them," I say, closing the browser. "The poems are gone, and the names. I'll get the rest after dinner, I swear." I chew on my bottom lip. "I didn't mean for this to happen." I look to Eric for any scrap of forgiveness, but he only shakes his head and scowls as he pushes past me on his way into the dining room.

"You didn't mean it," he mutters, "but you could have prevented it."

42. Something you should have done...

Kayla finally comes back to school, and for the second time in as many months, she's waiting for me when I get off the bus, except this time she's got nothing to say. We stare at each other, silent.

"You didn't return my calls," I say. "I was worried."

"*I* was worried," she says. "I did everything wrong, Cass. Every single thing." She looks terrible, her face all sallow and miserable. "I saw the blog," she says.

"Yeah. It's kind of all messed up, isn't it?" I hitch my backpack up onto my shoulder and make a face. "I'm sorry my church is being stupid about the carnival."

Kayla makes a face, her mouth quirked up on one corner like it does when she's being a smartass. "Yeah, my weekend antics didn't really help the cause." She stops, drags her toe through the layer of slop on the ground. "I wasn't really driving, you know."

"Were you... otherwise engaged?" I can't really look at her, so I make designs in the slush, too.

"Ew, gross, is that what they're saying? I was *asleep*." She giggles and pulls her coat tight, looking up at the sky. Her eyeliner is a mess, and to be honest, she looks like she hasn't slept in days. "Bryan was driving and he slid off the road, which is why we were found by the cops."

"Are you... okay?"

"Like, did I get hurt?"

"Like, are you *okay*?" I shiver. It occurs to me that it's not always such a bad thing to be the boring friend, the sane one. I start walking again, toward the school.

"I guess. Are *we* okay?"

Kayla has never asked me anything remotely similar to that in her life. "You're sure you didn't get a head injury?" I say.

As if on cue, a wet, sloppy snowball collides with my own head. "What the..." I look around, wiping nasty slush off the side of my face. "Ew, it got in my ear!"

"What the *hell* is your problem?" Kayla has identified the attacker and is giving him a hand signal that does not mean truce. Another snowball lobs toward us, but she opens the door to the school and blocks it. Splat! The wet mess slides down the safety glass.

"That was so gross." I shake the snow out of my collar and run my fingers through my hair. "And uncalled for."

"Cass?" Drew looks as though she's been waiting for me. She looks desperate.

"Oh, uh … hey." I busy my hands with my once-again-soaked mittens. "What's up?" *What's up.* As if I don't know.

"You … you didn't read Divinia Starr?" Her whole face is trembling like a beaten puppy. I want nothing more than to flee this conversation.

I fight to keep my tone neutral, thoughtful. "Hm, yeah, I think so. Britney showed me some comments or something last night when I was working on the newspaper. She said they were from Joyful News." I shrug, feigning cluelessness. "I don't really get into that stuff, you know." I try to walk away, to extract myself painlessly from this moment. Obviously she read the catastrophe. But what does that mean? How many other people read it? Do they really think I wrote those awful things?

"Cass. It's all over the school. Everyone's talking about it." She reaches for my elbow, but I feel her desperation and move past her, like an eel. A slippery eel.

"Stop this! Stop pretending you don't know what I'm talking about," she says. "The other comments, Cass."

I turn to see her face dissolve—in an instant, she's nothing but soggy despair.

"I only wanted some advice, and now everyone has seen my poetry, and … " She crushes her fists into her eyes and then searches my face desperately. "It wasn't you, was it? Look, I know it was stupid, to write to the blog about something I should have just talked to you about … "

"It wasn't me." I take a half step toward her, but then I stop. "Drew, I swear. Those poems … "

Out of nowhere, a crowd has formed—it's not exactly obvious yet that they're gathering to watch Drew and me, but the traffic in this hall has definitely slowed and people are milling around in clumps, their murmured conversations lulled. They stare, talking behind their hands. Are they talking about me, what a bitch I am, or are they talking about her, what a loser she is? It doesn't matter. "It wasn't me!"

Drew shakes her head. "But my poems—"

"Cassie!" The crowd parts for Annika and Britney, trailing their mechanical minions.

I turn to look at them, incredulous. Do they really think I'm going to act like we're friends after they set me up like this? They stole the poems and then ridiculed them on the blog *while pretending to be me*. They're evil in pink lip gloss, basically.

"It was them," I say to Drew. "It was Annika and Britney."

"Cassie, we *need* to talk," says Britney. "Seriously, this cannot wait."

"You gave them my poems?" Drew asks. Her voice is soft, hurt.

I shake my head. "You *wanted* me to give them your poems."

Her face is so covered with tears, it's no longer pitiable. It's gross. I take a step back. Of all the people in this school who could want to be my best friend, why Drew Godfrey? That "off" smell of her. The way she stands too close. All of this drama, over what? A heavy weight sinks into my stomach. Over me using her, that's what.

"Cassie, OMG, is this that creepy girl who's stalking you or what?" says Annika.

"Is this the loser from the Divinia Starr blog? OMG!" echoes Britney. A murmur of shocked voices from the robots.

"Cassie, we want you to know we don't blame you for telling her off like you did," Annika says, her pink nails digging into my arm. "I mean, it was deleted right away by Divinia Starr, but luckily someone got a screenshot."

"Yeah, it's basically gone viral. You're, like, a celebrity, Cassie."

"Whatever, I'm out of here," I say, looking around for Kayla. She's gone. Melted away into the crowd, like always. And here I thought maybe things were changing.

"I told you to give them the poems, but you *knew* I wanted to remain anonymous," says Drew. Her voice has a little hiccup in it now and her eyes look sort of bleak, like. Sort of dead. "I didn't want anyone to know they were mine."

Her words are a plea, but what does she expect me to do? So many eyes, all around us. The hands, the shoving elbows. What are they waiting for? They think...do they think I was the one who *posted* her poetry? Do they think I betrayed her on top of betraying her? I try to read their faces, but they only look hungry—waiting for more drama.

"Drew, I—" It doesn't matter. They don't care who gets hurt as long as there's something to gossip about. As long as they can pin a target on someone other than themselves.

Annika tugs on my arm. "Drew's disgusting, Cassie," she

says. Her perky tone is gone, and what is left is pure bitch. "It was funny, okay? It wasn't really about you. Just *look* at her."

I look at her. Her stringy hair. Her splotchy face. The ring of people waiting, grasping for details to gossip about later.

"I'm sorry, Cass," Drew says, barely louder than a whisper. She's apologizing to *me*, of all the messed up things on earth.

And I can't do this. I can't be Drew's friend, but I'm sure as hell not going anywhere with Annika. I can't believe Kayla abandoned me.

"I'll see you in study hall," I say to Drew, and then I turn away. I'm about to push past the ranks of kids to get to my locker, but through them from the other direction strides Mr. Dawkins, followed closely by Kayla, who must have run to get him.

"What's going on?" He walks into the center of the hall. Traffic moves along; people dissipate. Even Drew wipes her eyes and lowers her head, slipping past him toward the girls' bathroom. "Is she okay?" he asks us. I shrug and turn to go, too.

"Cass." His voice is sharp.

I stop. I don't turn back.

"Is she okay?"

I swallow, my head inching back toward him a little. "She's fine," I say, but my voice is hard to find, and he asks me to repeat myself. "She's fine!" I shout, and then I run toward my locker, away from the bathroom. I want to smash things, or cry. I want to go home.

"Write me some poetry!" Mr. D calls after me. What a tool. He has no idea what's going on in my life. This stupid poem... my fists shoot out on their own accord and slam into my locker door. Sharp pain stabs up through my arms. *Stupid everything.* I round my shoulders into the books I'm carrying and stumble off toward homeroom.

43. If you could have a second chance...

Drew wasn't in study hall seventh period, she didn't show up at school or youth group on Wednesday, and she isn't anywhere in the halls this morning either. Darin gives me a few questioning looks in English class but doesn't ask about the poem or anything else, and neither does Mr. Dawkins. Kayla and I manage to pretend like nothing ever happened, but the rest of the school is not as tactful.

"Did you hear about Drew Godfrey?" I overhear in one class. "I heard her parents shipped her away to a Christian camp to save her soul from sorcery."

Totally not true. Drew's mom isn't a church member, and they didn't say a word about the blog or anything at church last night. I keep my mouth shut, though. It's so cowardly, but I'm relieved they're leaving me out of it, that aside from a few strange looks, nobody's talking about me. Maybe people will forget my apparent part in all this. Maybe it will blow over once they get all the drama milked out of it, once some other gossip-worthy event pushes this into the dim recesses of our rather short-lived collective high school memory. I'm worried about Drew, though.

"That's not what I heard. She's not coming back; she's being homeschooled."

"It's like some kind of cult, anyway, that church."

"I heard she's switching schools."

"I heard she had a psychotic break."

Everyone has heard something, but when the assembly is called at the end of the day, nobody is talking about Drew.

"It's the carnival."

"They're gonna cancel it."

"How can they cancel it? It's *tomorrow*. Martin Shaddox is coming and everything!"

"It's that stupid church."

"It's those stupid snow sculptures in their underwear."

"It's the bonfire."

But it's not the carnival that the principal, Ms. Clark, is talking about. It's bullying. Groans echo from the bleachers of the gymnasium where we're all gathered. She starts by talking about how different the world is from the world she lived in as a teenager, and I feel every person in the room—teachers included—let out a sigh and settle back into their seats. Nobody is really listening until she finishes this preamble and breaks the real news to us.

"This past week, one of our very own, a member of the Gordon High community, was cyberbullied."

Loud fake gasps all across the room.

Ms. Clark gives us all a stern look and waits for it to get quiet again. "Cyberbullied," she continues, drawing out the word, "to the point of attempting to end their life."

There's a reaction, but this time it's smaller, more concerned.

"The Gordon High student and the student's family are in need of our positive thoughts and support right now, and I'd like the cooperation of each and every one of you. Although we can't release the student's name, our crisis intervention team decided to call this assembly because students at this school played a role in this traumatic event, which has left one of our very own in critical condition, hovering on the brink of tragedy. Some of you contributed significantly to this student's pain by making…"

Ms. Clark pauses, her voice breaking, and I can't breathe, waiting for her to finish. Is she talking about my blog? Is she talking about Drew? Oh *god*.

"Students at our school posted horrifying comments about this student on a website which has recently come to my attention. I want you to know that the administration at Gordon High will be enforcing a *zero tolerance policy* on harassment and bullying of all forms. This is a serious matter. A student's *life* hangs in the balance because of this website and the hateful comments, and as an administrator—as a *parent* —I hold every one of you who participated in this bullying responsible, whether you actively commented on the website or linked to it from somewhere else or even gossiped about it offline." She takes a shuddery breath and the room explodes in murmurs, questions, denials.

It has to be Drew, but I don't get it. Her life hangs in the balance? *Suicide?* I think back to the last time I saw her, those muddy eyes of hers, apologizing to *me*—as though it wasn't all my fault in the first place. I should have followed her into the bathroom, talked to her, let her know I was on her side. Was I on her side? *God,* I'm such an idiot. I should have moderated the comments before they got out of hand like that. But how was I to know it was going to get so nasty, or for that matter, that Drew would do something so extreme? I didn't know she'd try to kill herself. Was she depressed? Looking for attention? Okay, so that's an awful thought, isn't it. I'm an awful person.

And then, awful person that I am, my brain starts trying to speculate the method she might have used. How morbid is that? So morbid. But really. Wrists, maybe? Or pills, probably. Her mom does all that international travel, so she's probably got sleeping pills lying around. Or antidepressants. Seems like everyone's got some of those lying around. Not a gun, though. I shudder. Seriously, Cassandra, what is your freaking problem? This is Drew Godfrey you're talking about. A human being. A *friend.* At least, she could have been a friend.

"For the next few hours, certainly, and likely longer, all school computer accounts will be inactive," Ms. Clark goes on, "because we have reason to believe that at least some of the hateful activity on the website in question was occurring on our own servers. We will be retrieving IP addresses of individual commenters, and several members of the community have already come forward with some screenshots of comments that have been deleted. Our tech team will be working to help us isolate all accounts in question."

This statement is followed by an even louder reaction. A lot of kids have gone to Divinia Starr's blog while logged into the school network. Probably almost all of them.

Panic is a cold stone in my belly. Will they be able to uncover the admin of the blog, even though I started it from home? IP tracking, screenshots... I'm sure they'll also talk to Annika and accounts receivable and try to track down the ad I placed in the newspaper. The stone starts to rotate, slowly at first like a lumbering planet, but it's clear I can't stay here in these bleachers, listening to Ms. Clark lecture about bullying. I scramble to my feet, feeling the stabbing presence of a hundred sets of eyes at least, watching me as I flee to the bathroom.

So much for everyone forgetting about my involvement. Do they suspect that I'm the one behind the whole blog, too? It doesn't matter, since I'm in fact the heartless user who caused all the drama in the first place.

I'm staring into the bathroom mirror, trying to believe that I feel worse about Drew than about myself—about the potential of getting caught, or about people hating me. The truth is, my brain is racing back and forth between the thought of Drew dying, and the thought of Drew dying and it being my fault. Not *all* my fault, I tell myself, but, you know. Significantly my fault.

My hands shake. I run the cold water and stick my wrists under the tap. Then I bring my cool wrists up to my cheeks. My face is hot. Maybe I'm feverish? I gaze into my own eyes, looking for a reason to go home and hide under my covers, but I don't look sick, just guilty and terrified. I jump when the bathroom door swings open.

"Don't say one word to anyone," says Kayla. She holds up a hand to wave away my protests. "No, I know what I'm talking about, Cass. You keep your head down and don't say a word, and everything is going to be fine. These tech guys are talking tough, but they're using scare tactics. The truth is, there's no law against setting up a blog, and there's no law against accessing that blog from the school servers. If a site is blocked and you hack through the filters, that's one thing, but you haven't done anything wrong." She frowns. "Or at least, you haven't done anything against the technology use policy."

"Can you believe it, though? What if Drew dies? I...I should have gone after her." I shake my head. "Everyone's going to hate me." Oh god. What a pathetic, self-centered thing to say. I press the heels of my hands into my eyes until I see sparkles. "I just...I didn't know she would do something like..."

"Look, Cass. You're not responsible for all of this." Kayla indicates the bathroom, and I look around as if the blog comments are scrawled on the whitewashed walls. Knowing the way these things work, they probably are—scratched into the paint on the metal doors with safety pins, hateful conversations blossoming in black sharpie beside the toilet paper dispensers.

"I should have been nicer." The spinning stone in my stomach has dissolved into a swirling soup. Even if it's not my fault, I'm going to be the scapegoat. In like five minutes, the halls are going to be filled with people, and they're all going to be playing the part of the innocent bystander. They're all going to be looking for someone to blame.

"You wrote the blog post, and yeah, her email was about you, but you *didn't* write the mean comments," Kayla says. "You didn't plaster that girl's poetry all over the Internet." She takes me by the shoulders but I drop my eyes. I can't look at her. I don't even know who she is to me, anymore. "So maybe you were a shitty friend to Drew. It happens, you know?" Kayla hunches over, all awkward, and sticks her face in front of mine. "People make mistakes. People even act like really big jerks, and they say and do stupid things, but it doesn't mean they have to be really big stupid jerks forever, okay?"

I look up. Is she talking about me, or herself? Her eyes are all shiny, and she's blinking rapidly to keep from having a bad case of raccoon eyes.

"I should have at least invited her to come down to the Cities with us instead of making her lie for me and then sit home all alone," I say. It's not that I don't appreciate Kayla trying to make things better between us, but I can't think about that right now. "I should have—"

"*Cassandra*. You didn't make Drew try to kill herself. This goes beyond you."

I nod. "Yeah, but I didn't make her want to try to live, either." I press my cool wrists one more time against my cheeks and brace myself to leave the sanctuary of this bathroom.

Kayla puts her hand on my arm. "Wait," she says. "I know this isn't the time to talk about this, and I know it's not about me, but sometimes people can change." She nods to the door. "Whatever happens out there, I'm on your side. Where I should have been all along. Give me a second chance?"

I can't deal with that right now, honestly. I can't think about my friendship with Kayla or our future, not now. "I hope Drew gets a second chance," I say.

44. You would fight for . . .

I pause for a moment inside the bathroom door, listening to the thunder of feet exiting the gymnasium. You'd think maybe the sobering news of Drew's suicide attempt would subdue the several hundred Gordon High students as they ponder their own culpability or mortality or whatever, but no. They're almost unbearably loud, and when I gird my loins and merge into the flow of students in the hall, it's all I can do not to cover my ears with my hands.

And all of them are wailing about how it's not their fault.

"So, was that your idea of a sick joke, Cassie?" It's Annika. She grabs hold of my sweater sleeve and tosses her hair, making sure there's an audience to witness this public accusation. I admit it. I'm impressed by the audacity.

"Yeah, now the whole school is going to get in trouble," says Britney, but she sounds a little more subdued than usual, a bit of the shine worn off. It's tough to be perky after you almost kill someone.

"Do you realize that people are going to end up losing their chance to be accepted at their top colleges now, just because you wanted to start some kind of flame war on that stupid blog?" Annika's voice is getting shriller by the second.

"Yeah, go ahead and pin this on me. Whatever." Even if it's more true than she knows, I have no idea why other people saying shit that causes them to be passed over by their precious college choices has anything to do with me. "I didn't force anyone to go to that blog. I didn't make anyone say mean things to Drew." I try for a defiant tone, but my voice betrays me with a tremor. Why do they have this kind of power over me? I spin the lock on my locker and grab my binder for study hall.

"I can't even believe you have the nerve to stand there and judge other people for saying mean things to that poor girl when everyone here knows that the majority of those comments were from you, Cassie Randall. And all because that *poor girl* was brave enough to call you out on your bullshit act." Annika's face is the perfect mask of outrage, and she cheats her body away from me as though she's performing in a play. I glance over my shoulder and see that it's close to the truth. A crowd has gathered around us—and they don't look friendly. I pretend to check my face in the mirror on the locker door, though really all I see is a blur.

"Don't you have someone else's life to ruin?" Kayla's voice surprises me. She's still here, speaking up for once. Like a friend.

"Don't you have something skanky to do in a car?" Annika's perfect composure is dented, even if she's still on her game with the sharp tongue. I can see it in her eyes.

"What's the point of this conversation?" I hug my binder

to my chest, but today I'm standing up straight. If they want to make this whole thing out to be my fault, let them. I can own it. And as soon as I figure out a way to make it better with Drew, I will, which is more than any of these mechanical girls can say. I'm through being a tool.

"The *point*, Cassie, is that you're no longer welcome on the newspaper staff," says Annika with a defiant flip of her ponytail. "Britney and I feel absolutely *betrayed* by this—"

"They're saying Drew might not ever recover," says Britney. She looks scared, her mascara-coated lashes gummy with tears.

Annika glares at Britney for interrupting. "By this heartless act that could cause so many people in this school to suffer." She places a hand over her heart, looking the very picture of sincerity. "I thought you were supposed to be some kind of super Christian or whatever, Cassie. First you used her, and then you crushed her spirit. The poor, sweet, innocent girl."

I push past the huddle of gum-snapping girls and start walking toward study hall. Annika and Britney follow, trailing their minions. Now they're chasing me. I turn to look at them, and the sight of everyone gawking at this scene—like it's some messed-up reality TV show and they're the voyeuristic public getting their kicks from watching everything explode—makes me sick. Are they waiting for me to punch Annika, to come unglued and pull her hair and screech obscenities? Am I supposed to cry and beg her to forgive me? All the crowd really wants is to rid themselves of suspicion and guilt. Can they prove that I was the one who posted the mean things? Can pinning this on me make them feel better about how they laughed, how they passed on the link?

Would it make *me* feel better if they did? If I took the blame, all of it? I could go right now and walk into Ms. Clark's office, show her the blog, explain my intentions, admit my mistakes. Would she believe me?

She would tell my parents. I mean, obviously this is a big deal. Okay, so I'm a coward. I'm the biggest coward on earth, and I can't do that. My parents can't find out about this. My mom... *no.* I turn away from the mob, away from their sick hunger, but Annika throws one more barb at my back.

"Everyone here *knows*, Cassie Randall."

I look at her; she gestures to the crowd around us, which has grown—milling groups of interested eyes and ears straining to catch every word.

"What?" They know what? I try to catch Britney's eye, but she looks away.

Annika draws the crowd's attention with a precisely timed dramatic pause and then shakes her head like she's so ashamed of me it's rendered her speechless. She opens her mouth helplessly once or twice and then gasps out, "Oh come *on*, Cassie. The girl even said that she wrote those poems and gave them to you. Obviously she was in love with you, and you couldn't handle that." Once again she turns away from me slightly, speaking her soliloquy, "It's so terribly sad the way pathetic people will post such cruel things on the Internet. So many awful things they would never say in person."

My face burns. "She wasn't in love with me! She only gave

me the poetry because she wanted it to be in the school newspaper. You stole that poetry from me and passed it around to everyone and ridiculed it!" I gesture to the minions, and of course they all shake their heads. Nice little trained monkeys. People murmur to each other behind their hands. "And you're the ones who posted those comments—you and Britney!"

I feel Kayla's hand gripping my elbow. "Come on," she says under her breath. "This is a bad scene." Yeah, no shit, it's a bad scene.

"That poor, poor girl," says Annika loudly, dramatically, as Kayla tugs me into study hall. "I wonder if she'll ever forgive you, Cassie. I mean, if she lives."

I should say something. I should say something perfect and noble—something that will convince all these onlookers that I'm not the mean girl; I'm not the one to blame. But my throat is tight; my unshed tears have a stranglehold on my voice, and it's all I can do to walk away with my head up.

"That poor *girl*," says Kayla to the crowd, "is named Drew Godfrey. And she's what we should be focusing on, not all this stupid drama."

45. Something you could never do…

It's all anyone will talk about. The study hall monitor gives up trying to keep us quiet and instead settles in with a crossword puzzle or whatever study hall monitors do when they've thrown in the towel. Eric is the only one who will look at me, the only one who knows the whole score. "They don't really believe you wrote those comments," he says. "Anyone with half a brain can figure out you don't have anything to gain by posting the poems or signing your own name. Mostly they're just worried they're going to get into trouble for going to the blog on their school account."

"Maybe they should be more worried about whether Drew is going to be okay," I say, but I know I'm as guilty as everyone else, losing my sadness and horror at Drew's actions in my fear about facing the consequences of my own actions. Or inactions, when it comes right down to it.

About ten minutes into the period, I'm called down to Ms. Clark's office. It's my chance to spill all of this. Instead,

I sit mute in the chair across from her, tightly wound and clutching my own arms to keep myself together while she shows me screenshots of the comment catastrophe and clears her throat in an awkward sort of disgust. Obviously I'm here because my name has come up, repeatedly, both in the comment stream and by others who've warmed this chair before me, whose hands have reached for the tissues Ms. Clark provides at the edge of her desk, whose blotted tears are crumpled up in the wastebasket beside me. But I don't cry, and I don't tell her anything. I fight the urge to pull my knees up to my chest and feel the heavy stone spinning faster and faster inside my body. I imagine it polishing all of my insides to some kind of ugly, shameful iridescence.

"Cassandra," says Ms. Clark with a long sigh, "I understand this is a difficult situation. I've been studying the issue of bullying extensively for the last dozen years, and I know it's not a simple matter. It's no easy task to unravel the dynamics of an awful situation like this, and you have to understand that I'm trying to give everyone the benefit of the doubt. You understand that, right?"

I nod, but I don't know if I understand any of it. They talk about this in school a lot—saying we're a bully-free school and that we take bullying seriously—and it's true in a lot of ways, but it's always about these simple scenarios, like a big kid beating up a little kid for his lunch money. Even when they try to get more subtle in their examples, it's always very clear who's the bully and who's the victim. So is Annika the bully, and Drew is the victim, and I should be the helpful bystander who tells an adult what Annika has done so that she can be stopped? Okay, so if I go with that interpretation, what is Annika guilty of? I can't prove anything about the poetry or the comments on the blog, especially not while keeping my silence about the identity of Divinia Starr. Almost all of Annika's comments to Drew in public have been shrouded in that wide-eyed insincere kindness—it's not like she walks around spouting hate speech or pissing on cars or punching people in the face. It's all under the surface, invisible. And that makes it really easy for it to appear like I'm the bully and *she's* the bystander, doing her duty by reporting me.

And wasn't I, really, more hurtful than Annika's crowd and their snide comments when I took advantage of Drew's desperation and made her lie for me, without even seriously considering asking her to go along?

"I want to reiterate how important we as a school feel it is for bystanders to come forward, Cassandra. One of the students I've spoken with, of course I won't give names, has told me that you are no longer in possession of these poems, that you haven't had them for some time. This student doesn't believe that you are the one responsible for these comments."

I keep my face neutral and think about this. One of the marionette girls, afraid of losing her college of choice or whatever?

"I don't have the poems," I say. I'm not willing to give any more detail. "Why don't you trace everyone's computer accounts, like you said in the assembly?"

Ms. Clark sighs softly, and I get this sense that maybe they can't do it after all. Maybe because so much of what happened was after school, from students' own homes . . . maybe there are laws against that kind of snooping around. Whatever the case, I think Kayla was right that most of what she said in the assembly about the accounts and IP addresses was more of a scare tactic than a reality of their investigation.

"I'd rather get a sense of this crisis on a human level first," Ms. Clark says. "It's not as much about punishment as it is about processing this event and ensuring that our school community can heal and move forward with the certainty that something like this could never happen again."

"Is Drew…" I can't really finish the sentence because I'm not sure I want the answer.

"We don't know yet," says Ms. Clark, and she scoots the box of tissues a little bit closer to me. "We won't know for sure for some time, it seems."

I press my arms tighter around my middle, trying to slow down the spinning stone. "It doesn't seem real," I say. I don't mean to speak, but then I can't stop. "I saw her Tuesday morning and she seemed…she never seemed like she would do something like this, you know? I just can't…wrap my head around it."

"You two go to the same church," says Ms. Clark, her voice gentle.

I nod. "We have youth group together. I—I wasn't good to her." I gesture toward the screen of her computer, toward Drew's incriminating email.

"There are lots of reasons for people to attempt suicide, Cassandra. Loneliness, chemical imbalance, romantic problems, a feeling of hopelessness for the future. Bullying is one reason, and it could have been the only one, or it could have been the tipping point in a long list of reasons."

It still doesn't seem real. "But the blog...I didn't leave those comments." I almost reach for the tissue, but I can't stand the thought of Annika reaching for the same box, the idea of her weeping in this same chair.

"Your church has been quite upset about the blog. Your parents too, I would imagine. Am I right, Cassandra?"

There's something knowing in her tone, and I think again about those computer accounts, about what she says and doesn't say. The stone in my belly spins and I have to leave— I'm going to be sick. I lurch to my feet and run. I'm half expecting Clark to stop me, maybe even clap a set of handcuffs on me or fold me into the back of a police car, but she only calls after me, "My door is always open, Cassandra, if you come up with anything to help us with this investigation."

46. Something you didn't expect…

I cry in the bathroom stall like it's going out of style, which of course it never is. As long as there are high schools, there will be girls crying in bathroom stalls. When my eyes finally clear enough to see the writing on the walls, I wish I could cry more, but I'm empty, spent.

"Cassie?" The voice is tentative, a mere whisper outside the stall.

I don't answer. I don't know which one of them it is, but I'm not going to give any of them the satisfaction of seeing my puffy face. I won't have them thinking that I'm crying because of them.

"It's Britney," the voice continues, and I can tell by the sound that she's been crying too. "I saw you come out of Clark's office, and I … I want you to know that I told her the truth, when I was in her office."

The truth. So she was the one who told Clark I didn't have the poems.

"I guess you didn't want to get in trouble when your account showed you'd posted the poems from the newspaper office," I say, opening the door of the stall and stepping out to face her. "Did you throw Annika under the bus, then?"

"I didn't ever have the poems, Cass." Her face is pale, her makeup ruined. "I did go to the blog that night from the newspaper office, but I called her. Annika was the one who posted."

"You told Clark it was Annika? Seriously?"

She reaches for my arm, like I'm going to rush out of the bathroom and tell on her. "Cassie—"

"Cass." Might as well get one thing straight here.

"Cass." She nods. "I...I didn't tell her the other thing, though. I didn't tell *anyone*." Her perfectly manicured fingernails fly up to her mouth and she starts to gnaw away at them like a guinea pig with a fresh carrot.

"What other thing?"

"I promise, Cass, I won't tell. Annika's my best friend, but she's like this sometimes, you know? She goes too far." Britney bites a nail, spits, bites again. Gross. "It's like, she's under a lot of pressure at home, to be perfect, and sometimes...well, it makes her kind of mean. Not to me, usually, but when she finds someone with a kind of weakness...I think it's hard for her too. She's got this mother, see. Who, like, is always just so. Her house is just so. Her hair, her makeup, her family. And she's...she's *sharp*, like a weapon." She takes a long, shuddery breath. "Annika's never had anyone who wasn't trying to overpower her. I think she forgets, sometimes, how to stop."

"*What other thing?*" Why is she telling me this about

Annika? Like I need things to get more complicated in my head.

Britney startles, spitting another fragment of fingernail onto the floor and fixing me with her wide eyes. "I mean the thing where you're Divinia Starr."

47. Something you should get rid of...

I don't suppose things can get much worse if I skip the rest of study hall today. I walk out of the bathroom in a kind of numb stupor. Britney told me how I forgot to clear the browser history on my computer in the newspaper office when I left to go help the boys with the snow sculpture. How I'd actually forgotten to log out of my Divinia Starr account.

"I logged you out right away because I didn't want you to get in trouble," she said, and I guess I believe her, especially now, knowing what she told Clark. "I was trying to be nice. But I guess in the end, I wasn't nice enough."

None of us were.

I stand at my locker for a second, uncertain. Should I go and tell Clark right now, get it over with? Again, I think about my mother finding out about the tarot. I spin the lock slowly, still wavering, and as soon as I open the metal door, two triangular pieces of folded paper fall to the floor, shoved through the slats at the top of the locker for me to find.

I pick them up and weigh them, flip them over in my hand. Neither one has any identifying markings on the outside, and both are folded in the same style. I slide the flap of the first triangle and open it, but as soon as I unfold the final crease, I can tell that this is not a pleasant note. The handwriting slants violently across the page in thick black marker. My hands shake as I read—the note is nothing but a string of hateful words and threats. The anonymous writer promises that I am actually *the most HATED person EVER to walk the halls of Gordon High!!!* The bulk of the message—the theme, so to speak—seems to be the words that are scrawled across the top, down both margins, and in block letters across the bottom: *U BETTER WATCH UR BACK!!!*

For some reason, I carefully fold the note back up into its cutesy triangle before pocketing them both. I can't bring myself to open the second one, and, for whatever reason, I'm equally incapable of throwing them away. Unbelievable. I've never received a threatening note before in my life, and now I've gotten two. I'm out of here. I put on my coat and slam the locker door shut, a little loudly.

"Cass, hey!" I look up to see Darin waving at me from down the hall, near the drinking fountain.

"Hey." I wait for him to get closer. "What class do you have right now?"

"French," he says, holding up the stupid Eiffel Tower bathroom pass. "Which I'm failing."

I try to laugh. "You say that about English too, but I've seen you. You do plenty of work when nobody's looking."

He throws up his hands, playing innocent. "Who, me? No way. Too cool for school. That's me."

"Next I'll find out you have the top SAT scores in town. And I'll be like, I don't even know you!"

How can I be having this conversation when Drew Godfrey might be dying, when Annika's turning the whole school against me, when I'm on the brink of my parents discovering I'm the antichrist or whatever and disowning me or sending me off to some kind of religious boot camp for reprogramming?

"You have study hall, right?"

I nod.

"So let's skip. Let's go see if Eric's finished the sculpture."

"You're failing French." My heart leaps at the idea, even so.

"Yeah, so?"

"You have the Eiffel Tower."

"It's a traumatic day. Madame LeBlanc will understand." His eyes get serious and he reaches out a finger, touching my cheek lightly, below my eyes. "You okay?"

I brush the back of my hand quickly across the spot. It comes away black with eyeliner. "Fine. You know."

"Did you get my note?" He ducks his head, all shy hair hanging in his face, so he doesn't see a thing when my fist snakes out and punches him, hard.

"Oof! Cass, what the heck? *Ouch*."

It's only after seeing the shocked look on his face that I remember there are *two* notes. Two notes, only one of which I've opened.

"Oh god. It's a long story," I say. I dig through my coat pockets while we walk to his locker, and he busies himself with his own jacket and backpack while I unfold the *second* triangle of notebook paper and smooth it out against the lockers.

My cheeks tingle as I study the drawing, which certainly doesn't deserve a slug in the stomach. In his familiar black ink, he's sketched a spiky-haired girl in a kissing booth, lips puckered up and about to connect with those of a boy with shaggy hair and a pen in his hand. Behind his back is a sign that says, in Darin's adorable block lettering, "This lane closed. Please try next window."

"I'm so stupid," I say, and I show him the other note. "I guess I'm new to this whole hate mail thing."

"Oh, Cass. This is messed up."

He flattens the hate mail against the leg of his jeans, and I can't keep my eyes off his hand—an ordinary hand, clean fingernails, a light scattering of hair on his slender fingers. I try to recall what his hand felt like in mine. Speaking of messed up, how can I think about things like that right now? Am I completely heartless? *Stupid.*

"You should probably show this to Ms. Clark, Cass. It's evidence."

Evidence. A word that brings to mind other words. *Crime. Investigations.*

Guilt.

"Some freak hit me in the head with a snowball yesterday." I run a hand over the collar of my coat as though the slush is still there. "I feel like everyone hates me. Which I guess would be what I deserve."

He holds the door for me, and for a long time the only sound is our footsteps slogging through the mess on the ground.

More snowy silence, and then Darin speaks. "Cass, nobody hates you." He stops walking and surveys the scene ahead of us. Sterling Lake looks peaceful and pristine with its layer of fresh white snow, even though everyone in town knows the lake is a festering mess of mud and goose droppings.

"If they don't now, they will soon." Everyone needs a scapegoat, and as far as anyone knows, I'm doubly to blame, or triply—the girl who used Drew, the girl who started all the drama, the girl whose blog post exploded. It's not going to change even if I turn myself in, or even if there's proof I didn't post those mean comments. "The whole thing is my fault. Drew wouldn't have any reason for killing herself if it weren't for me."

"For *trying* to kill herself."

"I hope so."

"And you don't know that, Cass. You don't know what Drew's life was like, what her reasons were. You can never know what's going on inside someone's heart, what they might need or what might push them over the edge, over their limit."

"But you can *try*, you know?" That's the part I hate. I never tried—even when it occurred to me that I should. "I was too big of a coward."

"Do you think she's going to be okay?"

I shrug inside my heavy coat. "I hope so."

"I could have been nicer to her, too. I could be nicer to

everyone." He looks at me as we walk, and his eyes are so sweet. For the slightest second it pisses me off that he's so nice, so caring. It pisses me off that I'm not.

"Darin, I—" I should tell him, about the blog. How I screwed up.

"We've all been cruel to people, Cass. You didn't know it would lead to this when you asked her to cover for you to go that concert." And then he does it again—he takes my hand. He squeezes my fingers a little and leads me toward the edge of the shore where the Eric's snow pile stands.

"I…" I twist my hand away. I can't hold hands with someone while I'm planning my big confession.

"No," he says, and he takes my hand again, but this time he pulls me in close to him. Very close. I feel my body tense as he reaches toward me—my breath catches and his face gets so close. But he just tugs on my hat as he leans toward me, his eyes on mine. "You didn't mean to hurt Drew."

I shift away from his eyes, but I let him keep my hand this time, allowing him to lead me along, my eyes shrinking away from the glitter of sun on snow, settling on the slushy trail ahead of us. We're quiet again, approaching the sculpture area, and I'm excited to see Eric's version of Northstar. I bet the sculpture has come a long way since Monday afternoon.

I can't do it. I can't tell Darin about the blog, not right now. What if he thinks I'm one of those people who gets off on the drama? What if he can't see that my intentions were good, even if I made a huge mistake in not moderating comments, not predicting how stupid and mean people are? Eric told me someone would get hurt, and I should have realized that he'd have insight into how awful people can be.

"Oh." Darin stops in his tracks, sucking his breath in through his teeth, and I look up, raising my free hand to shade my eyes against the bright winter sun.

Oh god. We're both standing here stunned, our mouths hanging open. Eric's sculpture is almost done—the block of snow chiseled into the shape of the broad-shouldered comics hero, his one fist raised up, a star-shaped ice crystal connected to his glove. Eric has spent hours here carving away, perfecting his sculpture. It looks amazing.

And horrifying. Across the front of his sculpture, someone has spray-painted two words in red paint. One of them is misspelled.

The stone that has been spinning in my stomach since the assembly chooses this moment to eject itself from my body. I turn and puke into the snow.

48. One good thing...

Darin drives me home, his eyes flicking away from the road every couple of seconds to land on my face. "I'm worried about you," he says, for the third time in eight blocks.

I send a text to Kayla, letting her know I'm not going to be on the bus. I'm worried, too, but less about myself than about Eric, about Drew. Even about my parents and how this will hurt them—I've tried so hard to keep from hurting them all my life, and now I'm breaking their hearts all over the place. Lying to them, sneaking away to Minneapolis, dealing in sorcery, failing English.

Killing a girl. *Almost* killing a girl, I hope.

Darin pulls the car into my driveway and puts it in park. "Thanks for the ride," I say, but my hand rests on the door handle without pulling it open.

"You know, it might be a good thing," he says, and he reaches for me—his thumb lightly brushing my cheek. He leans over, his fingers curling into my hair, pulling me toward him.

Whoa, wait. What's going on? I can't seem to stop myself from moving closer. "What might?"

My voice sounds all stupid and breathy, but really, what might be a good thing? Telling my parents I'm the source of the evil they've been protesting all along? Telling Eric that someone spray-painted *DIE FAGGETS* across his sculpture, but that we couldn't tell Clark about it because then she'd call Mom and Dad? My mind races, but my eyes slide closed and my question dissolves in this kiss. *My first kiss.*

His mouth presses only briefly against mine, and then he moves up and kisses both of my eyelids, which are leaking stupid tears.

Of course I'm going to ruin the moment by crying. And, *oh god*, probably by having puke breath. My hand flies up to cover my mouth. I rinsed twice and chewed a piece of gum, but still.

"What might be a good thing?" I say again, and now I really want to tell him, about Divinia Starr—about everything. But what if he thinks I should turn myself in?

"It might be good for Eric. For your family. For everyone to be honest about who they are and who they love, and ... " He takes a deep breath and shakes the hair out of his eyes again. "And maybe even what they believe. They're your parents, and it's normal to follow their lead and stuff, but you're also allowed to have thoughts they don't have." His fingers are still tangled in my hair; his thumb still rests on my cheek. We're acting like this is all completely normal, like we've always paused mid-conversation to make out (okay, so that tiny kiss could not in any universe be mistaken for making out, but still), yet my brain feels like a pinball machine after a particularly successful round—all flashing lights and frenetic music. I try to drag my thoughts back to the moment, back to what he just said.

"I…" I look up at the front window. One lamp is on that I can see, but I can't tell if anyone's home or what. "I'd better get in there," I say. My voice is shaky and strange. I smile and lift my index finger at him, waving it back and forth even though this time there's no smiley face drawn on it. "Bye, Darin," I whisper, and I pull open the car door.

49. One way you like to "be yourself"…

"They're not home." Eric picks at the plastic wrap on a loaf of banana bread on the table. "Emergency meeting at the church. They picked up Dicey from school." He hands me the note, penned in Mom's neat script, but those are the only details she gives.

I hang my backpack on the hook behind the door. The emergency meeting must be about the blog, about Drew.

"Are you okay?" he asks. His hands fidget on the legs of his jeans.

What a stupid question. As if either of us could be okay. I'm so far from okay, and it's only going to get worse. I look at Eric, his eyes worried and maybe reproachful, and I can see those awful words in blood red against the brilliance of the snow, the sun shining on the day that Drew Godfrey tried to kill herself, and it doesn't make sense. *It doesn't make sense.* Maybe evil really is the only explanation—the presence of demons or sorcery or something truly wicked.

"Eric, look. I know Divinia Starr told you something else, but please don't give Gavin a ring at the carnival. Please."

"What are you talking about? I didn't..." He can't keep from blushing, and even now, he can't stop a smile from stealing over his face at the mention of Gavin and the ring.

"It's escalating," I say, pulling up the picture I took of his sculpture and handing my phone to him. "Please, Eric. I can't..." I can't bundle him in bubble wrap and keep him safe.

"Nobody's going to hurt me, sissy. I promise." But I see the way his mouth twitches down at the sight of the graffiti.

"Darin and I scraped it off," I say. "So nobody would see." Once again, I'm erasing the evidence of someone's hatred against my brother in order to keep his secret. Protecting him in one sense, but at the same time putting him in danger by not telling anyone who could help.

"Maybe people *should* see," he says. He twists his fingers around and around the space on his ring finger. There's a tension in him I've never seen before, as though a current of electricity is running through him. It's not fear, or even nerves. His eyes dance.

"You're...in love." As the words exit my mouth, I see it so clearly. I recall the looks he and Gavin save for each other during morning prayer circle, the way Eric seems so far away during dinner. "You really love him, don't you?"

"It's stupid, I know," he says. "High school sweethearts never last."

"That's not true," I say, though I think it might be.

"Doing this, giving Gavin a ring—don't you think it would

send a message to these haters? A message of support for Drew, too?"

I pull up a chair. "Will you let me do a reading?" Maybe I can ask, in general, what the carnival will be like, get a feel for whether or not I have anything to worry about. Maybe the cards can tell me what to do. About everything.

"Haven't you figured it out yet, Cass?" Eric's mouth tucks in at the corners as he studies my face.

"That's what I need the cards for."

He shakes his head. "Don't you think this has gone on long enough?" He lops off the end of the banana bread and pops it into his mouth, then cuts three more slices and stacks them on a plate.

"I'm not saying I'm going to put it on the blog." I pluck a piece of bread off his plate and take a bite, but once I'm chewing it up, the last thing I want to do is swallow it. My mouth is dry as dust.

"I'm not talking about the blog, sissy. I'm talking about the secrecy. You've got to come clean about this. Tell Clark about the blog. Tell Mom and Dad about the cards." He spreads the butter on his slice of bread carefully, avoiding my eyes. "For Drew," he says, after a pause. "Do the right thing."

I force the mouthful of bread down and toss the rest of my slice on the counter. "Like you should talk!" I'm not the only one around here who has secrets. I stomp down the hall and pull the cards out of my closet, not bothering to close my door.

I need to focus. I need to figure out what I'm supposed to do here, what I'm supposed to say. Am I going to tell my parents about the blog? About the cards? About me? I think of what Darin said in the car, about how I can have thoughts and beliefs that are different from theirs. I know that; I mean, obviously. That's what this whole card thing has been about, right? About me having my own thing. But can I tell them? Can I tell them I don't really believe in God? That I'm an *atheist*? The word is like some kind of curse word, and I don't know, I don't know if I can break their hearts like that. I could tell them about the blog without telling them all of it, right? People get led astray all the time—they give in to temptations or whatever.

My thoughts are everywhere—Drew, Darin, Eric, Kayla, my English grade, the carnival, the snow sculpture, betrayal, guilt, my duty as a daughter and as a person. The cards flip through my fingers in a comforting rhythm. Am I still the least interesting person I know? Do I care anymore? It seems so long since the New Year, since my birthday and that stupid survey.

One month. So much has happened. I started working on the newspaper and met a boy I like. I lied to my parents and went to my first concert. I got dumped by my best friend and then ... well. The next part is still in progress. I had a friend try to kill herself. *A friend.* My hands pause in their shuffling. I'm no friend to Drew, and it certainly isn't because of her hair or her skin or any other failing on her part.

"Cassandra." Eric knocks on the frame of my door, even though he's looking right at me.

The garage door rattles the far wall of my bedroom, and

I know they're home. "How can I tell them?" I fan the cards out across the carpet in front of me. "They'll be crushed."

"Cass."

I don't look up from the row of cards, moving my hand slowly from one end of the line to the other. "What should I do?"

I speak my question out loud, but I'm not talking to Eric. I'm talking to the cards, waiting for them to call me, for fate to guide my hand to the right answer, the correct path, the perfect card. The kitchen door opens; I hear the bells on the leftover Christmas wreath that's still hanging on the back door, the sound of Dicey kicking her boots off next to the hall closet.

"I told them," Eric says.

"What?" He *told* them? My hand drops, and without thinking I scoop the cards up and stuff them back into the box, my heart stuttering inside my chest.

"I told them I'm gay." His fingers tap against the legs of his jeans—I watch them for a stunned moment before I dare look up.

"What? Eric, when? How? Oh *god*." I have to put a hand over my mouth to keep myself from blurting out more questions.

He shrugs. "Right after the thing happened at the lookout." He gestures to the fading bruise on his eye. "It wasn't such a big deal in the end. Pastor Jake is helping, and I think…it's getting better. I don't know, Cass. I guess I'm trying to say that Mom and Dad aren't as delicate as you might think. They're pretty open-minded once you let them in."

I jump to my feet, and I think I'm going to give him a hug,

but once I'm standing, I don't know what to do with myself. Next to him I'm such a coward, and such a fool. I think about them talking in their bedroom, their voices so serious, and it all makes sense. "Why didn't you tell me?" I ask.

I hear the scrape of wooden chairs from the dining room, the sound of the television news. I'm still holding the deck of tarot cards, and I notice that I missed one card—it waits on the carpet, face down. Is it the answer to my question?

"You've been . . . " He follows my gaze to the card on the floor. "Preoccupied."

I look up. "It's time, isn't it?"

Eric smiles, a two-dimple smile. "It's time to be yourself, sissy," he says, and I feel brave, as though for the moment at least, I know what that means.

50. Something
you can't do...

My parents sit still and quiet, heads bowed, hands outstretched and clasped together on top of the shiny wooden table.

"Cassandra," says my father, but his voice sounds strange, like he's having trouble squeezing the word out past a lump in his throat or something. He raises one hand and beckons for me to sit in the chair between them. I go to them, and they take my hands. My resolve of a moment ago is flattened by a sense of dread.

"Father, forgive us for the things we have said and done, the things we have left unsaid and undone." Dad's eyes are closed, his prayer a mere whisper.

Why is he referencing the confession prayer? I don't think I've heard anything close to those words since we joined Joyful News. They make me uneasy, the part about things left undone. Is it possible to do every right thing, every good thing? But if there is no God, if there is no God, if there is nobody to forgive me for those things I neglect to do, then it's up to me to make them right on my own.

I can feel my pulse jumping in my neck, and I wonder if they can feel it in my hands. They squeeze tightly, as though they're terrified of me running away, but then they both drop my hands and I feel unmoored.

My father takes a breath, long and steady. In. Out. Then he opens his eyes and looks at me. Looks *through* me. "Lord, be with Cassandra," he says. "Amen."

"Mom! Are we going back...?" Dicey comes sliding in from the hall, wearing a church skirt. Going back to church? For what?

Mom doesn't look at my sister, just stares out the window.

"Did someone die or something?" Dicey spins her skirt out in a circle.

"Dicey!" I say, but I'm wondering the same thing. "Mom? Is it Drew? Did she...?" My voice cracks.

"Dicey, go to your room," my mother snaps, still without turning from the window. My sister and I exchange a look, and then Dicey scurries down the hall obediently. Mom doesn't ever raise her voice or just sit and gaze out the window. Something is going on, that's for sure.

Okay, so I'm the one who makes little, quiet waves. I forget my Bible. I stop participating in the morning prayer circle. I keep my eyes open while we say grace. None of these tiny rebellions has prepared me to be the kind of girl who can tell her parents that not only did she lie about going to a baptism, act uncharitably to a suffering girl, and dabble in the occult with disastrous consequences, but also she doesn't actually believe in their idea of God.

"Mom?" I can't quite figure out what to do with my hands, still adrift on the table, so I fold them in front of me. "Is Drew okay?"

"We don't know yet," says my mother, and her eyes fill up with tears. "She's in Duluth, in a hospital for teens with . . . her issues." Her voice breaks along the edge of the sentence.

A hospital for teens with issues sounds closer to okay than critical condition hovering on the brink of death in the intensive care unit. "But she's alive." I fidget, weaving my fingers together first one way, then the opposite.

"They showed us some pictures at the meeting," my father says. "Screenshots of the bullying. Some of the comments that were made on that website . . . comments that *you* made."

"We can't . . . we can't even trust you to tell us the truth anymore," says my mother.

"I didn't leave those comments, honestly. Mom, don't cry. Please." I can't handle her like this. "It wasn't me, I—"

"We stayed after the meeting to talk to Pastor," says Dad.

"About Drew?"

"About you."

My mom reaches over to the napkin basket and presses a cloth against her eyes, puts herself back together. "He has agreed to meet you for counseling, several sessions a month," she says.

"Counseling?" I'm not crazy. Drew's the one who needs a therapist.

"Spiritual guidance," says my dad. "Your mother and I both worry that you might be feeling a bit adrift—your faith needs an anchor, and Pastor Fordham is willing to give up his time and energy to help you."

And again with the anchor. Is that what they think? Like they can weigh me down with more dogma and everything will be all right. "That's not what I need," I say, but how can we finish this conversation? "I can't talk to Pastor Fordham. I can't…"

"You can't even try this?" says my dad.

"I can't," I say. "I can't believe in everything you believe. I *don't* believe."

There's a sound—maybe my mom draws in one breath, quickly, sharply—or maybe all of the oxygen is unceremoniously sucked out of the room. Either way, there is a small sound followed by silence, and I can't breathe. I can't speak. I can't take back what I just said.

"Young lady," says my dad at last, but his voice lacks its customary power. He, too, falls silent and brings one hand up to press against his chest, as though my words are physically breaking his heart.

"I'm sorry," I say, but it's not what I mean, and I don't try to make it sound like it is. "It's not like I'm trying to disappoint you. I'm *trying* to tell you the truth." And I squeeze my hands together so tightly I can feel my arms start to shake, thinking of all the truths lined up in front of me, still waiting to be told.

"What you *think* is the truth…" My mother whispers into her fist.

"This is exactly why you're going to talk to Pastor," says my father. A light sheen of sweat has broken out across his brow, and I remember the way his hand felt, the papery skin—how suddenly frail he seemed on the night Eric was attacked. I'm hurting him. I'm aging him. What if... what if he has a heart attack?

I can't tell them. I can take it all back, right now—tell them I was mixed up. I can spend an hour a week with Pastor Fordham, breathing through my mouth to avoid the sour smell of him; I can pretend, like I've done all along.

Except. It's time to stop pretending—time, as Eric said, to be myself. But also, time to take responsibility for all those things I've done and left undone. "I'm not talking to Pastor," I say. My voice is quiet but it's firm, too. I sit up a little straighter. "Look, I'm not trying to hurt you guys, I swear—"

"Cassandra." My father admonishes me out of habit. The hand on his chest moves to the bridge of his nose, pinching it between his thumb and forefinger as though he's trying to staunch the bleeding. He doesn't look at me.

"I started that tarot blog." I speak to my clasped hands, and I go on before they can interrupt. "I'm Divinia Starr. I'm the evil influence the whole church has been so worked up about, but I'm not... it's not evil. It's an advice column. It's a bunch of cards." I pause, but the room is silent, waiting. "I made a big mistake. I let the comments go unchecked, and it all got out of hand, and if I could go back in time and change things I would. I'd change everything, I *swear*." And one more thing. "Also I'm failing English."

Okay. So that's everything. I wait, my eyes still fixed on

51. Something you try to avoid ...

I keep waiting for her to barge in, to talk to me—even to yell at me. To tell me she still loves me. Dinnertime comes and goes, and I hear the sound of silverware being loaded into the dishwasher. I can't hear any evidence of normal conversation, and even Dicey doesn't talk in a voice loud enough for me to hear through the walls of my bedroom. My prison. I sit on my stupid pastel-rainbow bed and stare at the center of the floor, where a lonely tarot card still lies, face down.

Won't Eric stop in to relieve me from this solitary confinement? He could at least bring me my phone from my backpack behind the front door, even though the only person I could possibly call would be Kayla, and I don't think now is the time to talk to her. She wouldn't come close to understanding how much this sucks.

I don't know what to do with all the resolve I had to "be myself." Okay, so maybe I thought confessing would change everything, would open up this amazing dialogue between me and my parents while sappy music played in the background, or maybe it would throw us all into a time warp where none of this would have ever happened. At the very least, I guess I hoped that coming clean to my parents would make me feel better about Drew—like maybe she could someday forgive me for all the stupid things I've done—or perhaps I hoped I'd be instantly reinvented as a better person, the kind of person who takes responsibility for her actions and stands up for the weak and the oppressed.

Yeah. I'm that stupid. I roll off my bed and, still skirting the mystery card on my floor, I crouch down to say hello to Pumpkin and Nut, who squeak happily. I wonder if I could sneak out to the hall closet for some fresh bedding and clean their cage. It would feel good to do something right, something that doesn't ruin anyone's life or hurt them or disappoint them, and the sight of a joyful guinea pig in a clean cage is pretty much the greatest thing ever. I gather up their food and water dishes. "Be right back, girls," I say, and already, speaking in a soothing voice helps calm me. "I'll bring you fresh water and hay, sweethearts."

I press my ear against the door, but I can't hear anything, not even the evening news, which my dad almost never misses. Okay, so . . . did they all go out and leave me here? Like, who cares about Cassandra, she doesn't believe in God. Maybe they're out hiring an exorcist, or whatever non-denominational equivalent might be available to cleanse their home and their daughter from the evil spirits.

Whatever. They can't keep me in my room forever. My hand rests on the doorknob but I don't turn it, not yet. This is so dumb. Am I really cowering in my room, hungry and thirsty, afraid to venture out into the rest of my house? Stupid!

I open the door and stomp my way noisily to the bathroom across the hall, risking a look down the hallway toward my parents' room. The door is closed, no light visible underneath.

"Whatever." I drop my armload of bottles and dishes into the bathroom sink, fill it with warm water, and wash them quickly, relying on the night light so that I don't have to look at myself in the mirror.

I rinse and dry the bottles carefully and brace myself again for entering the enemy territory that has become my own home. Once again, all the doors in the hallway are closed, and everyone seems to be either gone or silently ensconced in their rooms. I tiptoe into the kitchen. "They could've at least brought me some food," I say, and then I find myself actually *crying* when I open the fridge and see the plate, neatly wrapped in plastic and waiting for me. I'm such a mess. I toss the plate into the microwave and watch it spin for a moment before my gaze falls on the cabinet under the sink.

The door is still equipped with child safety locks, even though Dicey's the youngest in our family. My parents always intended on having a whole series of children, stair-steps down to the babe in arms, but Mom had some medical stuff between me and Dicey, and then what happened with the baby, and I guess in some ways we've all been unwilling to think about it being the end. In any case, I'm so used to this that my fingers push the plastic latch down automatically and slide the door open. My heart is thumping. Why am I so nervous? They're my cards, after all.

I pull the trash can out of the cupboard and tilt it toward me. The cards should be near the top, but I don't see them, so I gingerly turn over some of the contents. There's the broccoli stems from last night's salad, some of my brother's morning oatmeal ... no cards. Which means my father must have removed them. Was he worried I'd dig them out? Or did he want to personally destroy them?

The microwave dings. I wash my hands and the lemon scent of the dish soap wafts up, bringing a pang to my chest as I think of my mom's eyes, the way they were closed off to me, so distant and hard. I've hurt her—there's no question, but if I do what she wants, I'm only going to be pretending again. I shake my hands into the sink and grab a fork from the drawer.

It doesn't work like that. I'm not just someone's daughter or someone's best friend or anyone's puppet, either. And I'm not going to spend all day tomorrow at the church. Just because I'm a teenager doesn't mean I should have to believe everything that my parents believe.

I take my plate out of the microwave, balance it and the guinea pig dishes in one hand, and pull the sack of bedding and the bottle of vinegar spray out of the hall closet with the other. I use my right elbow to open the door to my bedroom and then nearly drop everything when Eric clears his throat from inside my room.

"Sorry!" He jumps up to take some stuff from me. "I didn't mean to scare you, honest." Pumpkin, curled up against his chest, chirps at the disturbance, so he sits back down and cuddles her. "And I didn't mean to scare you, either," he whispers.

"Took you long enough." I sit down and sulk, nibbling at the chicken on my plate. "You said they would be open-minded."

"Give them time," he says, taking Nut out of the cage and settling both pigs on the floor under a sheet of newspaper. "They'll come around." He picks up the tarot card from the floor and tosses it at me. "You forgot one."

Once again I find myself with a mouthful of food I can't swallow. The card lands on my bed, still face down, promising me some glimpse of destiny. "Eric, I can't do this." I stare at the card.

"You can't do what?" He shrugs, noticing my face. "I'll wait until you're finished eating to clean the cage."

"No, it's not that..." I flip the card over. *The Hanged Man*, Major Arcana XII. The sight of the guy hanging there, upside down from a tree, makes my stomach plunge; the few bites of chicken I've managed to swallow threaten to come back up. The look on the man's face is so grim, like he's watching his own death.

"I can't stay here. I can't spend tomorrow at church. I can't let this happen." I have to be at the carnival tomorrow, even if it means defying my parents. Even if it means scaring them. "Look." I hand the card to Eric.

"Cass. What, do you think there's going to be a lynch mob at the school carnival? You think Ronnie and Blake are going to string me up for giving Gavin a ring in front of a gay snowman?" He shakes his head. "They're not killers. They're obnox-

315

ious little boys who don't have the sense to think their own thoughts."

"But the card—" I grab it out of his hands. "Darin told me about this other Cassandra. In ancient Troy." I trace my finger over the wounded face of the hanged figure. "She was a prophetess, and she was always right, but nobody believed her." I stuff the card into my pocket but my hand encounters a folded triangle of paper. My stupid hate note. I pull it out, unfold it, hold it up for Eric to see. *U BETTER WATCH UR BACK.* "I'm not good enough at reading the cards. This Hanged Man could mean anything, but don't you see? It has to mean *something*. What if something terrible happens and I can't stop it?" What if something terrible has already happened, and I can't fix it?

"Terrible things do happen, Cass. But so do good things. And sometimes we can't tell the difference between the two until afterward." He grins, as though he can erase all the bad things in the world with a flash of those dimples.

Maybe he's right, but what if he's wrong? "I've got to go," I say. I jump to my feet, making the piggies squeak in surprise. "Don't tell *anyone* I'm gone until tomorrow." And then I leave, before he can say another word.

52. Where would
you run to...

I feel totally conspicuous skidding on the icy sidewalks, running away from home. I'm certain that every approaching car is full of spies ready to report my whereabouts, even though I'm praying that nobody knows I'm missing yet. It's late, and it's cold, and I've been walking forever, with nowhere to go, stupidly. I'm also starving, but at least I thought to grab my backpack with my phone in it. I pull my hood up and burrow my face into my scarf, hoping Kayla got my text, hoping she'll find a way to come and get me even though she's grounded from her hearse. She hasn't returned my message, but she's my only hope.

I'm starting to lose that hope—and the feeling in my toes—when I hear the rattling exhaust of a car coming up the hill. It slows, comes to a stop beside me. I pull open the passenger door. "H-how?" My teeth chatter. "I d-didn't have your number."

Darin grins. "That's because I've been too lame to call you.

I figured you'd try to walk all the way to Kayla's. Insane, on a night like tonight, Cass. Now quick, get in before you freeze solid out there." He switches the heater to high and I climb in. "Are you okay?"

I'm still shivering. "I'm despicable," I say. I fiddle with the mittens on my lap. "And I kind of need a place to stay."

Darin takes his eyes off the road for a moment and studies my face. "Eric called," he says. "I told him I'd call him back when I found you."

I don't answer. I can't move, can't speak, not until he tells me I can stay.

"Cass, it's *January*." He keeps driving, heading into the country north of town. "If you're going to run away, you need to plan it for a summer month." We pass the turnoff to Plath's Lookout, and we both glance up the snowy road as though we could see, in the darkness, whose car might be parked at the barrier, the windows steamy.

Darin nods. "Ever been up there?"

My teeth have finally stopped chattering. "I like seeing the sunsets." I don't mention the last time I was there, but the thought of it is heavy and sharp, like I'm holding onto a bundle of those swords on the tarot cards.

"Yeah, me too," says Darin. He turns off the highway onto a narrow, snow-covered driveway and parks beside a neat wood pile. "So, Cass?" He glances over at me. "Uh…would you like to stay here tonight?"

I bite my lip. "In your tree house?" My voice is a tiny squeak.

He nods. "But you have to tell your brother," he says.

I rest my head against the seat, staring up at the star-studded sky, perfectly clear and freezing cold. "And I have to tell *you.*" My voice is too quiet to hear.

"Everything's going to be fine," he says, his voice soft in the darkness. "But we need to get you warmed up." And then he leans in toward me, and I close my eyes on the stars and the cold sky. This time his mouth lingers on mine, and I wrap my hands tightly around my seat belt, clinging to this moment, to this breathless kiss.

53. If you were a comic book hero …

The "tree house" is cozy once Darin builds up the fire. I sit on his bunk, wrapped up in an army-green sleeping bag, watching him prod the stove like an expert. "You open this vent if the fire gets low," he says, demonstrating. "Adding wood is simple. You don't have to freeze." He looks up at me with a shy smile, but his eyes are tired.

"Maybe you should stay," I say. "I mean, to keep me from freezing to death and all." Okay, so it's a bad time for awkward flirting, but I get something like a real smile out of him.

He stirs the fire again, ducking behind his hair. "Did you call Eric?"

"I texted him, and Kayla too." I didn't tell either of them anything except that I'm safe and I'll be at the carnival tomorrow.

"Your parents are going to be worried."

"My parents are asleep." I can deal with my parents tomorrow. "They want to send me to religious counseling."

He turns from the fire to look at me. "So you're running away?"

"You make it sound so childish." I pull the Hanged Man out of my pocket and study the guy's face, his red leggings, the one leg bent behind the other at a strange angle. "I had to do something." I keep my eyes on the card in my lap. "I told them everything. About not believing, and about the blog. I'm Divinia Starr, Darin. I'm the reason for all this stupid stuff happening."

"You could have told me." He looks back at the stove, into the fire, and then he slowly pushes the door on the firebox shut and clamps the metal handle down. "Well, that does make things messier." He stands up, and I've never really thought of him as being tall or anything, but it's like he's towering over me.

And I feel small, and mean, and hateful. So I start to babble.

"I'm scared, okay? I made a big mistake, and Annika is turning everyone against me, and Blake and Ronnie or whoever is vandalizing my brother's sculpture, and my parents took my cards away, but I sort of picked one card to tell me what was going to happen at the Winter Carnival, and this is it. The Hanged Man." I push it toward him.

He shakes his head, doesn't take the card. "What does it mean?"

"I . . . I mean, it's a *hanged man*." I didn't look it up. Couldn't look it up, actually, since by the time I saw it, my dad had confiscated everything. But look at it. What could be good about it?

Darin starts pacing, from window to door and back, and he looks so pissed. Does he hate me now? What happened to the freedom to not believe in anything? I scrunch my feet up on the bunk, still cocooned in the sleeping bag, and I pat the mattress beside me. "Hey," I say. "Sit. You're making me nervous."

I'm making *myself* nervous. What if all of this is my own twisted attempt to be like Cassandra of Troy, singled out by the gods with a stupid curse, a tragic superpower that makes me more interesting?

He sits, but he looks disappointed in me. "You should have told the school right away." He shakes his head and lets out a long sigh. "Damn, Cass. You should have moderated those comments."

"I know that, okay? So ... I've been living with that knowledge spinning inside me since it happened, and I've been trying ever since to figure out how to make it better, how to fix this awful mess." I hug my knees to my chest. "I couldn't tell Clark at school today because I knew she'd tell my parents, and it couldn't come like that, from the school. I needed to tell them myself."

"And it didn't go well." Darin leans against me, just a little, but it's enough that I know he doesn't completely hate me.

"I've never seen my mom look the way she did. My parents truly believe my soul is in terrible danger from this sorcery, or witchcraft." I flick my fingernails against the tarot card, sending it spinning across the little room. "They've already been hurt more than any parents should be hurt, and I've always done whatever I could to keep from adding to their burdens. But now they probably think their two oldest children are lost. That our souls won't be in heaven with them."

Darin takes my hand. "Your little brother," he says. "My mom told me."

"Caleb." I almost never say his name. "Yeah, he's a part of this." I can't bear the thought of seeing my parents hurting the way they did when my brother died, ever again. I think it would have been awful and tragic no matter how he'd died, but the fact that it was so unexpected and inexplicable—Sudden Infant Death Syndrome—made it so much worse for my mom, who'd researched everything and followed every guideline to the letter.

"His death...it was like it cemented my parents' belief in God's mysterious ways," I say. Caleb was perfect. A tiny, nearly translucent vision of perfection. Those skinny purple legs jerking this way and that on either side of the giant puffy diaper. The tiny hand, a miniature red fist stuffed into his perfect, slurping mouth. I couldn't believe God would want to take him from us, but I can appreciate the comfort that the church offered to my family. "We wouldn't even be part of Joyful News if it weren't for what happened with Caleb. They were so kind, so *embracing*."

Darin produces a small sketchbook and one of his trademark black pens from a shelf above our heads. He pulls his feet up onto the bunk and sits with his back against me, drawing. I feel the weight of him, solid and warm against me—a sign that he, at least, can forgive me for my stupidity.

"It was the first time in my life, I think, that I looked

at my family and saw that they were different from me," I say. "Their reactions, their beliefs. What they needed to feel strong." I yawn. The little studio is cozy and warm now that Darin built up the fire, and I'm feeling sleepy and heavy. "What're you drawing, anyway?" I let his weight tip me over, curled on my side in the bag, my heart jittery against my ribs. I'm here, in this moment, in this *bed*, with this boy. What if he were to lie down here beside me, scrunch himself into this narrow space? What if he put his arms around me? What if . . .

It hurts, to be happy. Right now, how can I be feeling this? I force myself to think about Drew, about her stricken face in the hall the last time I saw her—I make myself imagine her opening a bottle of pills with shaking hands. Lying in a hospital bed.

Darin laughs. "No big deal, I'm just drawing you in your underwear," he says.

"*Whaaaaat?*" I sit up fast and make a grab for the sketchbook, but he holds it out of my reach, and I'm all tangled up in the sleeping bag. I shove him, and we grapple for a moment, both of us laughing. "Let. Me. See!"

He holds his hand up, grins, and shakes his hair out of his eyes. "Relax, Cass, I'm messing with you." The book has fallen closed in his hand, so he flips it open and holds it out to me, a shy smile on his face. "All comic book heroes wear their underwear on the outside," he says. He chews on the side of his bottom lip and watches my face. I look down at the page.

"It's me!" It's his spiky-haired version of me, except I'm wearing a cape, and . . . yeah, it pretty much looks like I'm wearing my underwear. I blush.

"It's us," says Darin, "saving the day." The two heroes are flying, hand-in-hand, over a field of snow sculptures, ready to swoop down at the first sign of danger.

He takes my hand in real life, gives it a squeeze. "I'm glad you're different, Cass." His voice is soft. "Your family is stronger than you think." Gently, he pushes me back down onto the bunk and leans over me, his lips brushing my forehead. "You can have this sketchbook," he says, setting it beside my head. "My studio is always a good place for inspiration."

I roll my eyes. "Are you talking about the English poem again?" Tomorrow's the deadline, but it's not like it matters now.

He smiles, stepping into his boots. "I would never," he says. "Get some sleep, and I'll be in to wake you up for the carnival." He turns off the lamp and leaves me to the dim glow and the quiet crackling of the fire in the stove.

I roll toward the wall, hoping my mother is sleeping now, hoping she's oblivious to my disappearance. Hoping I can make amends in the morning.

54. What are you waiting for…

When I wake up, it's not quite light, and the world is fuzzy and all one color. Darin is tapping softly on the door. "Hey, good morning," he says when I hop over in the sleeping bag to let him in. "My sister wants to talk to you."

I grab my backpack and pull on my coat and boots, shivering, and follow him to the house. The snow squeaks under my feet—a sign of the deepest cold—and Darin turns and smiles as we get to the door. "Did you stay warm enough?"

I nod, but I'm afraid to speak. What if I have morning breath? We step inside, into a high-ceilinged hallway paved with tile. "Be right back," I whisper, and I scurry into the bathroom to clean up. I'm queasy, running on very little sleep.

When I wander out to the kitchen, Darin is perched on a tall chair at the granite breakfast bar, and a curvy girl with long, dark hair stands beside him on one bare foot, cradling her other foot in front of her like a tiny, pink baby. She wears pale blue silk pajamas, and when she turns to smile at me (still on one leg), her eyes are identical to her brother's—a calm, steady gray. "I'm Claire," she says, then tucks her foot against her standing leg, yoga-style. "You look like you could use some coffee."

Kicking her foot out, she twirls her way over to the coffee pot, filling a brown ceramic mug. She hands it to me, black, not asking if I take cream or sugar. I don't.

"Tell Cassandra what you told me," says Darin, and I watch as Claire sets her coffee on the granite countertop and performs a flawless backbend in the middle of the kitchen, her dark hair falling to the floor. One by one, her legs spring up into the air, the legs of her pajama pants bagging up around her knees, and she stands on her hands for a moment before twisting down and returning her feet to the floor.

"Are you a gymnast or something?" I'm still holding my coffee cup halfway to my mouth.

She smiles, tossing her hair. "Nah, my boobs are too big." She sticks her chest out proudly to show me. "I want to run away with the circus, but my parents are making me do community college first."

Darin throws a wadded-up paper napkin at his sister. "The freak show, maybe," he says. "Tell her about the Hanged Man."

Claire wrinkles her nose. "I'm sorry to hear about that girl who got bullied on your blog. I heard what happened to her. Mean people suck." She reaches up and rummages through the cupboards above her head, pulling a box of cereal out.

"Hungry?" She reaches in with one hand, pulls out a fistful of cereal, and offers the box to me.

"You know about the Hanged Man?" I take the cereal, but I'm not sure what to do with it. My mom would *kill* me if I reached into a box like that.

"I *love* that card." Claire shoves the rest of the cereal from her hand into her mouth and holds up a finger while she chews. "It's one of the few cards I can always remember, mainly because the meaning is so much better than what it looks like."

"Really?" I stare at her, my hand snaking into the cereal box on its own. My stomach rumbles, and I toss a handful into my mouth and pass the box to Darin.

"Claire's been talking up Divinia Starr since the beginning," says Darin. "She's way into things like that." He slides a book over to me, already open to the page. The sight of the man hanging from the tree makes the cereal and coffee churn inside my stomach.

"It's a card of change," Claire says. "Life in suspension. Like this guy is hanging there, meditating. They talk about it being like a rebirth, like, you know, how babies turn upside down before they're born?" She twirls.

"Life in suspension." I look at the guy hanging there, except this time I try to imagine it as a good thing. Can he get down from the tree and move on? Be reborn? I stare at the picture, the tree, the man's face. Is it serene, rather than stoic? "The leaves!" I notice that the tree is more than a gallows. It has green leaves sprouting out of it.

Darin passes the box of cereal back to me and I munch absent-mindedly, pulling out my card and holding it beside the black-and-white picture in the book.

"Oh, hey," says Darin, reaching into his own backpack. "This is actually for you. I totally forgot, with all the craziness. It's from Dawkins. He stopped me in the hall yesterday after lunch and told me to give this to you. He said to tell you that you're too smart for this shit."

My eyes widen. "He did not." I look at the crumpled paper. It's Mr. D's email address, scrawled in his familiar green ink.

"Paraphrased," says Darin with a shrug. He stuffs an extra hat and gloves into his pack. "But he did say, 'Friday midnight, final offer.'"

"Damn him." My fingers fiddle with the scrap of paper. "I could easily lose this address before midnight," I say, but then I turn the paper over and catch more of his green script. *You're making too much of this, Cassandra. Hang in there, and maybe try to look at the assignment from a different perspective.* The word "hang" is underlined twice.

"Did you know," says Claire, "in the early days, this card was called the Traitor. Because that's what they did with traitors, I guess. Hung them by one foot."

"Traitors?" My face is hot. I skim the explanation in Claire's book, which is much more in-depth than my guide-book with its little list of single-word meanings. With a book like this, Divinia Starr could...I shake my head. No. Divinia Starr is finished. I read how the Hanged Man card seems to have little to do with tragedy and everything to do with self-reflection, a change of perspective, a sacrifice, and ... my eyes land on one word, written in all capital letters: *REPENTANCE*. I try to force a swallow beyond the giant lump in my throat.

"Oh." The word hits home, slugs me right in the guts. It's what I'm searching for, a way to repent, to make up for being the traitor. But how can I, when I can't see or speak to Drew? And even if I could speak, what could I possibly say that could begin to make up for everything I've done? *And the things I've left undone.*

Claire smiles cheerfully, but she leans down on the counter so that her eyes can find mine and hold them. "Maybe you need to hang upside down for a while," she says. "Change your perspective."

I feel stupid, but maybe she's right. I spin around and hook my legs over the top of the chair and lean back—not graceful like Claire, but at least I'm upside down. I look around. Stone tile, chair legs, cabinets with glass fronts so I can see the dishes and things inside. Claire's bare feet dancing around, pink polish chipping off her big toes. In the gap between the stove and the refrigerator, a little tumbleweed of dust moves slowly along the floor in the current of air from the heat registers. The blood is pooling in my head, and I'm trying to capture that serene feeling of the baby waiting to be born, but really all I want to do is to figure out the least awkward way of getting myself upright again.

A note flutters past my face, escaping my pocket and

landing on the tile below me. *Try to look at the assignment from a different perspective*, the note suggests. The assignment.

"Repentance." I flop around until I'm upright, digging out the sketchbook that Darin gave me last night. *Write something*. Make something right.

55. The song you can't help singing …

The Winter Carnival is in full swing when we arrive. Darin and I sneak past the kissing booth and head toward the snow sculptures, hoping to evade my parents and anyone else who might want to interrupt my plan.

Kayla is in her element, leading Martin Shaddox around by the arm, pointing out all her favorite sculptures, and flirting —of course she's flirting. Martin takes it all in stride, geeking out right beside her about all this comic book stuff.

"Cassandra, what the hell?" she says by way of greeting. "Here, Martin, excuse me for a minute. Tell Darin about the evolution of gay comic book heroes after Northstar." She grabs me by the arm and drags me behind a stack of speakers next to the pavilion.

She looks over her shoulder. "Your parents have been *freaking*. They made this huge announcement, and they were, like, crying and asking everyone to look for you. Seriously, your mom looked awful." She shoves me a little, on the shoulder.

"Where the hell *were* you? My sources said you stayed with sketchy-boy last night, but I told my sources you were way too lame for that."

"My parents—where are they now?" I need them to be here when I do this, and Eric too.

"They're with some pastor guy. Your church put up a hot-chocolate-slash-Bible-study tent on the other side of the park." She points.

Some pastor guy? I can't believe they'd bring Fordham here. Like they're planning an all-out intervention for me, dragging me kicking and screaming back to Jesus. My hands start to sweat, but I have to do this. "You've got to do me a favor, Kayla," I say. "Before Martin announces the winners for the sculpture contest, I need him to give me the microphone, for just a minute."

Kayla hesitates. "I don't know, Cass..."

"Please. It's for Drew."

She nods, still looking uneasy. "Be ready, then. The awards ceremony starts in fifteen minutes, right here at the pavilion, and then the dance starts."

Fifteen minutes. The sketchbook feels heavy in my hands, and my lungs constrict as I look up at the tall stacks of speakers and think about what I'm going to do.

"It looks really nice," I say, nodding at the decorations, the paths winding among the snow sculptures lined with glowing jar lanterns. "You did a great job."

Kayla smiles, but she looks surprised. "Thanks," she says, and turns to the stage.

"You've got a plan," says Darin, sidling over to me. I glance over his shoulder to see Kayla standing on tiptoe, leaning in to whisper something in Martin's ear. Her friend's crazy request. It takes a lot for her to trust me, since she's obviously on shaky ground here with the carnival, and I appreciate it. Appreciate *her*. It occurs to me, watching her eyes light up as she talks to this famous comic book illustrator, that it wasn't all her fault. Our friendship falling apart, I mean. Okay, so I've always followed her lead, but did I ever really try to understand her excitement about this kind of thing? Did I ever try to really be interested, instead of reciting my best friend lines?

"I don't know if it's a good plan." I shift the sketchbook to my other hand, my sweaty fingers leaving a dark smear across the blue cover. I can still back out, run away again. I could make up with my parents, be a better daughter. Finding a new perspective could mean so many things.

Darin puts an arm around me and reaches over, flips open the book to my song. I clear my throat. "'Song of Myself: The Hanged Man Remix.'" It sounds so stupid. "Darin, I can't..."

"'For Drew, with Repentance,'" says Darin, reading the dedication over my shoulder. He waves his smiley-faced finger at me. "You can," he says. "I'll go get your family."

56. The self you wish you could be …

The microphone that Martin Shaddox hands me slips in my fingers, and my nervous breath puffs out in a cold billowy cloud as I look out at the students and teachers assembled around the pavilion. They're talking, laughing, shoving each other—gathered here because they've been told to assemble, not because they're terribly concerned with who won the sculpture contest or the ski race or whatever. I search the crowd for Darin, for my parents. For Eric or Gavin. But it's like my eyes have frosted up and everyone in front of me is slightly blurry.

I raise the mic, but it's no good. I can't. The crowd loses interest, starts talking more loudly. Someone shouts, "Come *on* already!"

I blink, wipe my eyes with my sleeve, blink again, and their faces swim out of the crowd and stare at me, scornful and mocking. Annika and her robot chicken army. Perfect. I stand up straighter, tap the microphone lightly with one finger.

"Okay. So I know this isn't what you're here for," I say. My voice trembles, my breath catching awkwardly in my chest.

A teacher I don't recognize starts moving toward the stairs, a frown on her face and an official spring in her step. She's coming to get this show back on its pre-approved track, to remove the unpredictable. My eyes flicker over to her and then back to the audience, which is actually quieter now, waiting. I can feel them restlessly pulling together, into a solid mass. A wall. I take a deep breath.

"I—" I glance at the approaching teacher again, but now Mr. Dawkins is standing next to her, his hand lightly resting on her arm, asking her to let the unpredictable happen, like poetry. Or fate. "Wait just a moment," he says to her, though of course I can't hear him. A moment. This moment.

"I know you've all heard about what happened on the Divinia Starr blog," I say, and I can almost hear the crowd draw in a breath. "I can't take back what happened, the hurtful things that were said about Drew Godfrey, or the awful result."

"You're the one who posted all those mean things about her!" A shout from the back of the crowd, and heads swivel to see who it is.

"No, I—I didn't say the mean things about her, but…" My fingers fumble with the sketchbook, which slips from my hands and falls open on the floor in front of me.

"She thought you were her *friend*!" shouts someone else.

"Traitor!" This time I'm almost sure it's Annika.

I bend down to pick up the sketchbook, which has fallen open to the page where Darin drew the two of us as heroes, saving the day. *Traitor.* Hanging from one foot. I stand up and take a shaky breath. "Yes. I wasn't a good friend." I resolve to say it all, no matter who shouts at me. "I didn't post those terrible things about Drew, but I could have stopped them, because the blog they were on was mine. I was Divinia Starr, and I *knew* there was a possibility of the comments turning mean. I knew that because they'd gone over the line once already, but…I didn't moderate them."

This part is hard to say, but at last the crowd is silent, letting me speak. "I've told myself that I didn't moderate the comments because I didn't think people would be that mean, but the hard truth is, I think part of me enjoyed seeing the drama." This isn't in the script, even though there isn't a script, and I'm as surprised as any of the kids in the crowd by what I'm saying.

"I guess probably a lot of us have that reaction when we see crazy Internet drama," I continue. "It's easy to laugh, or hit share, or post some anonymous comments of our own." I sigh. "I wish I could say I'm braver in person. That I never laugh at the mean things people say to get a laugh, that I never repeat those things to get a laugh of my own, later."

I have to wrap this up before I start crying or something stupid like that. "Okay, so…I'm failing English class." I risk a glance at Mr. D, who smiles and gives me a nod of encouragement. The woman beside him nervously scans the group of students, but she lets me continue.

"It's stupid, really, but we had to write a poem, and I couldn't do it. I couldn't write a poem celebrating myself and singing myself because the thing is, I'm not always sure what my*self* is, you know? Like with Drew. Was I the kind of person who could be her friend? The kind of person who *would* be her friend, even when it was difficult?"

I look at Britney, who kept my secret, and at Annika and her mechanical girls. "I guess I couldn't write a poem to celebrate who I was because I was so many different people, depending on who was leading the way. So I wrote this poem, to celebrate the self I *wish* I was. The self I hope I can be."

It's quiet. The crowd is still, leaning forward. I search for Darin and find him at last, see my parents on either side of him—my mom with her hand pressed up against her mouth, my dad with his shoulders drawn in tight, his fingers plucking at the stubble on his cheek. I think I see him start to smile. "So this is my song," I say, and my voice is clear and strong. "For Drew, and for myself." And then I read, but in my heart, I sing.

Song of Myself: The Hanged Man Remix
For Drew, with Repentance

I celebrate myself, and sing myself,
a traitor hanging in this tree
and what I assume you shall assume.
I'm life suspended at seventeen,
uncertain and undeclared,
free, as you said,
to believe in nothing—
nothing at all.

I celebrate myself, and sing myself,
the self
I want to be—
the self who doesn't need a tragic superpower
to be interesting
the self who would welcome you.

I thought I could hide behind another name,
walk behind someone brave enough to take
    the first step,
but they led me away from myself.
Hanging here, I find a new perspective.
I see the leaves are making a comeback—
little tendrils snaking around my ankles,
and it's not enough, to follow.

I don't want to get lost, carried away
in a crowd of gossiping mouths
and stony eyes.
I celebrate the self
that steps down
from this tree
and steps up
and stands up
for you.

57. What forgiveness
is to you...

What doesn't happen after that:

I don't stage dive into the arms of all my adoring fellow students and crowd surf my way over to my parents, who don't weep and tear their garments and don't tell me I'll never again have to eat tater-tot hotdish or go to church or do the dishes if I'll only come home. That doesn't happen.

I do not have a miraculous epiphany that results in me finding Jesus and being born again and speaking in tongues and ascending to heaven in a chorus of angels.

I don't look up as the music swells to see Drew Godfrey standing backstage with tears in her eyes, and she doesn't run to me and hug me and tell me she forgives me for everything now that she's heard my beautiful poetry. That definitely doesn't happen.

And I guess I can't say for certain, but I'm pretty sure that all of the students at Gordon High do not undergo an instant transformation into super-tolerant, inclusive, and supportive individuals who turn away from drama to link arms and sing together or something.

Okay. So that doesn't happen, but there is a smattering of applause when I finish my song and hand the microphone back to Martin Shaddox, who does announce that Eric's snow sculpture of Northstar wins first prize, and when he does, the crowd cheers like crazy. And when my brother runs up onto the stage to pick up his trophy, they do start to chant and stomp their feet—"GIVE HIM THE RING! GIVE HIM THE RING!"—until Eric's face is a deep red color and my hands are sore from clapping, and Darin pushes Gavin up onstage, and Eric does give him a nice silver Claddagh ring and a big hug. My parents do applaud, if a little hesitantly, from their spot at the back of the crowd. Mr. Dawkins does pull me aside and shake my hand; he tells me he knew I could do it and that he'll be changing my grade before he leaves for the weekend.

"You know I have to take off points for lateness, but that was A work, Cassandra." His smile fades. "I'll put in a good word for you with Ms. Clark, but I think you'd better go talk to her right away."

Ms. Clark does explain to me, in great detail, all of the articles and sub-articles of our technology use code and anti-bullying policy that she feels I've violated by creating the blog and allowing it to get out of hand. However, she acknowledges that, since I created the blog from my home computer, and since I (allegedly) didn't actually post any of the hateful messages, that I will not be suspended from school. Instead she explains how I will have to pay back the ad fee for the space I stole in *The Gordon High Gazette*, a considerable sum of money. I do agree to work long hours at Joyful News in order to pay it back, doubling up my church newsletter hours with filing and cleaning duties. Ms. Clark also does admit that she admires what I said out there, at the carnival, and that she hopes people were listening.

"It's easy to talk about bullying," she says, "but it's hard to connect that talk to all the little moments in life where you really could be the person who steps up."

My parents, one sitting on either side of me, each put an arm around me and squeeze, and it's not a squeeze of "all's forgiven," or even a squeeze of "we're so proud of you," but, at the heart of it, it's a squeeze of "we love you anyway," and that's one thing that does happen.

58. Right now you are…

March comes in like a lamb, and Darin convinces my mom to let me leave the house unsupervised—for driving lessons, of all things. "Cass needs some sun," he says, smiling that bashful smile of his and shaking the hair out of his eyes. He quirks an eyebrow. "It would help her mood, don't you think?"

I roll my eyes, but he's right, and my mom knows it too. I've been imprisoned for exactly a month, confined to my room with no phone and no computer—no contact with the outside world except at school and during my "counseling sessions" with Pastor Jake Marshall, my brother's mentor and, it turns out, a pretty good listener. He's also a pretty good racquetball coach, which is sort of a strange context for religious counseling, but it works surprisingly well. Also, I'm getting good at racquetball.

"Oh, fine," says my mother with an obligatory sigh, but I see the way her eyes soften toward Darin, and I think she's starting to like him, despite his role in my recent disobediences. "*Safely.*"

Darin catches my hand as we walk out to his car but he

keeps quiet, and for a while the only sound is our shoes in the slush. The sun feels nice on the top of my head, warm in a way that feels forgotten, and even though I know we're not done with winter yet, the smell of the breeze is enough to convince me we're on our way to spring.

"I've been thinking about Cassandra of Troy," I say at last. "I wonder if things could have been different for her, even with her blessing and her curse. I wonder if she could have made her *own* future. Her own truth."

Darin smiles and opens the driver's door. My hands are sweaty, but driving isn't the only thing making me nervous. Today is Drew's first day back at home, and it'll be the first time I've seen her since...since she swallowed a bottle of anti-depressants and didn't wake up for several days.

"She wouldn't make a very interesting tragic hero, in that case," says Darin. He leans in close, pretending like he's going to show me how to adjust my mirrors. Instead he kisses me, and he smells like sunshine.

I laugh, pushing him away. "My mom's probably watching!"

"I'm keeping you safe," he says, and makes a big show of tugging on my seat belt. "Now check your mirrors, shift it into reverse, and look over your shoulder as you back out. Let's do this."

Let's do this. I drive slowly, my first time on the actual streets by myself, and Darin directs me in a soft, patient voice until we pull up at the curb beside Drew's house. Then he takes my hand and draws a little stick-girl on the inside of my wrist. She has spiky hair and she's flexing her muscles, which bulge from her right arm in goofy bumps. "You're stronger than ever," he says, and we both laugh as he pokes me in the arm. He's been teasing me for weeks about my racquetball arm. "You can do this."

I nod, and I unbuckle and get out of the car, but I have no idea *how* to do this—how to walk up to that front door and make things better. I march up to the porch, wishing I had something to carry.

Drew opens the door before I ring the bell, so I know she saw the car pull up, and I'm glad that she had a moment to prepare for my arrival, to gather up her own strength. She looks different, her stringy ponytail gone and the rest of her hair cropped close and uneven. Her eyes are different, too—she looks directly at me, no more of the wavering hairline gaze. She has a steadiness about her that's new.

"Hey," I say, and then I lose track of all the things I thought I might say. "I ... I'm glad you're okay." The gravity of what could have happened is heavy all around her, and I'm drawn in, throwing my arms around her in an awkward hug.

She hugs me back. It's not a made-for-TV moment, but she smiles and squints up at the sun. "Yeah, I'm glad too," she says. Then she nods. "I really am."

"Drew, I had no idea. I wish I'd known ... I wish ... " I trail off, struggling to find the words.

"I know," she says. "I read the poem you sent."

"I was hoping you would—"

"I read it a lot." She glances over her shoulder and gives a little nod, as if to reassure someone she's okay, and I catch a glimpse of her mom hovering nervously in the hall. "Sorry,

Cass, I'd invite you in, but...we're in the middle of packing, and..." She pulls her sleeves down over her hands and crosses her arms in front of her chest. "Everything's a mess, you know."

I know. "You're packing?"

She shrugs. "Yeah, my mom doesn't want...well, it's not really working, with her gone all the time and stuff. We're getting a condo in the Cities, and I'm going to try the traveling thing again. I'm doing online high school for the rest of this year, and probably senior year too."

"Oh." We stand there, and I realize that, even though I've never wanted to be Drew's best friend, I'm disappointed she's not coming back, that she won't be at youth group, that she won't be a part of the graphic novel Kayla and Darin are writing and I'm doing layout for, that she won't get to see how Britney has started sitting with us at lunch.

I step back, onto the porch, taking my leave. "I'm sorry, Drew. I'm going to miss you." It's the truth.

"Bye, Cass. Thanks for stopping by." She starts to close the screen door, but she stops halfway and looks me in the eyes again. "I think there are good things in the future, for both of us," she says, and then she smiles. "Truth."

I smile back, and then I turn before she can shut the door, before I can lose sight of her face, and I walk toward Darin, who's standing by the gate. The wind has picked up, bringing with it a soft muddy smell of new beginnings, and his shaggy hair whips around his face. I reach into my pocket for the card I've been hanging on to all month.

"Knowing the future is useless if you don't understand the truth about right now," I say. I lean in, my eyes locked on his until we're too close to focus, and we both close our eyes, our foreheads touching.

"I'm glad you're not a tragic hero," he says.

I lift my hand, feeling the card flutter against my fingers in the wind, and then I let it go.

59. You celebrate yourself …

60. You sing yourself …

Photo by David Hoole

About the Author

Elissa Janine Hoole bought her first deck of tarot cards as a birthday gift to herself when she turned twenty, and even in the privacy of her own apartment, she felt like she should hide them. The three words she uses to describe herself are *curious, caring,* and *contemplative.* Suggestions from her husband and two sons include *crazy* and *cantankerous.* Elissa teaches middle-school English and sometimes makes her students write poetry that celebrates and sings themselves. She also wrote the YA road trip novel *Kiss the Morning Star.*

Visit her online at ElissaJHoole.com.

If you could change one thing . . .

For Cassandra Randall, there's a price to pay for being a secret atheist in a family of fundamentalists—she has nothing good to write on an online personality quiz; her best friend is drifting away; and she's failing English because she can't express her true self in a poem.

But when she creates a controversial advice blog just to have something in her life to call her own, there's no way she can predict the devastating consequences of her actions. As her world fractures before her very eyes, Cass must learn to listen to her own sense of right and wrong in the face of overwhelming expectations.

$9.99 US / $11.50 CAN
ISBN 978-0-7387-3722-5

50999

flux

www.fluxnow.com

NW